The Stork

A Shelby McDougall Mystery

Nancy Wood

Cover design copyright © 2019 by Niki Lenhart
nikilen-designs.com

Published by Paper Angel Press
paperangelpress.com

ISBN 978-1-953469-31-1 (Trade Paperback)

10 9 8 7 6 5 4 3 2

Dedication

For Hansie

Acknowledgements

After *Due Date* was published in 2012, I thought that the second book in the Shelby McDougall series would be a snap. One year, tops. Hah! It's five-plus years later and, finally, *The Stork* is ready for publication. It's been a long road.

Once again, I must thank writing coach and editor extraordinaire, Mary Carroll Moore. She helped transform the manuscript into a novel, guiding me through the ins and outs of storyboarding, helping me find and expose the threads of Shelby's story, and making sure I picked up all those loose ends.

I really appreciate the support of friends and acquaintances. You always ask about my writing; you supported *Due Date*; you supported me as an author. You invited me to your book clubs and came to my reading at Bookshop Santa Cruz. It has been truly magical.

A thank you to the early readers of *The Stork*. You helped shape the novel by pointing out those places where the story dragged or didn't make sense, or where the characters' actions didn't quite match up with their personalities. I'd also like to acknowledge the members of my book club, the Aunties Brigade, for reading an early draft and for sharing a passionate love of books.

Santa Cruz is a real place, and, again, I must ask for the indulgence of readers when the imagined landscape doesn't quite match up with reality. As for the science: any errors are mine and mine alone.

A thank you goes to my family: my husband and now grown-up kids, my parents and in-laws, my siblings. I said it before and will say it again: thank you!

And a huge shout out to readers everywhere. Keep reading! Reading is a miracle.

INTRODUCTION

Many thanks to Paper Angel Press for picking up *The Stork*, the second book in the Shelby McDougall mystery series, and for providing it a new lease on life. Though this edition does not have plot, character, or setting changes, I was able to fix a few things that needed attention.

As with *Due Date*, I'm delighted with the new cover and hope you are too. Paper Angel Press is a phenomenal press that supports authors one hundred percent. The press has a great reach; provides promotional assistance; and publishes in paperback, hardback, and digital formats. Thank you, Paper Angel Press, for this opportunity.

Happy reading!
Nancy

DAY ONE

TUESDAY, JULY 17

1

THE CALL CAME AT TWO IN THE MORNING, the shrill ring startling me from a deep sleep. I bolted upright, grabbed the cell off the bedside table, and flipped it open.

A woman's voice, high-pitched, insistent, and on the edge of hysteria blasted from the speaker, cutting off my greeting mid-sentence.

"Hello? Hello? Is this the P.I. agency? I need to leave a message for Shelby. For Shelby McDougall."

I replied cautiously, "This is Shelby."

The woman drew a long, shaky breath and started to cry. "You answered," she said. "You're there." Another breath. "You have to help me. You're the only one who can. Please, help me." Her voice cracked in anguished, ragged sobs, and she breathed heavily, as if trying to get a grip. As if steeling herself so she could continue.

She started and stopped, started and stopped again. Then, in a low almost inaudible moan, she said, "My baby. He's gone. Someone took him. He's been kidnapped."

Blood roared in my ears. Sweat dotted my forehead and fear, as bright and sharp as the honed edge of a razor, parked itself low in my belly.

"Who is this?" I asked as I swung my legs to the floor and fumbled for the light, trying to catch my breath, trying to remember how to breathe.

The woman's moans ratcheted to a shrill, inhuman wail.

"Who is this?" I repeated; my voice now loud, sharp, demanding.

"L … L … L …," the woman managed, before dissolving into frantic weeping.

"Please," I said, trying to soften my tone. "Talk to me. Who are you? Where are you?"

But her sobs grew distant, as if she'd put down the phone, and a cascade of notes signaled the end of the call. I listened to empty air, imagining a woman in a darkened room, curled in a fetal position, weeping for her lost child. I'd received calls like this before, but it had been years. Calls from grief-stricken women teetering on the edge of sanity, hoping I could help. Thinking that because I'd tricked fate, because I'd been able to save my babies, I'd magically be able to do the same for theirs.

I never could.

The number was local, from the 831 area code. That didn't help — 831 covered three counties. The woman could be anywhere, from right next door, here in Santa Cruz, California, to Gorda, on the Big Sur coast at the southern edge of Monterey County. I called back, but the phone on the other end rang and rang, the sound tinkling into emptiness. No greeting, no voicemail.

I dropped the cell on the bed and massaged my temples where the headache lurked, wishing I hadn't had those beers earlier in the evening. I picked up the phone and redialed. Again, no answer.

I hopped out of bed, rifled through the clothes piled on the floor, found the sweatshirt I'd peeled off a few hours earlier, and pulled it over my head. Two Advil and a glass of water later, I was back in my room.

Calling, letting it ring ten times, disconnecting, calling again. Turning the small flip phone over and over in my hands, willing it to ring.

The Amber Alert system was enabled on the phone, but nothing had come across in the last few days. If I was in the office, I could use the scanner to listen in on the police frequencies. At the very least, I should be able to find the address through reverse lookup.

But the cell rang before I could get started.

"Shelby?" This time, a man spoke; his voice a low and gravelly rumble.

"Who are you?" I asked in return.

A slight pause, followed by: "Ryan Boyd."

Boyd? Ryan Boyd? I felt like the air had been knocked out of me. I doubled over, muffling the gasp that threatened to spill out, giving me away.

But he wasn't fooled. "You okay?" he asked.

I slowly sat back up, feeling the headache now. The Advil hadn't touched it; it felt like a six-inch-wide steel band was wrapped around my skull radiating a pulsing, punishing pain.

I didn't answer. Instead, I asked a question in return, my voice small and disbelieving. "One of the twins was taken?"

Taken. Why had I used that particular word? Not kidnapped or abducted or snatched, but taken. As if something had been taken from me. As if the twins I'd given up for adoption five and a half years ago were still cleaved to me, still part of my life.

"Yes," Ryan replied. "Justin was kidnapped."

Justin. My son.

"It happened sometime Saturday night. Lisa checks on the kids every morning when she gets up around six. Justin's bed was empty. He wasn't in the house. His sister had no idea he was even gone." Lisa, I knew, was Ryan's wife. The twins' real mother.

Ryan's voice caught and he blew out his breath in a sigh, a sorrowful rattle that made me shiver. "Lisa's hysterical. Beside herself."

Completely understandable, I thought, and then asked, "What are the police doing?"

"They were here all day Sunday. All day yesterday. And will come back today. Interviewing me, Lisa, the neighbors, Justine."

Justine. My daughter.

After a beat, I asked, "Is she safe?"

"Yes," Ryan replied. "I just checked on her. She's fine."

"Why didn't I see this in the paper?"

"The police wanted to wait. To see if we'd get a ransom call." He paused. "We haven't."

"How come there was no Amber Alert?" I persisted.

"There was no information to post," Ryan replied. "We don't have anything to look for."

"But why call me?" I asked.

"Lisa thinks the world of you. She showed me the article that ran in the paper last month, about you taking down the baby trafficking ring and what you've been doing since then.

"She was so proud, she wanted to cut it out and put it on the fridge. Then, when this happened, we decided to contact you."

My jaw dropped in surprise and I snapped it shut, feeling like it'd been opened and closed by some external force. As if I were the dummy and the universe was the ventriloquist.

Ryan's voice dropped a register as he added, "We thought we'd be calling an answering service or a machine, and you'd get the message in the morning. I'm sorry to have woken you."

"It's okay. I have the backup work phone this week," I said. "I'm the answering service.

"But why me?" I repeated. "What can I do that the police can't?"

"Please," he replied, his voice pleading. "Lisa insists that you're the only one who can help us."

One of Grandpa Stearns' sayings popped into my head and I could hear his measured voice: "No good will come of this, Shelby. No good."

A warning? Or just the jumbled thoughts of someone yanked from sleep in the middle of the night?

But, unable to refuse, I said, "I can come in the morning. Early, before work, say, around seven-thirty?"

"Thank you," Ryan replied. "Thank you."

2

LONG AFTER WE'D HUNG UP, I stared at the flip phone, the after-hours backup for the P.I. firm where I was working. I was thinking about how easy it had been for them to find me.

As an aspiring P.I., I was hired to find people. And once I found someone, it was my job to discover everything there was to know. I knew how to tunnel into a life and excavate details, the daily routine that cascaded into a full-blown existence — family and friends, jobs, income, addresses, cell numbers, social media accounts, vehicles, credit score, purchasing preferences, workout schedules, eating habits, medical history. To dig even deeper and ferret out the intangibles that created an inner life — the joys and sorrows, loves and lovers, disappointments and dreams.

I'd done some research when I'd moved back to Santa Cruz, California three years ago; wanting to find out as much as possible about the couple who'd adopted my twins. But once I'd unearthed the basics — names, ages, employment history, income, and address — I'd stopped. Much more would be stalking. So I'd written it all down and had forced myself to forget. Though I hadn't been one hundred percent successful. Right away, when Ryan Boyd had said his name, I'd known who he was.

I used to think about the babies all the time. At one time, I even considered them my babies. Even though I wasn't the one waking up in the middle of the night to feed them or change their diapers. I wasn't the one wrestling them into car seats and taking them to play dates and doctor appointments. I wasn't reading to them or restricting their screen time.

In the last year, the twins had finally fallen from my consciousness, pushed to the back of my mind by more immediate concerns. School, work, friends, family. It was as if that chapter in my life no longer belonged to me. As if it had happened to someone I'd read about in the paper. Or in a book. But not to me.

It had happened to me, though. A younger me. A much more naïve me. A much more trusting me. The phone call brought it all back — a roaring, thundering mess of fear and panic, mingled with still-fresh disbelief and a small nut of pride.

Too jittery to sleep, I grabbed my laptop off the desk and opened it as I sank into bed. I studied the ad that had caught my attention earlier in the evening, the one I'd found on a message board called *Surrogate Moms Classifieds*.

The ad read: Gestational surrogate wanted. First time moms encouraged. You will be well rewarded.

I'd seen this exact phrase just once before, years ago.

The sum of it held an implicit promise. If you answered this ad, something besides money waited for you. Something exceptional. Life-changing, even. I'd fallen for it — hook, line, and sinker. And my life had changed, in more ways than I could have possibly imagined. Not all of those changes were good. Most of them were downright terrifying, plunging me into a world of evil I'd only seen in the movies or on TV.

I angled the screen back and read it again:

Gestational surrogate wanted. First time moms encouraged.
You will be well rewarded.

You: Willing to relocate. Have a healthy BMI. Don't use
drugs, meds, alcohol. Don't smoke.

Us: A happily married traditional couple living in northern
California.

All expenses associated with the pregnancy and delivery will
be covered. You will be well compensated for your time and
efforts. Please email. We'd love to hear from you.

Gestational surrogate. Such a clinical, sterile term. I'd been a straight-up surrogate mom. My eggs were used, making me both the biological mother and the birth mother. A gestational surrogate was a step further down the technological path. Eggs were taken from either the intended mother or another woman and fertilized in a lab. Embryos were then inserted into the uterus of the gestational surrogate, the woman who would carry the babies to term. The surrogate had no biological link with the fetus. She was just the incubator. The carrier.

No fee was given in this listing. Often, payment for services was announced first thing: twenty-eight thousand, thirty thousand, forty thousand. The most I'd seen was a cool fifty grand. Don't let anyone say money wasn't a factor. It was. It always was. The typical couple, usually in their mid-to-late thirties or early forties, were lawyers, doctors, engineers, executives. Couples who'd married late, focused on their careers, and had forgotten what later became their urgent biological imperative.

The surrogates, of course, were always younger. Often broke. Surrogacy offered a year's salary or a down payment on a house. In my case, I was looking for a quick fix to crushing college debt.

I read the ad again, chilled by the phrase, First time moms encouraged. This was unusual. With the wisdom of hindsight, I could see why agencies and legitimate intended parents wanted a surrogate with a previous full-term pregnancy. The woman would know what she was getting into. There would be no messy emotional ties. Less chance the surrogate would balk. After I'd uncovered what was planned for my babies, I'd briefly flirted with raising the twins. Even though I had no money, no job, and no place to live, I'd wanted them. I'd yearned for them, ached for them with every cell of my being.

But I'd done what was right for me.

I copied the data from the ad and pasted it into my Stork spreadsheet, my private and obsessive catalog of the hundreds of ads for surrogate moms I'd discovered since my babies were born. I still believed that the intended parents I'd contracted with, Jackson and Diane Entwistle, along with their delivery man, Frankie Browning, hadn't acted alone. In my gut, I knew there was someone else. A mastermind. A boss. A mythical Mafia-like overlord, who I'd nicknamed The Stork. The person who orchestrated baby trafficking in central and northern California.

The Stork theory held traction, at first. Diane had insisted that The Stork existed, but claimed she'd never met him or her. She'd maintained that all communication was by old-fashioned letters, delivered to a PO box and burned after reading. The investigators had pegged Frankie for a time, but that never panned out. As the leads thinned and the investigation stalled, the detectives had concluded that Jackson, Diane, and Frankie were operating completely on their own. My brother, Dexter, agreed with this theory; as did my best friend, Megan Fitzgerald; my parents; the district attorney; and my lawyer. But I'd never given up. I was sure The Stork was still at work. An ad for a surrogate mom might take me to a set of intended parents just like Jackson and Diane — intended parents who had no intention of keeping the baby. Intended parents who were frauds, driven by greed. Intended parents who would adopt a baby in a closed adoption, send the birth mother on her way, and deliver the baby elsewhere. All details arranged by The Stork.

Just like I always did, I shot off an email from the bogus email account I'd created just for this purpose.

Long after I shut down the laptop, I lay in bed, awake. Remembering —

The gun. The bite of the rope against my ankles and wrists. The duct tape covering my mouth. And the infant squalling: a relentless, frantic mewing.

3

WHEN LIGHT FROM THE PALE DAWN SNUCK IN through a crack in the curtains, I knew it was time to get out of bed. I quickly gulped a cup of black coffee, showered, and then downed another cup while I munched a piece of whole wheat toast smeared with butter and jam. No matter how little I slept, the combination of bitter and sweet always jolted me into some kind of functioning state. Before leaving, I scrawled a note for Dexter, my brother and roommate, and propped it against the coffee pot:

Don't forget that Megan is coming for dinner tonight.

My not-so-subtle mission to set up Dexter, separated from his wife three years ago, with my best friend Megan, was going slowly. I knew they'd be perfect for each other. They just hadn't realized it yet.

The Boyd family lived in Watsonville, the second largest city in the county. About twenty miles south of Santa Cruz, it was surrounded on all sides by the fertile fields of the Pajaro Valley, planted with strawberries, raspberries, blackberries, cauliflower, broccoli, artichokes, and decades-old apple orchards. But the relentless pace of progress had chipped into the acreage devoted to agriculture. Every time I went to Watsonville, it seemed like another housing development or mall had sprouted overnight, hiding the rich, brown soil under pavement, storm drains, sidewalks, and buildings.

I took Watsonville's Main Street exit off the freeway and turned right onto Ohlone Parkway, named for the Native American people who'd lived along this part of the California coast. I passed the entrance to a shopping center on the left, deserted at this early hour, save for the addicts swarming Starbucks for their morning fix. To my right was a trailhead into Struve Slough, one of the few remaining wetlands in this area. Glossy red-winged blackbirds perched on slender marsh grasses and the liquid tumble of birdsong filtered through the closed car window. A flock of mud-colored ducks congregated in the middle of the open water, while a blue heron waded slowly in the shallows, fishing. As I drove past, it flew off, its silhouette reminding me of centuries-old Japanese etchings.

Rows of identical townhouses lined the streets in the Boyd's neighborhood. When parking places became scarce, I knew I was close. The police must have announced the kidnapping. I parked two blocks away, next to a trailhead that led back into the slough, and walked quickly along the carbon-copy streets, slowing when I turned onto the Boyd's block. The lawn in front of their small house was crammed with equipment, reporters, cameramen, and technicians.

The noise increased as I shoved my way through the crowd and ran up the porch steps, ignoring demands for information. I prayed that my picture would not end up in the paper.

A police officer stood in front of the door, feet spread, hands clasped behind his back. "No visitors allowed," he said, raising his voice over the rabble.

"Ryan, Mr. Boyd, called me and asked me to come over," I yelled.

"He didn't mention it," the officer shouted in return.

"Try. Please?" I asked.

Without answering, while keeping his eyes on me, he banged on the door. A few long moments later, the door opened a crack. The police officer turned around and leaned in, saying, "This woman here says you asked her to visit."

The door swung wider and the din from the reporters on the lawn rose. "Has there been any contact from the kidnapper? Any ransom demands? When will your son be returned?"

After a confirming nod from the person inside, the police officer pushed me through the door. It slammed behind me and the cacophony outside dulled.

I stood in a dimly lit foyer facing a narrow staircase. A hall jogged to the left, toward the back of the house. The living room, as dark and quiet as a parlor in a funeral home, was to my right.

For an instant, I couldn't breathe. I felt like I'd just fallen from a great height and had landed on my back, the breath knocked out of me. My knees buckled and I grabbed the banister, steadying myself.

"Shelby," Lisa Boyd was saying, offering her hand, "I'm Lisa. Thank you so much for coming."

As I reached for her hand in return, I felt flighty and untethered, barely resisting the urge to tear through the house, tunnel into every room and closet, every crevice and corner, searching, stopping only when I found her — my daughter.

"And this is Ryan," Lisa continued, gesturing to the man standing behind her.

Reluctantly, I forced my attention to Lisa and Ryan, my ears pricked for the tiniest sound, for any movement from an active five-year-old.

Lisa was a short, wide woman, flowing out of the blue sweat pants and black sweatshirt she'd probably pulled on Sunday morning and hadn't taken off since. Her blond hair was sculpted into a glossy helmet that appeared sprayed to her skull. Dark-framed glasses slid down her small nose, and she had a nervous habit of pushing them back up by the left temple. Despite her red, puffy, bloodshot eyes, her face was smooth and her skin translucent, making me wonder if her weight gain had been recent.

Ryan, as thin as a store mannequin, towered over his wife. Short graying hair lay close to his skull and his skin was sallow, as if he hadn't slept in weeks. He wore rumpled khakis and a blue button-down, with the buttons mismatched, leaving one side of the collar higher than the other.

"Thanks for coming," he said as he grasped my hand. "The police seem to have stalled. And they say that the first twenty-four hours in a kidnapping are the most important."

I repeated what I'd said on the phone. "I really don't know what I can do for you. It's well past that time period."

Ryan said, "When Lisa read that article in the paper, she was so glad to learn that you were back in the area and that you'd landed on your feet, after …" He hesitated, shrugging. "She always wondered what happened to you."

I glanced around, looking for Lisa, wondering why Ryan was talking for his wife. But she'd disappeared. "She knew you went back to Portland, but then lost track. Anyway, when she saw that article, she wanted to call you. To invite you over; to get to know you." He shrugged again. "We never did. And then this happened."

That article in the paper. A three-part, front-page story in the Lifestyle section of the Sunday edition. It had been published last month. I didn't want to be interviewed, but Dexter had lined it up for me and Kathleen, my boss, thought it was a great idea. Picture and everything, along with information about my enrollment in the Criminal Justice program at De Anza Community College in nearby Cupertino and my apprenticeship with Private Investigator Kathleen Bennett, one of Santa Cruz County's finest. The article, titled "Shelby McDougall: Local Heroine," laid out the entire case, starting with my surrogacy arrangement six years ago.

Part two of the article followed the chain of events that led to me cracking open the baby-brokering scheme and, months later, discovering skeletal remains in the crawl space under the cottage I'd lived in for four months. And part three reported on the final chapter, when I'd ended up outside of a wrecked car on a twisty Santa Cruz mountain road, frantically jiggling a catatonic infant, trying to keep the baby alive. Inside that wreck was delivery man Frankie

Browning, the monster I'd handcuffed to the steering wheel. The same man who delivered babies from intended parents Jackson and Diane Entwistle to their final destination. The man who'd become my lover and my confidante — and the psychopath who'd been hiding everything from me.

Everyone, except me, thought it was a great article. I winced when I read it. I sounded so young. So trusting. And so embarrassingly naïve.

But at least I had some sense now. When the reporter had asked if I was still involved, I'd politely shaken my head and said, "No. No way."

Until I had proof that The Stork existed, I'd keep my theories to myself.

4

"WE FOLLOWED YOU IN THE NEWS after we adopted the twins," Ryan said as he walked out of the foyer toward the living room. "When you found that skeleton and when you almost got killed." His voice fell and he glanced at his hands, clearly uncomfortable. "Lisa meant to call at a decent hour," he continued, "and we even talked about it, but she chickened out. I know she thought she would be leaving a message." He gave a small, tired smile. "I woke up to her voice on the phone."

Ryan gestured for me to sit and I maneuvered to the small sofa, pushing a pile of *People* magazines to one side. As I tucked my backpack on the floor underneath the side table, I took in the living room. It was cluttered. More than cluttered. The room was overflowing with furniture, knick-knacks, trinkets, and tchotchkes. Even though it was the middle of summer, Christmas decorations still graced the room. A wintery village of illuminated cottages, circled by a train with a red engine and three red and green cars, sat on a card table by the door to the kitchen. The thick thatch roofs of the tiny porcelain cottages were covered in fake glittery snow and a Christmas sleigh, pulled by eight miniscule reindeer, sat on a rooftop. Santa, with his sack of toys, stood next to the chimney.

Other than this homage to Christmas, there was no sign of the two almost first-graders who lived in this house. No messy jumble of kids' books was piled on the sofa. No dolls, balls, board games, hot rod cars, stuffed animals, crayons, dress-up clothes, or blocks were strewn across the floor. Not a shred of kid-sized clothing was draped over the furniture. And no colorful finger paintings or scribbles hung on the walls.

Where was she? Wouldn't a five-year-old be up by this hour, clinging to her parents for dear life? And, given the situation, wouldn't her parents be clinging to her in return, not wanting to let her out of their sight?

Ryan caught my stare and misinterpreted it. He pointed to the train set and said, "We kept that up for Justin. He liked it so much that we didn't have the heart to take it down." His voice caught.

Justin. My heart stopped. To hear his name, right from his father's mouth, made it real.

Lisa erupted into a wail. She stood in the kitchen at the sink, doubled over, arms braced against the counter for support. Ryan jumped up and reached her in a few steps, pulling her into his arms. "Shh, shh … Get a grip, baby. Okay? Shelby's here. She's going to help us."

Ryan reached around his wife and grabbed a dish towel off the counter. Lisa wiped her face and blew her nose while her husband cradled her, wrapping his arms around her from behind. With one last shaky sigh, she tossed the towel into the sink, turned around and smiled at her husband, and then at me, a thin smile that raised her round cheeks. But her eyes were panicky, and I was sure her mind was moving a million miles an hour, going all the places that were best left alone.

She surprised me, though, as she took a breath and settled her face into a steely mask. Her eyes focused. "Coffee?" she called, as if I were just a normal visitor, on a normal day.

"Sure," I replied. "But don't go out of your way."

"It's fine," she said as she opened a cabinet. "Good to have something to do."

Ryan returned to the living room and eased into one of the chairs across from me. In addition to the delicate faux-Victorian red velvet sofa where I sat and Ryan's straight-backed wooden chair, two small armchairs that matched the sofa flanked a bookshelf. Side tables, jammed with porcelain figurines, were wedged between each piece of furniture. A squat coffee table, covered with magazines and newspapers, sat in the middle of the room.

A few minutes later, Lisa appeared, holding a tray with three mugs and spoons, napkins, a sugar bowl, a coffee carafe, and a small pitcher. Ryan jumped up and tossed a pile of magazines from the coffee table to the floor. Lisa seemed composed as she set the tray down, but a slight tremble gave her away. The mugs she'd picked were cheerful things, decorated with Christmas scenes. They probably reminded her of happier times. One of the mugs sported a bright-eyed snowman chomping on a corn cob pipe, wearing a straw hat and striped scarf. Green sleighs and red holly berries ringed another. Dr. Seuss-like Christmas trees, with crooked tops and shiny silver ornaments, were stamped on the third mug.

"We love Christmas," Lisa stated, picking up the carafe and filling the snowman mug. She handed it to me, gesturing toward the sugar and cream.

Smiling, I accepted the coffee and waved off the extras. In between sips, I noticed the Thomas Kinkade paintings. There must have been three dozen of them. Landscapes of homey cottages nestled in mist-covered valleys hung so close to each other that the frames almost touched. Paintings from Kinkade's Disney Dreams series, great moments from classic animated Disney movies, like *Bambi, The Lion King,* and *Beauty and the Beast,* covered the opposite wall.

I recognized them all. During my first semester of college, when I was sure that I wanted to surround myself with art and the people who created it, the only art-related job I could find was working as an associate in a Thomas Kinkade gallery. I'd lasted exactly a month before the gallery went under and took my job along with it.

Lisa caught me staring. "You like him?"

I nodded. "Yes," I replied, "I do."

That was no lie. In spite of myself, I did.

She smiled. Her entire face lit up, as if she'd won the lottery. This might have been her first smile in days. "I knew I would like you," she said.

Smiling in return, I reached over to put my coffee cup down on the end table next to me, finding an open spot between a Bambi figurine and a small Disney castle.

Hands shaking, Lisa picked up her mug. Coffee sloshed from the top, staining her blue sweats. She started to cry, tears coursing down her cheeks in unashamed streams.

"Shh, baby. It's okay." Ryan reached over and deftly took the mug from her hands and put it back on the tray. He handed her a napkin, and then turned toward me, saying, "We need help. We have a team working with us; they'll be here at eight-thirty." He glanced at his watch. "They asked to camp out here twenty-four seven, but we just couldn't handle that. So we compromised and have the officer on the porch. They say there's a pair of undercover detectives watching the house, but we haven't discovered them yet. They must be very good.

"I know they've tapped the phone," he added.

I flinched. I didn't want to end up on their short list of suspects.

"Don't worry," he reassured me. "We called on our cell phone."

Nodding, my mind already racing ahead, wondering how this would turn out, I picked up my mug. "Is your daughter home?"

Lisa pointed upstairs. "She's asleep. Napping."

But a low voice, as sophisticated and sultry as Ingrid Bergman's in *Casablanca*, contradicted her. "No, I'm not, Lisa. I'm right here."

"Justine, she's your mother. Call her Mommy please," Ryan said sharply. At the same time, Lisa said, "Justine, honey? You need to go back upstairs."

Justine? I held my breath and craned my neck, emotions seesawing between excitement and dread. I wanted, needed, had, to see her.

"But I'm not sleepy," she said. "You know that. I'm never sleepy. Besides, I want to see who you're talking to." The voice drew closer.

Years ago, I'd spent hours dreaming of this moment. Wondering what it would be like. Wondering if I'd feel an instinctual pull, the primal force, the genetic connection between me and the babies I'd given birth to. The babies I'd given up for adoption.

I was about to find out.

5

A CHILD ENTERED THE ROOM, head high, shoulders back, posture and poise as perfect as a queen's. She stopped right in front of me, her toes almost touching mine, and looked directly at me.

Without hesitating, she asked, "Are you going to find my brother?"

The child resembled me in some ways; but in others, not at all. Her coloring was fair, like mine, and freckles spread across her nose and cheeks like an accent, whereas on me, they were the main show. Our hair was the same: thick, chestnut locks. Hers frizzed past her shoulders to the middle of her back, while mine was shoulder-length, just long enough to pull into a ponytail. Our noses were similar; classic Roman schnozzes, supposedly a sign of a headstrong personality. And her body was just like mine at that age — squat and stocky.

But it was her eyes that grabbed my attention. They were nothing like mine, a blue that was remarkable only in the right light. Instead of a solid pigmentation, both of Justine's eyes were rings of color — amber, brown, gray, green, hazel — circling a yellow-brown pupil that glistened, cat-like. Predatory. The effect was both unsettling and bewitching. I found myself staring.

I remember wondering, in the muddled days of my pregnancy, who the twins would look like. I'd hoped and dreamed that they would look more like me than Jackson, the intended father. But on the night Diane had almost killed me, the night she'd spilled everything, she'd told me, her cold voice touched with pride, that Jackson was not the biological father. My eggs had not been fertilized with his sperm. The vial had been switched out at the fertility clinic, replaced.

Still staring at Justine, I could see this truth. There was nothing of Jackson Entwistle in this child.

"Are you?" she repeated.

I swallowed, surprised to find myself almost speechless. "Am I what?" I couldn't even remember what she was asking.

"Going to find my brother," she repeated.

"I'll try," I blurted. I wanted so much to please her.

"You didn't say who you were." It was hard to believe this child was the same age as Megan's daughter, Annie, a bubbly kindergartner who could only sit still when she was in front of the TV.

"I'm a friend of your parents," I said. "My name is Shelby."

"But I've never seen you before," the child protested.

"I've been away."

"Oh, okay." Justine drew her pink terrycloth bathrobe around her and pulled her tiny foot out of her sheepskin slipper. Still studying me, she rubbed the top of her foot against the calf of her other leg. She hadn't blinked.

She slipped her foot back into the slipper and shifted her head. The spell was broken.

"Bye." She waved at me as she turned around and walked toward the front hall and the stairs.

"Bye."

Sweat had collected under my arms and my shirt stuck to my back. I was disappointed. Ridiculously disappointed. The connection I'd yearned for hadn't materialized. No sparks. No fireworks. No Hallmark moment. The child had no clue who I was.

"She's a bit unusual," Lisa offered. Her husband shot her a look I couldn't read. "There's something different about them," she continued. "When they were three, we put them in day care, but it didn't work. They don't get along with other children. They're very much their own unit." Her smooth brow furrowed as she glanced at her husband. "They're actually not very good with other kids. The director asked them to leave because they refused to participate in the group."

But Ryan shook his head, contradicting her. "It's those other parents," he said. "They're way too protective. At some point, children have to learn that it's a tough world out there."

I wondered what had really happened and how difficult it would be to find out.

"The director, who said she was an early childhood expert," Ryan air quoted the word "expert", "recommended that we take them to a psychologist. For testing. After we tried two more day care centers with the same results, we did. We could barely afford it. Those tests ran us several thousand dollars."

Justine's voice, coming from somewhere out in the hall, interrupted. "That man wasn't very nice to me, Ryan," she said.

"Justine," Lisa said, "please go back upstairs," just as Ryan interjected that his name was Daddy, not Ryan.

"Okay," the child sighed, petulant. But I didn't hear any movement.

Lisa compressed her lips into a thin, straight line. "Can you take her to her room?" she asked Ryan.

Ryan nodded, stood, and put his hands in the pockets of his khakis. "You'll tell Shelby everything?" His eyes were fixed on his wife's. "All of it?"

Lisa bobbed her head in agreement, and Ryan turned, saying, "Come on, Justine. Upstairs."

Two pairs of feet climbed the stairs. As soon as the footsteps receded, Lisa leaned over to me. Her lips were drawn thin and her eyes were hooded.

"What do you want to tell me?" I asked, as gently as I could.

"The psychologist basically told me my kids were freaks." She spat out the word "freaks" as if it were a piece of rotten food. "Justine's IQ is two hundred and ninety and Justin's is three hundred. Do you know what percentage of the population has that kind of IQ? Zero. No one. And I have two of them?" She leaned closer. "He told me that Justin and Justine were unusually gifted. That they had no chance at a normal life in school, in relationships, in work. In anything.

"He wanted to work with them, but we said no." She gestured to the cramped room. "Look at us. We're about as normal as you can get." As her eyes wandered to the Christmas train, she added, "Maybe a bit fixated on Christmas, but otherwise pretty normal.

"I had to quit my job as a medical receptionist, so we're living on Ryan's salary as the service manager at the Toyota dealership. It's tight. They need things. Our biggest expense is books. Those two demand books. Books, books, books. They are reading books for college kids. Advanced math. Science. Philosophy. Justine's reading the dictionary for the umpteenth time."

I didn't see a book in the room and wondered if Lisa read at all.

"Sometimes they talk to each other in a code that sounds like gibberish to me. And they don't sleep," Lisa confided. "I've given up. I used to think that maybe they slept a few hours every night. But now, I think they don't sleep at all. At first, Ryan and I would take shifts. Four hours each, so that one of us would always be awake with them. Last year, we gave up. Now, we go to sleep at ten and get up at six. Lord knows what they do all night. The computer is in our room, so I know they don't use that. For all we know, they might be out wandering the neighborhood.

"We took them to the doctor. Perfectly healthy, he said. Said he'd never heard of anyone not sleeping." She sighed. "It was almost like he thought we were making it up."

She sat back and picked up her mug, holding it with both hands. "And they want to eat all the time. Protein. Half-cooked meat." She shuddered, shifting her mug to her right hand and gesturing to her midsection with her left. "Look at me. Before we adopted them, I was tiny. Petite. Fit. But now, I've given up. I can't exercise. I'm with them all day. I eat, I worry, I eat. I used to have friends. And now, it's just me and them."

Lisa took a sip of her coffee, put the mug back down, and placed her hand on my knee, as if pulling me toward her. "The questions," she continued. "They're always asking questions. Always those 'Why?' questions that are impossible to answer. One starts, the other picks it up, and they go back and forth like they're playing ping-pong. But real questions, not typical *why-is-the-sky-blue* type questions. Justin once asked me to explain why Einstein integers are unique factorization domains. 'Huh?' That's what I said to him. I had no idea what he was talking about." She gave me a wan smile. "I still don't, even after I Googled it."

"Never heard of it," I interjected.

"When they were one," she went on, "just twelve months old, they could recite the alphabet. Backwards. I'd never even mentioned the word 'alphabet' to them. They learned to read when they were two. We never got to read them baby books. Justin laughed when I tried to read *Goodnight Moon* to him." She teared up again, pulled a tissue from the pocket of her sweats, and dabbed her eyes.

"But they're my babies," she said, gulping back a sob. "I love them. I want my Justin back."

I paused, trying to wrap my head around what I'd just heard. Geniuses. Oddballs. Freaks. I asked, "Did you ever notice anyone following you? Or watching your children with unusual interest?"

Lisa blew her nose. "No. Nothing. Once people overheard Justin and Justine talking, they tried not to stare. But people were curious. Curious in the way someone would be of zoo animals. They'd watch them, fixated, and then look away really fast when they saw me staring back.

"One time, I caught this woman watching us. She was around my mother's age. We were at the playground just down the street. She came up and gave me her card. She said she was a psychiatrist."

"Do you remember her name?"

She shook her head. "No. I threw the card out right away. I didn't want my children to be studied like they were scientific experiments."

"What did she look like?"

"I don't know," Lisa replied, shaking her head. "Gray hair. Glasses. Nothing remarkable."

"How long ago was this?"

Lisa stared up at the ceiling. "Maybe six months?"

"Did she say how she knew about your kids?"

"No," Lisa replied. "I assumed she was from the same office as the psychologist we'd been to."

"Can I get the name of the office?"

"Sure." Lisa stood, walked to the kitchen, and returned with a business card. "You can take it. I have another."

I glanced at it, a name and phone number only. I slipped it into my back pocket. "Anyone else you can remember?" I leaned in, placing my elbows on my knees.

"No. No one."

"What about your husband? Would he remember anyone?"

Shaking her head, she replied, "No. Ryan never, ever takes the kids out without me. He gets overwhelmed."

I sat back. "I don't know what I can do," I said. "It seems so, so …" my voice trailed off.

"Hopeless?" Lisa started to cry again and just for a second, I wished she'd rage instead. Scream. Howl. Throw things.

"I'm sorry," I said.

We sat in silence for a few minutes, and I stared at a photo hanging on the wall across the room, right next to a Kinkade sunset. The twins were infants and they lay curled next to each other in a crib. One of them, presumably Justin, was cocooned in a blue blanket with a blue nylon cap squinched on his head. The other was wrapped in the same style, burrito-fashion, but in a pink blanket with a pink hat. Their milky blue eyes were wide open, taking in the world.

The phone rang and Lisa rose, walking as quickly as she could to grab the receiver off the wall in the kitchen.

Where had that genius IQ come from? Not from me, certainly. I was about as average in intelligence as you could get. Math problems were as incomprehensible to me as a foreign language. Philosophy? Never could understand it. Sometimes, even trying to decipher a newspaper article from *The Wall Street Journal* or *The New York Times* seemed out of my league.

A few minutes later, Lisa returned to the living room, barely containing her tears.

"Everything okay?" I asked.

Lisa shook her head. "The team is on their way. They'll be here soon. Bringing the FBI. Again." Her voice rose. "They'll be here all day. The FBI guy asks so many questions. He sits here and waits. Watches.

"And I'm such a wreck, that every time I talk to them, I remember something else. I know they think I'm lying about something. But I just can't remember. Everything is such a jumble." She dissolved into sobs.

I looked at her, wishing I knew her well enough to offer a hug. Instead, I asked, "They can't possibly think you had anything to do with this, do they?"

Lisa shook her head, muttering, "I don't know." She blew her nose, and looked at me, pleading, tears streaming down her face. "Please," she said. "Please. Find Justin for us. Just find him."

"I'll try," I replied. Lisa fought back tears.

"I'll try," I repeated, wondering if I was trying to convince myself as much as I was trying to reassure her.

6

A T THAT MOMENT, RYAN ENTERED THE ROOM, hands shoved in his pockets, back rounded, shoulders down; defeated, tired, bewildered. "She's fine," he said before Lisa had a chance to speak. "Back in her chair, reading the dictionary." He gave a tired smile and shrugged. "Her favorite thing to do." His voice trailed off and he sank down onto the sofa next to me.

"Will you help us, Shelby?" he asked.

"I'll try," I said, echoing my earlier statement. "I don't know what I can do, but I'll try." I hesitated, and then added, "Before I go, would it be possible for me to talk to Justine? To see what she remembers?"

"Sure. The police have already interviewed her," Ryan said. "She says she went to the bathroom and when she came back, Justin was gone." Ryan sighed, stood, passed a hand over his face in utter exhaustion, and extended his hand to his wife.

I wondered why she wouldn't have woken her parents.

The house was quiet now; the din outside had diminished. The refrigerator kicked on, sounding unusually loud. I wondered if the house was always this still. On a regular day, would Lisa be playing music, have the TV on, be chatting on the phone? She'd already told me she had no friends. But where was the extended family? The heavy weight of this silence, the absence of quick footsteps, chatter, and small, excited voices would be a constant reminder of what was missing.

A single carpeted hallway ran the length of the second story. The walls were adorned with family photos, from the two infants wrapped in their hospital pink and blue blankets with matching hats, to a recent one of the four members of the Boyd family posing in front of a staged fireplace. The last photo in the series showed Justin and Justine, arms linked, standing between two oversized crayons. They looked like preppie twins: Justin wore chinos, a lime polo shirt, and topsiders. Justine was dressed in a knee-length khaki skirt, a yellow polo shirt, and black flats. Brother and sister were mirror images of each other, with the same fair skin, chestnut hair, and compact body.

"When was that taken?" I asked.

"Just a month ago," Lisa said. "We go to the photo studio at Sears once a month. Sometimes we're in it, but most of the time, it's just the two of them." She gazed at the picture wistfully. "I like that one. The photographer did a nice job. Justin looked like that. So, so," she seemed at a loss for words, "confident," she finally said.

I stopped by the photo, absorbing every detail. Truth be told, the twins looked like adults and nothing like their actual age. In all the photos I'd taken or seen of Annie, her age was always obvious. Her rounded cheeks and lingering baby fat gave her away, as did her cautious grin and tiny teeth, her wispy hair clasped with a plastic pink headband, and her awkward proportions.

But Justin and Justine had none of that little kid charm. Justin looked just like his sister; same stocky body, same serious demeanor, same nose. Same hair, just shorter, styled in a Supercuts standard male cut. Same cat-like, predatory eyes. They both stared directly at the photographer, with lips drawn back in a forced smile that revealed a full set of glistening white teeth.

I turned as Ryan rapped his knuckles against one of the closed doors, while at the same time turning the handle. "Justine, honey," he said, "our friend would like to talk to you."

"Come in," a bored voice replied.

The girl sat in a pint-sized red armchair in front of the window. A matching brown armchair was right next to it. A child's bed, with a bright pink quilt pushed down to the foot, was in the far corner of the room. Another small bed, against the opposite wall, was made up with a dark orange quilt. Two dressers, both piled with books, were placed against the wall between the beds. A framed poster of the number pi, with the first digits in huge numerals, growing smaller down the poster until almost invisible, hung above the dresser I assumed was Justin's. A second framed poster, titled "Periodic Table of World Literature," with images of authors from around the globe and throughout history, hung above the other dresser. The remaining wall space was lined with bookshelves. Shelf after shelf of books, just like the public library. Not a single toy or stuffed animal in the room.

Justine stared at us as we entered. She looked so adult that I almost expected her to whip off a pair of reading glasses. A thick hard-covered book dominated her lap and I wondered how she had wrestled it up to the chair.

The child looked past me, at her mother. Her ringed eyes seemed to suck in the available light. "Lisa," she said, "did you bring me some food? I'm hungry."

"You just ate, before Shelby got here," Ryan said. "Remember? Two eggs, toast, bacon. After you talk to Shelby you can get your own food. There's plenty to eat in the fridge."

"Your mother is not your slave," he continued. "And you call her Mom."

Justine stared at him as he spoke and then turned her attention to me. "You're a friend of Ryan and Lisa's?" she asked.

"Yup." I sat on the floor in front of the chair, putting me closer to her level.

"I've never seen you before." She repeated what she'd said downstairs. I wondered if her genius took a literalist bent, where things always had to make sense and fit together in a logical stream.

"I've been away," I answered as I pointed to her book. "What are you reading?"

She angled the book down. "The dictionary," she said. I could see the two columns, the small text, and the indents in the paper along the edge where the letters were embossed.

"You read that a lot?" I asked.

She shrugged. "Sometimes."

"Do you ever read anything on the computer?"

She rolled her eyes. "When I can. Justin is always on the computer."

"What does he like to look at on the computer?"

"He found some college websites where the professors had posted their assignments. He was studying."

"Studying what?" I asked. It was hard to wrap my mind around the fact that these kids weren't even six.

"Math," she said.

"Did he ever talk to people on the computer? By typing?"

"No." There was no hesitation. "Justin doesn't like people very much."

"I see." I turned around, toward Ryan and Lisa. "Can I look at the computer? I want to find the websites Justin visited."

"Sorry," Ryan answered. "The police already took it."

Trying to conceal my disappointment, I turned back to Justine and asked, "So what happened on Sunday? Can you tell me?"

7

"THAT BED IS MINE." She pointed to the bed with the frilly pink quilt. "And that one," she gestured across the room to the bed with the dark orange blanket and pillow, "is Justin's. Every night at ten, Ryan and Lisa come in to say goodnight and close the curtains. After they leave, we read or talk." She glanced at the dictionary, eyes moving. "That night, we read until three or four. We like to rest a little before dawn."

Lisa gently kneed me in the back, her unspoken confirmation of how little her children actually slept.

"We got in our beds, and then I realized we hadn't turned off the light. I went to turn it off, and decided to go to the bathroom." She stopped and looked at us.

"Then what happened?" I prompted.

She looked back at the book in her lap. "When I came back, Justin was gone."

"Did you hear anything?"

"No," she replied, "not a thing."

"Why didn't you get your parents?"

She gave Lisa a sidelong look as she said, "I just figured Justin had gone out for a walk. Ryan and Lisa have forbidden it, but we do it anyway."

I turned around and glanced at Lisa who was giving her husband an *I-told-you-so* look.

Still looking at Ryan and Lisa, I asked, "How do you know Justin hadn't gone for a walk and been …?"

My voice trailed off and Ryan said, "We found a rag at the bottom of the stairs."

Justine continued, "So I lay back down and picked up my book. Then it started to get light and I realized that the red eye was gone."

"What's that? The red eye?"

"Justin used to make fun of me for talking about it," Justine said. "Some nights, I would see a red light on the top of the bookshelf. I called it that, the red eye, because it sounded more dramatic. It was over there." She pointed to the bookcase across the room. "But whoever took Justin took that also."

I stood and spied an adult-sized wooden chair next to the door. "May I?" I asked.

Ryan nodded and I pushed the chair to the bookshelf and then climbed up on it. I peered at the top shelf and turned around, asking, "Do you have a flashlight?"

"Sure," Lisa replied. "There's one by my side of the bed. Ryan, can you grab it?"

Ryan nodded as he left the room, throwing a confused look in my direction. When he returned, he handed me a slender flashlight. "Here you go."

I switched it on. The compressed plywood bookshelf had been painted white. "How often do you dust?" I asked, playing the light across the smooth surface.

"Dust?" Lisa looked bewildered and stared at her husband. "Dust?"

"When was the last time you dusted up here?"

She returned my question with one of her own. "Never? I don't dust, ever. At all."

"There's no dust on the shelf. Someone wiped it clean." I turned the light off and climbed down. "What was up there?" I asked.

Without looking up from the dictionary, Justine sighed and said, "It was a teddy bear. When its eyes lit up, they were red. Hence, the term 'the red eye'. I assumed that Lisa set up a nanny cam so she could watch us." She glared at her mother.

Ryan and I turned to Lisa, who was shaking her head vigorously. "I didn't do that. I would never do that. And besides, I never even noticed it."

Ryan chimed in, "Me neither."

I crouched in front of Justine, asking, "What did the teddy bear look like?"

"A teddy bear. Brown. Fuzzy. Cute. I didn't pay much attention since I figured Lisa had put it there. It just showed up one day."

"Mom," Ryan interjected. "She's your mother. Call her Mom."

"Do you remember when?" I asked. "That might be important."

"I do," Justine replied, nodding solemnly. "About a month ago. The day we went to get our picture taken at Sears. It wasn't there when we left, but it was there when we got back."

"You didn't tell your parents about it?"

Justine shook her head, clearly irritated. "No. I told you. Sometimes Lisa just does that. Puts things in here. It was too high up for me to reach anyway. I thought it was just for show."

"When did you see the red light?"

"At first, it seemed to be on all the time, but then it stopped and I kind of forgot about it."

I nodded. "If I come back tomorrow and show you some pictures of teddy bears, can you show me one that matches?"

"Sure," she answered, returning to her dictionary. "Whatever."

"Attitude," Ryan warned.

"What word are you learning?" I asked, more for conversation than anything else.

"Telophase."

The word stirred a vague recollection of high school biology.

She lifted her head and gazed at me, reciting, "From the Greek *télos*, end, and *phaínō*, stage. One. The final stage of mitosis in which the spindle disappears and two new nuclei appear each with a set of chromosomes. Two. A stage in meiosis that is usually the final stage …"

Ryan interrupted her with a sharp, "Enough," but Justine ignored him and continued, her voice high and clear, her mysterious eyes fixed on mine: "… the final stage in the first and second meiotic divisions that may be missing in the first and that is characterized by formation of the nuclear membrane and by changes in coiling and arrangement of the chromosomes.

"Next word," she continued. "*Télos.* Greek. An ultimate end."

She actually smiled.

Back in the living room, as I reached over to pick up my backpack, I said, "Is it okay if I come back tomorrow with some photos of nanny cam bears? I don't know if identifying the bear will get us any closer to anything, but you have to start somewhere.

"You should also tell the police to dust the shelf for fingerprints. And, it would also help to know the date you went to Sears. So we can figure out how long the bear was in your house."

I gave a half-hearted smile, feeling like a fraud. I knew the type of bear wouldn't matter. The date wouldn't matter either.

Truth be told, I had to see Justine again.

•   •   •

It was almost eight-thirty when I left the house. The police officer guarding the porch gave me a curt nod. A few news crews remained, packing up gear. The lawn was trampled, strewn with bits of trash. No one bothered me. The reporters must have filed their stories and left to scout out the next tragedy.

Tears collected in the corners of my eyes and I scrubbed my face with my hand. The connection I'd dreamed of for years had been just that, a dream, a fantasy, a product of my overactive imagination. There was no instant recognition, no magnetic attraction, no feeling of completeness. It was as if I'd just met a random child on the street. The child of a stranger.

But time would surely change things. I could cling to that.

The sun was already bright and the day hot. A heavy, expectant silence hung in street, leaving me open and exposed. I walked to the end of the block and turned the corner, imagining the neighbors staring at me from behind their drawn curtains.

I sat in the car, my right hand poised in midair above the ignition. With my other hand, I yanked down the visor to try to block the light reflecting off the paint on the hood of the car. It didn't work. I started the car and opened the window. A breeze came in, stirring my hair, and I pressed the switch to open the passenger window. I drove slowly through the development, thinking.

The children I had given birth to were geniuses. Beyond geniuses. Savants, child prodigies. Miracles. Or freaks, depending on how you looked at it.

A hundred years ago children like that would have ended up in a sideshow tent. In today's world, they might enter graduate school by the time they were ten, have their PhDs by the time they were fourteen, and change the world by the time they were twenty. The media would pursue them, relentlessly. Their lives would be public, and the public would be vicious. How could someone parent these kids?

And how could they have come from me?

I stopped at a corner, waiting until a young mother holding the hand of a toddler reached the other side of the street. They walked slowly, the woman's steps matching the small steps of the child next to her. Once they reached the opposite sidewalk, the toddler stopped abruptly and squat down, heels square to the curb. The mom bent over, and they peered toward the ground, likely examining the wonders of an ant or a stink bug. I was sure that Lisa had never done that with her kids.

At the next red light, I picked up my water bottle, unscrewed the cap, and took a swig. The water, bitter and warm from sitting too long in the steel container, made my stomach churn.

8

I ARRIVED AT WORK BY NINE-THIRTY. My boss, private investigator Kathleen Bennett, worked out of an office in a two-story building by the Santa Cruz harbor. It was an unlikely spot for a private investigator to set up shop, but as Kathleen pointed out, an office was just an office. Why not be located in a nice place? And this office, on the building's second story above a café and restaurant, overlooking the beach and harbor mouth, fit that bill. When I was sick of the computer, I'd take a quick walk. There was nothing like sand, surf, and salt air to clear your head.

Usually I walked to work, a fifteen-minute stroll from home, but today I had to maneuver the tight, practically full parking lot.

Tourists, I thought as I followed someone slowly inching through the lot in an enormous van. I found a spot in the upper harbor, a good five minute walk from where I needed to be. As I fed the meter, I made a mental note to return at lunchtime to put in more change.

My heart started to flutter as I crossed the lot. Craning my neck, I looked for Cody's car. Cody. My current, burning crush. I met him every morning at the coffee kiosk, a small shack at the edge of the parking lot. Our break was not at all scripted and, at this stage in our relationship, we didn't make plans. But Cody didn't know that I watched for him. I only left the office for my morning break when his green and white Sheriff's cruiser pulled into the lot.

Today I got lucky. He was already here.

I waved as I drew close, shouting, "Hey, Cody, over here."

He waved in return and pointed to the cup sitting next to him on the bench. "Hi, Shelby. How are you?" He gestured to the long line. "I decided to save you the wait. Black coffee, right?"

"Perfect. Thank you," I said as I sat down next to him. I didn't know what Sheriff's Deputy Cody Wilson knew about me. I'd told him the basics: that I was a student at De Anza Community College studying Criminal Justice and that I worked for Kathleen as an apprentice. He knew about my brother, my parents, and Megan. I hadn't told him my age. With thirty in sight, it wasn't something I shared willingly.

I'd also skated over my past. He hadn't mentioned that article in the paper and I wouldn't either. For now, anyway. Details like that might scare a person off.

Cody was mostly unknown to me, too. About six months ago, he'd transferred to Santa Cruz County from Fresno County in the Central Valley. His patrol assignment stretched from Live Oak, an unincorporated area just outside of the Santa Cruz city limits, south to the Monterey county line. I knew he took his job seriously. Even though the harbor was not in his jurisdiction, Cody was always on duty. Always scanning, watching.

I'd met Cody earlier in the summer when I'd waited in line behind him and found myself admiring the cut of his khaki shirt, how it strained across his broad shoulders. After he'd paid and picked up his coffee, I'd snuck sidelong glances, noticing his crew cut, as short as a Marine's, his brown eyes, a cleft in his chin, and dimples so pronounced that they showed themselves when he spoke. The man was bulky, as if he lifted weights, but not dense in the way of a serious bodybuilder.

"How's your day going?" he asked. "Are you just getting in?"

I nodded, cradling the warm paper cup between my hands. "I had an appointment this morning."

He looked at me, concern in his eyes. "Everything okay?"

"Yes, fine." I removed the plastic lid from the cup and blew on the hot liquid. My visit to Watsonville would also be my secret. "How are you?"

"Good, I've been on shift since six this morning."

"Anything exciting?"

Cody glanced at me and shook his head. "Nothing. I helped a mom with a stalled car who was trying to get her two kids to camp. That's about it. Otherwise," he set his coffee on the bench between us and stretched his arms along the back, "just keeping the public safe." He grinned. His radio crackled and he cocked his ear, listening. What sounded like gibberish to me must have meant something to him, for he leapt up, saying, "Gotta go, Shelby. I'll see you tomorrow?"

"Okay," I said, but he'd already taken off. I stood, noticing his coffee. "Cody," I yelled, "Cody?" But he was gone.

I tossed his cup into the nearest trash can, grabbed mine, walked over to my building, and headed up the outdoor stairs. Due to the high transient population and the ever-present tourists, the door at the top of the steps was locked with a security system that involved a badge and a keypad.

The building housed a collection of people who had enough money to afford a beach view and who preferred to work alone: two attorneys, a graphic designer, a CPA and bookkeeper team, and two software engineers — plus me and my boss and mentor, P.I. Kathleen Bennett.

Her large office was at the far end of the hall, on the beach side. Mine, directly across the hall from hers, was much smaller and had a view of the parking lot.

When I'd moved back to Santa Cruz, I'd directed my life to a new track, one that was impractical, difficult, and expensive. For the second time, I enrolled in college. I already had a Bachelor's in Art History. But my years in the arts were well behind me. I could get excited by an art exhibit, inspired even, but I no longer felt the urge to dig deep and unearth every last nuance about the artist and their paintings. My visceral need to understand art, relate to it, own it, and share it: all gone, wiped clean when that gun was pointed at me and my mouth was sealed with duct tape. Art seemed irrelevant. Catching criminals didn't.

I'd thought about enrolling in the police academy, but knew I was already too old. Instead, I wanted to be a private investigator. I wanted to catch bad guys. I wanted to find missing people, serve papers, assist with court cases, ferret out fraud, follow people, and find people. And I wanted to do it in California, a state with extremely difficult licensing requirements.

The timing for my career move had worked out perfectly. Dexter had just signed a lease on a two-bedroom apartment he couldn't really afford. And Megan was a student at the university in Santa Cruz, living in family student housing, somehow making it work as a full-time student and a single mom.

When I'd interviewed with Kathleen, I had four quarters of criminal justice courses under my belt, plus a two-month internship the previous summer at the San Jose police department. I thought I knew everything.

The day had been hot, and I remembered the tug of my blouse against my skin as I drove to her office in my car with the barely functioning air conditioner. When I walked into Kathleen's building, I immediately excused myself to use the restroom and dab tendrils of sweat from the back of my neck and my face.

Her handshake had been firm; her offer of a glass of water a godsend.

"Please," I'd replied, plucking an imaginary thread from my skirt. Nerves.

"So you're Shelby McDougall," Kathleen had said, sizing me up.

I nodded slowly.

"That was quite a case," she said as she shook her head and picked up a pen. Holding it between her hands, she twirled it, clicking it on and off. On and off.

"I often wondered about you," she said as she stared at me. "Dumb luck or something more?"

I blushed, but managed to smile and shrug. I knew people thought that. I could tell by the way they looked at me, with a mixture of awe, doubt, and disbelief. But here was someone who was asking me outright less than a minute into our conversation.

"You could have gotten killed."

"I almost did." I said, and then added, "Twice."

Kathleen stood, walked around to the front of the desk, and leaned back against it, just a few feet from me. I realized she was older than I'd originally thought. Maybe in her sixties, maybe as old as my dad. But, unlike Dad, this woman was fit, in tip-top shape, with a strong, tough demeanor. Someone with enough experience to know when she was being fed a pile of shit.

Kathleen stared down at me as she spoke. "I'm retired from the Gilroy police department. I've been a private investigator for ten years now, so you can figure out how old I am, if you know how the retirement system works in most police departments around here. I thought I'd seen it all and then I heard your story.

"Did you leave California? After?"

"I did," I replied. "Went back to Portland. To my parents. Came back here a few years ago. I worked and established residency and as soon as I could, I enrolled at De Anza in the Criminal Justice program. I want to be a P.I."

"Why not a cop?" Kathleen asked.

I smiled. "By the time I decided on my career change, I was too old. Besides, I'm not sure about wearing a gun. I don't like them."

Kathleen didn't smile in return, but nodded slowly. "Well, those are good enough reasons, I suppose. I don't carry a gun, though I do have a license and have a gun safe here in the office. If you are successful at jumping through all the hoops and completing all the apprenticeship hours for your license, a gun is something you'll have to consider."

After a pause, she leaned in, saying, "So tell me how you did it."

By the time I finished my lengthy story, I was a sweaty, strung out wreck. I laid out everything, starting when I signed my surrogacy contract with Jackson and Diane Entwistle and relocated to Santa Cruz, and continued to the fertility treatments and the pregnancy, my move to the cottage on Jackson and Diane's property, the growing pile of clues I was too dense and too trusting to read, to the night it all came down. I continued with my spectacular act two, finding the bones under the cottage where I'd been living, falling in love with Frankie, who I didn't know was connected to Jackson and Diane, and then discovering the truth in one horrible moment —

His gun aimed at me; the butt of the pistol as it slammed into my face; the stuffy truck, reeking of sweat and cigarette smoke; the tape, slick with saliva and fear, covering my mouth. The way my shoulders burned, shackled to the door handle.

Then, I'd launched into my current hobbies: trolling the internet, my suspicions about The Stork, my spreadsheet.

Kathleen had interrupted me a few times. Once to brew some coffee. The second time to pour two cups. And the third time for a bathroom break.

When I was finally done, two hours later, she looked straight at me, her eyes clear. "You're hired."

"I am?" I must have looked surprised, Kathleen had laughed.

"I'll set you up for a test run. If it works out, you can continue to work me for me as long as it's mutually beneficial to both of us." She'd extended her hand and I'd shaken in agreement.

9

K ATHLEEN'S DOOR WAS CLOSED AND I KNOCKED, mindful of her privacy.

"Who is it?" An unusual greeting for Kathleen, usually she was all business — she'd drop whatever she was doing, come to the door, and open it.

But given the hour, she probably figured it was just me.

"It's Shelby," I replied.

"Come on in."

I pushed the door open and slipped in. Kathleen sat at her desk, staring at her laptop. "How are you?" she asked, glancing up.

I shrugged and gestured to the chair in front of her. "Do you have a minute?"

She threw me a puzzled look. "Sure. Have a seat."

As I sipped my coffee, I filled her in on the recent events, from the early morning phone call on the backup cell to my visit to the

Boyd's. When I reached the part about the nanny cam, Kathleen put up her hand, saying, "Hang on a sec." She stood, quickly walked to the closet next to the safe, and opened it. She muttered to herself as she pushed aside hangers and rummaged through boxes. Seconds later, with a triumphant "ah-ha," she emerged, holding a teddy bear in her right hand.

"Here's one of those nanny cam bears," she said as she walked toward me with the cuddly bear. It was golden brown, about a foot tall, with stiff arms and legs that were permanently splayed outward. The bear wore a red sweater embroidered with an off-white heart pattern. Button eyes and a smile stitched into the white muzzle promised innocence.

"The camera lens is behind the right eye," Kathleen said, pointing, "and the microphones are concealed behind the paws." She handed me the bear.

It was soft and fuzzy, just like a regular teddy bear. No sharp edges. No extra weight. In fact, I couldn't even tell that the stuffed animal hid a recording device so sophisticated it could be used by Homeland Security.

I held it up and stared.

"You can't tell, can you?" Kathleen asked.

"No, not at all." I turned it over and examined the bottom, asking, "What does it have inside?"

"For starters, it has an HD camera that captures a one hundred forty-five degree view of a room. The camera adjusts to any light level, including night. Its range is about fifty feet, so it can easily get an entire room. In addition, the bear has an audio setup that would rival any serious mixing studio. The microphones can pick up sounds up to fifty feet away. You can set it up wirelessly so it sends the recording over a network. It also records to an internal SD card."

"Does it have a timer?"

She threw me a surprised glance. "You haven't had the tech class yet, have you?"

"Nope," I replied with a small smile.

"It's got a sensor, like a security light in your back yard at night," Kathleen explained. "When there's movement within the field of view the camera switches on. It records until there's no activity in the field for three minutes, which I believe, is configurable."

"Someone really wanted to watch those kids, didn't they?" I asked.

Kathleen nodded. "They must have. And they probably did, until the battery died.

"So the girl said the bear was removed the night her brother went missing?" she asked.

"Yes," I replied. "She was very definitive on that point." I sipped my coffee. "Can I borrow it and show it to her?"

Kathleen shrugged. "Not sure what difference that will make, but sure. You can get these things all over the internet. If you're really tech savvy, you can build your own. Obviously, someone knew what they were doing."

"Would it be possible to figure out where the video was sent?"

"I doubt it," Kathleen replied. "Whoever it was wouldn't have used the Boyd's wireless connection. They probably just connected to the cell phone network." She paused. "Were you able to get anything from the computer?"

"I couldn't look at it," I said. "The police had already taken it. Justine said that her brother looked for websites where college professors posted course work. For advanced math."

"Wow," Kathleen muttered. "Wow." Shaking her head, she glanced at her laptop, and then asked, "You're on track to finish those background checks today?"

I nodded. Kathleen had an ongoing contract with a tech company to screen all potential employees. Doing a background check was like surfing the internet, but with tools that took me a layer deeper than what was on the surface. I could ferret out decades-old infractions and photos that would make a mother blush. Digital footprints could never be deleted. If you knew how to look, they'd turn up, eventually.

Kathleen's desk phone rang, and she picked it up, saying, "Kathleen Bennett, P.I. One moment please." Placing her hand over the receiver, she said to me, "I need to take this. Can you get your laptop on your own? Borrow the bear if you want.

"And check your email. I forwarded you something."

I nodded as I reached in my pack, fished out the backup cell, and placed it on her desk. A few minutes later, I was in my office, having retrieved my laptop from Kathleen's safe. Every day, at the end of the day, I uploaded my files to Kathleen's secure network where they were encrypted, backed up, and automatically deleted from the laptop. I then locked the machine in the safe. Kathleen took no chances.

While my laptop booted and files were restoring, I picked up the bear. I found a tiny switch on the bear's backside and turned it on. Even in this light, I could tell that the bear's right eye flickered the tiniest bit. I put the bear on a shelf and turned out the light. As I circled my small office, no bigger than a cubicle, I studied the bear. When I moved, the bear's eye flickered red. But there was no sound. Other than the red flash, there was no indication that it was doing anything. No hint that it was anything but a golden, fuzzy bear.

I turned off the bear and opened my email, curious to see what Kathleen had forwarded. The first email in my mailbox had come from someone named "Lavender Farms". I clicked, hoping Kathleen had vetted it. I was sure that the article in the paper had prompted all kinds of mail, ranging from psychics convinced they could find missing babies to nut jobs claiming to be behind it all. I didn't need to read any of that.

But this email was not what I expected:

Dear Ms. McDougall,

My name is Michelle. My husband and I bought the property on Ice Cream Grade a few years ago. We remodeled before we moved in, starting with the soundproofed office. We removed the walls and opened the room up to the house. When we did that, we found something tucked into the framing. An envelope, which we never opened.

We kept thinking we should call the police, but we just never got around to it. The idea of investigators swarming all over our home frightened us.

We didn't know what to do with it, and just forgot about it. But when we read that article in the paper, our answer was clear. Please let me how you'd like to proceed.

--Michelle
Lavender Farms, Bonny Doon

I sat back, stunned. An unopened envelope. It could hold the key; the answers I'd been searching for. But it meant returning to Ice Cream Grade. Where I'd lived all those months, blissfully naïve, completely trusting, completely ignorant of what was being planned for my babies. Completely unaware of what was buried in the crawl space below me.

And where I'd found Megan that fateful night, a prisoner in a cage —

Rain pouring from the dark sky in relentless buckets. The steep trail a river of mud. The light from Jackson's flashlight shining on the smooth leather surface of his steel-toed shit-kickers. Megan's agonizing screams. The shiny gun. And Jackson's stinky, garlicky breath when he grabbed me and leaned in, close as a lover, trying to strangle me.

I shook my head, willing the memory away.

I swore I'd never go back there. Megan would warn me against it. PTSD, she'd say. Dexter would tell me I was crazy. I could hear him now: "Just have her put it in the mail, Shelby."

Suddenly, I wanted to jump into my car right now and drive up to Ice Cream Grade, to get it over with. But I had no idea if anyone would be at home. And besides, I had work to do. I emailed her back, thanking her, telling her I'd love to pick up that envelope as soon as possible. I left my cell number, my work email and number, and my personal email. To make sure I wouldn't miss the call, I added Lavender Farms to my contacts.

There was one more thing to do before settling in for a day of background checks. I pulled the business card that Lisa had given me from my pocket and Googled the psychologist. Just as I'd thought, he worked alone. The older woman who'd approached Lisa that day in the park was not affiliated with the psychologist. Who was she and why was she interested in Justin and Justine?

•　　　•　　　•

Later in the afternoon, I put the background checks aside and spent fifteen minutes surfing the internet, looking for anything related to Justin Boyd. The story had hit the news, big time, showing up in state and national news feeds. But other than the basic details, location, parents' names, dates, there was nothing. No report of a ransom call. No leads.

A knock on my door interrupted me; I looked up as Kathleen walked in. "How's it going?" she asked.

"Good," I nodded. "Thanks for forwarding that email."

"I read it," Kathleen replied. "What will you do?"

"Go up there," I replied.

Nodding, Kathleen picked up the bear and held it, closing her eyes as if weighing it. "Strange how it just feels like a regular bear, isn't it?" As she placed the bear back down, she asked, "Care to join me for a client meeting?"

Twenty minutes later, I was perched on the chair in front of her desk, as eager as a kid on the first day of kindergarten. Kathleen had angled the blinds downward and the room was dim. A pile of folders was stacked on the desk to her right, with a folder open in front of her. "We're going to meet Claire Rutherford," Kathleen said. "She suspects her son-in-law is up to something, but she can't figure out what. She wants us to follow him, get some photos. Should be an easy case."

She looked back down and squared a piece of paper in the file open on the desk. "How are the background checks going?"

"Good. I finished two of them. All the findings are in the folder called Background Checks, with a subfolder for each person, by their full name, last name first."

"Did you use the new template?"

I nodded.

"How did it work?"

"Very well," I replied. Kathleen had been experimenting with new ways of feeding the background check results to the client.

"Find anything?"

"Yup. One of them, now twenty-five and a college graduate working on his MBA at night, was arrested just after he turned eighteen for selling pot to his seventeen-year-old friends. All dismissed when the other parents decided not to press charges."

"Good job, Shelby," she said, but her mind seemed elsewhere.

I sat, waiting.

A few seconds later, Kathleen squared her shoulders as if making up her mind about something and looked up. "Do you want to try some surveillance?" she asked. "It's nighttime work." Shaking her head, she said, "I'm too old for that. Apparently, the woman's son-in-law goes out around ten at night, two or three nights a week, and returns around one in the morning."

"Absolutely," I replied, unable to hide the huge grin spreading across my face. "I would love to."

Kathleen opened a desk drawer, reached in and took out two yellow, blue-lined legal pads. The woman loved paper. She didn't use an app on her smartphone for notes. Or keep track on her computer. She used paper, just like my parents. But I suspected it wasn't because Kathleen preferred the simplicity of paper. She just wanted to avoid a digital record.

10

K ATHLEEN HANDED ME ONE OF THE LEGAL PADS along with a blue pen. At the same time, the intercom on Kathleen's phone rang and she pressed a button that unlocked the outside door. I walked to the office door and held it open, watching the woman walk toward me. Her step was confident and she looked like money: black slacks, red twinset, and a chunky gold necklace with matching earrings. Her hair, dyed a rich dark brown and styled in a short wedge, shone with the luster of expensive hair products. I couldn't even begin to guess her age; her perfectly applied cosmetics smoothed her skin and hid any wrinkles.

I stood to the side as the woman entered the room. "Kathleen Bennett," Kathleen said as she stood and shook the woman's hand. She pointed at me, saying, "My assistant, Shelby. She'll be working with me on the surveillance."

As the woman's eyes slid over and past me, I noticed that the almost-translucent foundation could not hide the pull of her cheeks and the pinch of her mouth.

She sat in the chair in front of Kathleen's desk, placed her black leather purse on the floor next to her feet, and settled her hands in her lap.

I took the chair on the woman's left, pushing it slightly behind her as I sat down, so she wouldn't be able to see me out of her peripheral vision.

"What can we help you with?" Kathleen asked.

Focusing her attention entirely on Kathleen, the woman began to talk. "My name is Claire Rutherford. My husband, Harold, and my daughter, Melanie, my only child, died three years ago." She shook her head, covered her eyes with her hands, and choked back a sob. "In a plane crash. They were flying to Aspen for the weekend, a father-daughter thing, but the plane went down. It was a charter."

Kathleen offered the woman a box of tissues. Claire pulled one out. Dabbing her eyes carefully, so as not to smear her makeup, she continued, "Melanie left behind a daughter, who was four at the time, and is now seven, and a beautiful boy who was only one. He's almost four now. Sarah and Randy Junior."

She paused. "My son-in-law, Randy, has a big ego. His full name is Randall Stephen Vinson the Second. He's named after his father, an admiral in the navy. I met his parents just once, at the wedding." She sniffed. "We weren't military enough for them, I guess. My son-in-law is career military. He's stationed at the Naval Postgraduate School as a professor in the Defense Analysis department. He's very, very smart. Intense. And passionate.

"But after Melanie died, something in his intensity shifted. He never seemed to get past the anger stage. You know, the five stages of grief," Claire said in response to Kathleen's questioning look. "Denial is the first one," she said, as she ticked them off on her fingers, "then anger, bargaining, depression, and, finally, maybe, you get to acceptance.

"I'm still in the depression phase," she added, taking a deep breath.

"Anyway, Randy is an angry man. I'd seen it some, years ago, before the children were born, but the last few times I saw him," she shook her head, "he was seething. Raging. It didn't seem to be directed at the children so much," her shoulders rose and fell as she shrugged, "but it is there.

"I have seen it seep out on occasion." She stopped and corrected herself. "I did see it seep out on occasion." Her emphasis was on the past tense. "I did see it," she repeated.

Kathleen asked, "You don't see them anymore?"

"He refuses to see me or let me see the children. It's been six months now and I have no idea why."

"Did anything happen?" Kathleen prodded.

"Not that I know of. I invited them over for dinner, and they were all set to come, but he called that afternoon, a Sunday, saying that Randy Junior was sick. We rescheduled for the following week and I didn't think anything of it. The next Sunday rolled around. This time, Sarah was sick.

"I decided to take her a present, and bring the food over to their house, so I just showed up on the doorstep at dinnertime. But they weren't home."

Kathleen shook her head, frowning.

"So I waited, figuring they'd gone out for a prescription. But after an hour, I left. I put the presents on the doorstep — a book for Sarah and a small car for Randy — and the next morning the bag was back on my doorstep with a note that said 'Please don't contact us anymore'." Claire choked back a sob. "I figured it was delayed grief, delayed anger at Melanie's death. That was six months ago. I call every week and leave a message and drive by. Sometimes I drive by Sarah's school and I see her at recess or waiting to be picked up by the nanny."

Kathleen leaned forward. "Maybe he's in a new relationship. Or maybe he's falling apart and he doesn't want you to know."

"But I want to help," Claire protested. "I want to be in my grandchildren's lives."

"I understand," Kathleen agreed. "So what can we do for you?"

"Follow him. I want you to follow him and tell me everything he does. Start with his nighttime outings. Of course," she added, "I don't want him to know he's being watched."

I was scribbling furiously, trying to keep up.

"Tell us more," Kathleen prompted.

"Melanie was thirty-two when she died. Randy is a bit older. He was thirty-five when Melanie passed away. He's thirty-eight now. Melanie met Randy after college, when she took a job at the Monterey Institute for International Studies in the HR department. She called it her starter job."

Claire paused and put her finger to her lips, swallowed, and continued. "Anyway, Randy was studying Arabic at the school. They met in the park one day, when Melanie was eating lunch. After a whirlwind romance, they married and moved to Germany. Four years later they moved back, and Randy started teaching at the Postgraduate School. Next thing we knew, Melanie was pregnant. She was so happy. We were all so happy."

The woman shifted in her chair, crossed her legs, and took a shaky breath. "I live in Pebble Beach, not far from my grandchildren. After Sarah was born, I came over and helped out a lot. Once or twice a week. Melanie went back to work, part-time, and I filled in so Sarah wouldn't have to spend as much time in day care. It worked. At least, I thought it did."

Kathleen was watching the woman intently, rolling her gold-plated pen between her fingers. I knew that expression well; I could tell she was analyzing everything the woman was saying, combing through her expressions and inflections, trying to sift out the truth.

Claire continued, "Randy travelled a lot in between semesters at the school. Afghanistan and Pakistan. He's considered an expert in that region. After Melanie died, he still had to travel, and I'd come over and stay with the children. But over time, things changed. For one trip, he got a nanny. For another trip, his parents came. Then, on some of the days I was scheduled to pick up the kids, he'd call in the morning, saying that it was the nanny's day, or that the kids were going to friends' houses after school. I was a wreck, too, so it was hard to keep track. Over the course of the first year, he gradually pushed me out of the daily routine. And by the end of the second year after Melanie died, I was just a weekend grandma. And now, my grandson probably doesn't even know who I am." As she dissolved into sobs, she leaned forward and grabbed a few more tissues from the box. "Sorry," she said. "Sorry."

Kathleen gently asked, "So why are you here now? Has anything changed?"

"Sort of," she said slowly. "I decided to watch him. I've been parking in his neighborhood for the last few weeks, just to see. And for three nights in a row, he's left his house around ten in that ratty old van of his. I didn't follow him. I knew he'd see me. But there's something fishy about it. I just want to know where he goes." She looked up. "And I want to make sure that the children are safe."

"Do you suspect that they aren't?"

Claire shrugged. "I just think it's strange that he'd push me out so completely. It makes me wonder if he's hiding something."

A new relationship was my guess. But it could also be a case of an overbearing grandma; a lonely woman suffering such a tragic loss, clinging to her grandchildren like a lifeline, suffocating them.

Nodding, Kathleen asked, "Who stays with the children when he's out?"

"They both go to school," Claire replied. "Sarah is in second grade and Randy goes to preschool. As far as I know, they get picked up by a nanny. She lives in. I've never met her." Claire's fingers worried the delicate tissues, rolling and coiling them into a small string, like a rope of licorice.

Kathleen stood. She walked to the small water dispenser in the corner of the office, pulled a glass from the nearby shelf, placed the glass under the spigot, and filled it. I recognized this tactic too. It gave her time to think.

Kathleen drained the glass, placed it carefully on the shelf to the left of the water jug, and turned toward us. She asked, "Have you ever been scared of your son-in-law? Did Melanie ever say anything?"

Claire's head snapped up. From my skewed vantage point, I could see that her brow was furrowed, as if she were really thinking about the question, as if that thought had never occurred to her. To be frightened of the man who'd married her daughter. She placed her elbows on the chair's armrests and her sleeves slid up past her wrists, revealing a thin gold bracelet on her right wrist and a watch with a large round face on the left.

"There was one time," Claire said quietly. She crossed her legs, right over left. The pant leg shifted upward, revealing tan hose. "Melanie had a black eye once, after Randy Junior was born. She said she'd fallen. Sometimes, I'd call, and she'd tell me not to come over, saying she wasn't feeling well. Another time I decided to drop by, it was in the afternoon, and I heard a keening wail coming from the living room. A mournful, desperate cry. I rattled the knob and the sound vanished. The house went completely quiet. No one answered the door. Or the phone.

"And, a few weeks ago, I drove by the school and saw Sarah's arm in a cast." She leaned down, reached into her purse, and pulled out her cell phone. "Here, I can show you a picture."

Kathleen returned to her desk and slid into the chair. Shaking her head, she said, "A cast on an arm doesn't prove anything."

Claire sighed, saying, "I know," as she dropped the phone back into her purse.

"Anything ever directed against you or your husband?" Kathleen asked mildly.

"Sometimes, he'd pop out with unkind verbal jabs. Barbs."

"Guns in the house?"

Claire shrugged. "Probably. He's in the military."

Kathleen asked, "Are you sure you want to do this?"

"Yes," the woman replied, nodding. "I'm positive."

"We'll follow him for you," Kathleen said, "but it's not cheap and it may be a waste of your money."

"One thing I do have," Claire said, "is money. My husband had a substantial life insurance policy and there was a settlement from the accident."

My mind wandered as they went on to discuss specifics. I glanced at my watch, almost five. I'd planned an easy meal for dinner tonight: pasta, sauce from a jar, cheese, premade garlic bread, and a salad. Cooking had never been at the top of my list of fun things to do. I needed to stop by the store and pick up beer and a bottle of wine. If I left by five-thirty, I could swing it.

I snapped back to the present when I heard my name. "Shelby here," Kathleen was saying, "will do the surveillance. Randy won't even know she's there. Right, Shelby?"

I nodded. Claire didn't even glance at me.

"We'll need some information from you before we get started: the address, a photo, any identifying features, description of his cars."

"I'll be out tonight, but I'll get them to you by noon tomorrow," Claire replied.

After Claire Rutherford left, Kathleen looked at me and then started shuffling papers on her desk. "What do you think? Is she genuine?"

"I don't know," I answered. "She might just be too overwhelming for her son-in-law. Or, she might be on to something."

Kathleen nodded. "That's my assessment also." She glanced at her watch. "I need to go, Shelby. Your laptop is put away already, right?"

"Yes," I said as I stood.

"See you in the morning," Kathleen replied. "Sleep well. Tomorrow, after you finish the background checks, start on Claire Rutherford and Randy Vinson. We're going to find out everything about both of them, and I mean everything."

11

MY PHONE RANG AS I WALKED TO THE CAR and I glanced at the display before answering. Unlike the firm's backup old-style flip phone, I had an iPhone. And, like everyone I knew, I depended on it for everything.

The display read Lavender Farms. Eagerly, I tapped the answer button and said, "This is Shelby."

"Hi. Michelle here, from Lavender Farms. We emailed earlier today?" Her voice lilted to a question.

"Yes," I replied. "I was surprised to hear from you. And yes, I would be very interested in that envelope."

"Can you come tomorrow?" she asked, her voice eager, as if now that she knew what she was going to do with it, she couldn't wait to get it out of her house.

"Sure," I replied, thinking about my day tomorrow. "Is it possible to come early, around eight? I have to be at work by nine."

"Yes," Michelle agreed. "That works. I know you know where to find us, so I'll see you then."

•　　　•　　　•

Our small apartment was empty when I got home. Dexter had said he'd be cutting it close for dinner, something about a late meeting.

By the time I'd moved back to Santa Cruz, Dexter had left his pushy, uptight wife. I was glad he'd moved out, even though it meant divorce and a shattered childhood for their daughter, Ashley.

No matter how hard I tried, I could not think of anything positive to say about Jessica, his ex. Everything was someone else's fault. Jessica pinned it all on Dexter: He never had enough money. Or ambition. Or taste. Or smarts. I was also on her list. She'd never forgiven me for being a surrogate. The very nature of the arrangement, as she used to call it, had tarnished my niece's perception of the saintly job of motherhood. Jessica even tried to pull Ashley's visits when I'd moved in with Dexter. I used the b-word sparingly in life, but she did fit the bill. Though I'd never say that to Dexter.

I put on my favorites playlist, a random mix that included music from my parent's generation — Motown, Joni Mitchell, Carole King, Carly Simon, James Taylor, Bob Dylan, Van Morrison, the Grateful Dead, Eric Clapton — as well as my brother's blues preferences and my collection of female artists: Lana del Ray, Rihanna, Adele, Kelly Clarkson, First Aid Kit, Regina Spektor, with a little Lady Gaga and Beyoncé thrown in to keep me relevant. I sang along as I filled the pasta pot with water and set it to boil and then started chopping tomatoes, cucumber, and avocado for salad.

Smiling to myself, I remembered what this place had been like when I moved in. A card table with four folding chairs had served as the dining room table. The boxy TV was perched on an overturned milk crate. A board across two additional crates served as the coffee table and an identical set up functioned as the side table. Bricks and boards formed a bookshelf. Dexter's room had been more like a bicycle repair shop than a bedroom. And the second bedroom, for Ashley when she came to stay, was as spartan as a monk's cell, with only a dresser and a bed. The kitchen contained just two sets of silverware and one pot that did it all: kettle, frying pan, pasta pot, wok. It was like living in a place you were about to move out of, with everything already packed and in the moving truck. We'd added to the household since then, and now, our home even impressed our mom.

When Ashley visited, we had a slumber party. At eight years old, she wasn't at the age where she demanded privacy. In fact, she hated to sleep by herself and loved our sleeping arrangements. We'd all bunk in the living room for a giant sleepover, pulling out the futon sofa and setting up an air mattress on the floor. She wasn't an easy child to sleep with; she tossed and turned, kicked and flung her arms out to her sides. But it wasn't a hardship. Dexter barely saw her. The custody agreement allowed Ashley to stay with him every other weekend and on Wednesday nights, from four in the afternoon until bedtime.

Though I never said this to Dexter, I suspected that Jessica's agenda was straight-forward: to get full custody and move back to southern California. I shuddered to think of my niece growing up as a Valley girl. I could see Jessica moving back in with her parents, wealthy right-wing Republicans, as conservative as they come. I'd met them a few times while I was staying with Jessica and Dexter during my pregnancy, and though we'd been cordial, our conversations had skittered on the surface, loaded with unspoken judgments from both sides.

The front door opened, and I looked up from the lettuce I was shredding into the salad spinner. "Hey," I said as my brother came in the door. He dropped his briefcase onto the sofa and reached down to switch on the lamp on the side table.

"Hey, Shelby. How was your day?" he asked.

I shook my head. "Busy. Very busy," I replied, deciding to save the story of Justin Boyd for another time. "And yours?"

"Another train wreck waiting to happen." Dexter eased his way into the small kitchen and pulled open the refrigerator. "I need a beer."

"Go for it," I gestured. "I got some."

He grabbed one, found the opener in the drawer, popped off the cap, and took a long sip. "Want one?"

"No, not yet. Thanks. How's the Iron Lady?"

The Iron Lady was our nickname for Dexter's boss, Ms. Alexandra Grey-Woodman. She was new to the city's Parks and Recreation Department, hired over Dexter, the long-standing Assistant Manager, after a national independent search committee recommended her. The woman was promoted as an expert in city government, with an emphasis in parks management. Her only prior job experience had been running a parks department in rural North Carolina. Dexter always complained that she was not qualified to lead a parks department in an urban setting with a large transient population. After six months, she hadn't even visited most of the parks in the city. She still didn't know anything about how the city's numerous summer programs operated. Dexter suspected an ugly truth: the woman didn't even like kids or the outdoors.

"I'm off work," Dexter snapped. "Don't need to talk about her."

"Sorry," I muttered. I ran water into the spinner, grasped the handle, and started twirling. I glanced over at him, gave the lettuce one last spin, and scooped it into the salad bowl. "You remember that Megan and Annie are coming over, right?"

"Yup. When?"

"Should be here in fifteen."

Dexter grunted and left the kitchen. "You mind if I turn on the TV?"

"Go for it," I answered. Dexter silenced my music, replacing it with the perky chatter coming from the evening news sports segment.

•　　　•　　　•

When Megan knocked on the door a few minutes later, I set the knife on the cutting board next to the half-chopped tomato and yelled, "Come in."

The TV snapped off and I heard Dexter stand and open the door. As I rounded the corner to the entryway, I caught Megan stepping back from Dexter. Had I interrupted a hug? Or something more?

I'd first met Megan, another victim of Jackson and Diane's baby-brokering scheme, about five and a half years ago. The night I'd figured it all out, when I realized that my babies would not stay at the house on Ice Cream Grade, I'd followed Jackson through a raging storm and found Megan locked in a cage, a prisoner. Though I'd emerged from that night relatively unscathed, at least physically, Megan had been shot in the leg by Diane at close range. That bloom of red on her jeans still haunted me in the middle of the night. We'd both been pregnant. Megan's daughter, Annie, was delivered the following day. My babies were born a few weeks later.

Like me, Megan had moved back to Santa Cruz after the attack. And, her mother, like mine, thought she had made the wrong decision.

I leaned over and pulled Annie into a hug. The child's full name was Shelby Anne Fitzgerald, Shelby for me and Anne for Megan's mother. The child had been called Annie from birth, which I suspect was due to Megan's mother's influence.

"Hi pumpkin," I said.

Annie smiled; a fleeting beam that disappeared as quickly as it had come, and held up her doll, a sturdy, tall plastic thing, with hair practically down to her shins. The doll was dressed in a riding outfit, complete with cap, jodhpurs, boots, and a riding crop.

"Her name is Tiffany," Annie said. "We left Rainbow, her horse, at home. Rainbow had a long ride today and is resting." Annie galloped across the living room, clucking her tongue and mimicking the sound of horse's hooves.

"Wow," I said, speechless.

"Grandma," Megan mouthed, and I smiled.

Dexter sank back onto the sofa and laughed as Annie cantered, galloped, neighed, whinnied, snickered, and clip-clopped around the living room.

I followed Megan to the kitchen. "You okay?" I asked, noticing how she favored her left leg.

Megan shrugged, her fragile shoulders rising and falling. She ran her hand through her short haircut, a pixie-like bob that showed off her perfect bone structure, petite nose and mouth, her gray eyes and full lashes. "Some days it's worse than others. I love my apartment, but it always feels damp and cool inside. Even on hot days like today. And me and damp don't do so well."

I nodded. "I'm sorry."

Dexter got down on all fours and gestured for Annie to climb on his back. She laughed, a high, tinkly chime. Dexter loved Annie. In fact, he loved kids in general. Most of what he did at work was for kids, even though he spent all day with adults, office politics, and city brass. Dexter crawled across the room and then sprawled on the carpet, moaning about his back.

Megan stood at the counter and picked up the knife but I waved her off and pointed to one of the tall stools at the breakfast bar. "Sit." I knew how much Megan hated special treatment, but some days, it was justified. I walked to the fridge, pulled out a beer for myself and offered her one. She shook her head and replied, "Just juice, thanks. I need to study when I get back. My midterm for my summer seminar is next week."

"How's it going?" I asked.

"Difficult," she replied. "Really difficult. Some nights, I find myself wondering what I'm doing. Me, a biochemistry major." She shook her head. "What was I thinking?"

I held up the bottle of orange juice. She nodded and I poured a glass and handed it to her.

Megan took a long thirsty gulp, and said, "Mom's been hounding me for months about going to see another doctor. So just to get her off my back, I drove to San Francisco yesterday after my morning seminar to see a specialist. Mom met us there and watched Annie during the appointment."

"And?" I added the salad toppings to the bowl of lettuce.

"Total waste of time. The doctor said they could do another surgery to try to straighten out my leg. Another surgery. Just the thought of it makes me want to cry." She stood, walked around the bar, and pulled her left pant leg up to her knee. "Look."

I glanced down. Her leg, from knee to ankle, seemed withered, smaller somehow than when we were at the beach earlier in the summer. Maybe it was just that her golden tan had worn off and her skin was now white and puckered.

"Mom thinks I should go to Sonoma State or some other place where I could live with her. The climate is a lot drier in Napa. It would be better for my health, I guess." Megan let her pant leg slither back down. "But I love UCSC. And I love it here — the beach, the redwoods. And I don't want my mom telling me how to raise my child."

Rubbing her eyes, she hobbled to the breakfast bar, lowered herself onto the stool, and picked up her glass. After taking a sip, she said, "I need to get a decent grade in this biochemistry class. It's so interesting, Shelby. I can't believe that I'm enjoying it so much. This coming semester," she continued, "I'm taking Human Genetics, math, and a laboratory techniques course. And to think that before," she waved her hand, "I was a theater major."

We both laughed.

"I have to ace everything this year. Everything. I want to work in one of the genetics labs next summer. One of the professors is researching a genetic disorder called Fragile X syndrome and how it affects people over fifty." She sipped her juice. "The real work is given to the graduate students, but apparently they keep one opening for an undergrad. The undergraduate does the easy stuff — categorizes the data that comes in and does the routine work on the cheek swabs." She laughed. "I'm already buttering up the graduate student who runs the lab. I drop by every couple of days and hang out. Soon enough, I'll start taking him cookies."

Dexter walked into the kitchen, carrying Annie, interrupting us. "Cookies?" he asked. "Did someone say something about cookies?"

Megan laughed again.

"Anyway, is it time to eat? We're starving." He drew out the word, turning it into a Cockney slang that emerged from the back of his throat like a song.

"Starving," Annie mimicked, her arms squeezing Dexter's neck. The two of them dissolved into giggles. My big brother Dexter looked so natural there, holding Annie. As if he were Annie's dad. And Annie clung to him in return, sticking to him like you'd hang on to a lifeboat in a storm.

"You could set the table," I suggested.

"Okay," Dexter put Annie down and winked at her.

He maneuvered around Megan and me in the small kitchen, handing the child four forks and four paper napkins. Annie ran over to the table and arranged them in a row.

"There," she announced. "Ready."

I heard a smile in Dexter's voice as he said, "Looks great." He ferried the plates and glasses to the table.

"How's work?" Megan asked.

"Good. Busy. Kathleen's given me a boatload of background checks. And, I'm going to do some surveillance this week," I turned off the stove and picked up the pot to drain the pasta. "Hey, after dinner, let's see if Dexter will watch Annie for a few minutes. I want to talk to you about something. We can go for a walk."

That popped out without thinking about it. In addition to damp, Megan and walks didn't do so well either.

12

W ITH RELUCTANT AGREEMENT FROM MEGAN, we left Annie and Dexter on the sofa after dinner, watching *Toy Story*.

"Great movie," Megan said as we left the apartment, "but I hate to just park her like that. Even though I do it all the time," she added with a smile.

"This will be quick," I replied, pulling the door closed behind me. "I just need to talk to you about something." Walking behind Megan, I could see the hitch in each step as she swung her left leg forward.

"We're going to that bench." I put my hand on her shoulder and pointed toward the edge of the lagoon behind the apartment complex. "See?"

Megan stopped, looked, and nodded. "Sounds good." We continued to walk in silence. The lagoon was a swampy backwater that, at one time, might have been home to a variety of fish species or migrating birds. On the whole, especially at this time of day, it looked picturesque enough, framed by a drooping willow and small feathery acacias. But a slick mat of algae covered the surface in places and the bright green water looked like it harbored enough nutrients to qualify for a Superfund site. A single duck slowly paddled through the algae, carving a narrow, curving channel. A chunky yellow rowboat followed the duck, several boat lengths behind. When it pulled too close, the duck flapped its wings, nimbly ran along the top of the dense algae mat, and flew to shore.

We slipped onto the bench. A few yards out, a takeout container bobbed on top of the algae like a small dinghy.

"What's up?" Megan leaned over and rubbed her ankle, and then crossed her leg so her foot dangled over her knee. She continued the massage.

I turned toward her. "I saw the Boyd family today."

"And the Boyds are …?" She eyed me.

"My babies. I saw my babies. One of them," I faltered. "I met their parents. Went to their house."

"You did?" Megan asked, surprised. "Why? Where?"

Night had almost fallen by the time I finished my story. I fell silent, hearing the occasional shouts from people in the apartment complex and the roar of tires on the road.

"So how do you feel?"

I shrugged. "I don't know. Sad. Regretful, relieved, worried, freaked out."

Megan laughed. "The whole ball of wax."

I smiled, "Yeah. That."

"What are you going to do?"

"Find Justin."

"How?"

"I have no idea. No idea at all."

"Did Kathleen have any suggestions?"

"No, not really."

Megan stopped rubbing her leg and turned to me. "You know, Shelby, it happened five and a half years ago. Annie will be six in December." She extended her leg, pointed her toe, and started lifting her leg up and down. "My stretches," she explained.

She was quiet for a minute and then said, "In a weird way, I'm glad it happened."

I shot her an *are-you-out-of-your-freaking-mind?* look.

Off to our left, a frog croaked and out in the pond something plopped, a fish jumping or a turtle slipping off a log. Save for the traffic noise and the glow from the lights of the apartment complex behind us, we could have been out in the country.

Megan nudged me. "If it hadn't have happened, I would have given Annie up. I wouldn't know where she was. And who knows where she would be …" Her voice trailed off and I shuddered.

"I know," I replied. "It's too awful to even think about."

But I did think about it. I always thought about it. The images that ran through my head were always the same and always grim. Babies, especially girls, living who knew where, forced into who knew what. And as they grew older, what would happen to them? On the good days, of which there were more and more, I could forget all of it and pretend those babies were living with loving parents who were unable to adopt legally. On the bad days, all I could see was sexual slavery, forced medical donations, and death.

I drew in my breath sharply, leaned over, and put my hands on my knees. Staring straight ahead, I said, "Someone else contacted me, too."

Megan threw me a sidelong glance.

"The people who live on Ice Cream Grade," I said. "The people who bought the property did extensive renovations when they moved in. They found an envelope in a wall. Never opened it."

"Shelby," Megan's voice was sharp. "Tell them to take it to the cops. Don't get involved." She turned to face me. "Let it go. Just forget it, Shelby. It's not your problem."

"But …"

Megan put up her hand and interrupted me. "I know you think there has to be something more. But there's not. You answered the wrong ad. I answered the wrong ad. There's no scheme. No Stork. Nothing.

"This obsession of yours is not healthy, Shelby. It won't get you anywhere." After a beat, she said, her voice softer, "I just don't want to see you get hurt, that's all. Either emotionally or physically. You're my best friend."

"Thanks," I replied.

She reached for my hand and squeezed it.

A few stars glowed above. Darkness had fallen and I could feel the dampness settle in, along with a hint of cool air, a promise of the fog that would surely blow in and embrace Santa Cruz in a cottony mist.

"Ready?" I stood.

Megan pushed herself up and we slowly walked up the sloping lawn to the apartment. Before we reached the halo of lights, she turned to me. "You'll find Justin," she said. "I don't know how, but I know that you will."

I was grateful for her confidence. I needed that. Someone had to believe in me, because right now? I sure didn't.

•　　•　　•

Dexter brought the dishes into the kitchen. I rinsed and put them in the dishwasher. "Annie is really attached to you," I said.

He grinned. "She is adorable. Reminds me of Ashley."

I smiled in return. Maybe my plan to set them up would work out. Eventually. In the last few months, in particular, it was as if Dexter had turned a corner. He seemed more relaxed, happier, less anxious. As if his ex, in her absence, wasn't ruling his every minute. Even though he was the one who left, he'd pined for her and had wanted her back. Hoped she would change, which, in my unasked-for opinion, was as unlikely as the virgin birth.

"So what are you doing with Ashley tomorrow night?" I asked as Dexter handed me Annie's bowl with a mound of pasta still glued to the bottom.

"First I pick her up at camp," Dexter replied. "Then, I'll take her to the park, followed by a visit to Mission Hill Creamery for a very small scoop of ice cream. After that, we'll have a picnic on the beach. Then, it's back to her mother."

"No mac and cheese?" I asked, laughing.

It seemed like the only thing Dexter ever fed that child was boxed macaroni and cheese. What was it about kids and pasta?

He shook his head. "Not tomorrow."

"She has to be back home at eight?"

"By eight, Shelby. On the dot."

I stopped the snarky comment hovering on my lips. "Sounds great. I love my niece."

"The more love, the better," Dexter replied.

"Does she come this weekend or next?"

"Next weekend, but I'm actually going to have her on Sunday. Jessica is taking a class."

My eyebrows rose, but I kept it to myself. Jessica allowing Dexter to be with Ashley when it wasn't a court appointed time: well, hell just might freeze over after all. I slipped past Dexter to wipe off the table.

"Want company tomorrow for your picnic?" I asked.

"Sure," Dexter said as he walked across the room and flopped onto the sofa, with his feet at one end and his head at the other.

"Mind if I invite someone?" I asked, hoping my voice sounded stronger than the quivery timbre I was hearing in my head.

"What?" Dexter sat upright and looked at me, remote frozen, pointed at the TV. "Who?"

"A guy," I said, stopping as I crossed back to the kitchen, sponge in one hand, a fistful of crumbs in the other.

"What's his name, where did you meet him, and what does he do?" Dexter asked.

"His name is Cody. I met him at work." I left out his job, on purpose.

"At work? You don't work with any men."

"I met him in the parking lot. At the coffee kiosk," I said defensively. The tone in my voice warned Dexter away from any more prodding.

"Sure, Shelby. That's great." Dexter's voice sounded bright, happy, as he slid back down onto the sofa.

"Good," I replied. "I'll see if Megan and Annie can come too."

Dexter stopped me. "Already done," he said, a lightness in his voice. "We're meeting at Seabright Beach at six."

My heart lifted. I smiled, and decided it was time to ask that question that I hadn't asked for months now. "Has your divorce gone through yet?"

"Shelby," Dexter twisted in the sofa to look at me, "you promised you'd stop asking."

"I know," I replied, "but you just need to get on with it. Get on with your life. It's time, you know?"

Dexter snapped on the TV and I knew our conversation was over. But he surprised me.

He muted the volume, turned to me and said, "Just thought you might want to know. It's done. Two months ago. I'm a divorced man."

My jaw must have dropped. I was usually the one with the bombshells, not Dexter.

"Got ya," he said.

The TV burst back into sound and I knew that Dexter would be smiling.

DAY TWO

WEDNESDAY, JULY 18

13

I WOKE EARLY, AT FIVE, NOT AT ALL RESTED. I'd stayed up late, way too late, surfing the internet. Browsing for ads for surrogates. Checking my email for a response to last night's inquiry. Hunting for anything related to Justin Boyd. But nothing meaningful surfaced. Not a word. I'd researched child savants, coming to the conclusion that, no matter how it played out, Justin and Justine would never be normal kids, going to after school soccer and spending Saturday mornings in front of the TV.

Images of Justin had stalked my dreams. Justin chained to a bed. Locked in a cell. Or dead in a ditch, discarded like a piece of trash.

Now, I snuggled under the covers and tried to get back to sleep, thinking of good things: Cody. Kathleen and work. Annie and Megan, Dexter and Ashley. School. But then, the negative thoughts took over again and I knew it was time to get up.

Standing at the sink with my first cup of coffee, I stared outside at the darkened lawn with the solitary streetlight planted in its middle, like the mythical lamppost in *The Lion, The Witch, and The Wardrobe.* I showered and ate my customary toast with jam sitting at the table, checking email until my brain cleared. Placing my used mug, plate, and knife in the dishwasher, I poured a second cup of coffee in a travel mug, changed, and headed out. I wasn't due at Lavender Farms for another two hours and it was too early to go to work. With Kathleen's system of keeping my laptop in her office, I couldn't start on anything until she was in. And Kathleen never arrived before nine.

Once in my car, I put on my driving playlist, a random mix of upbeat, high energy, indie folk hits, including "Home" by Edward Sharpe and the Magnetic Zeros, "Ho Hey" by The Lumineers, and "I am Love and You" by The Avett Brothers. Belting out the lyrics, I drove north on Highway 1, through the small town of Davenport, population four hundred and eight. Three restaurants, an inn, and a gallery lined the highway, angling to sweep in the ever-growing number of tourists travelling along the coast. The Whale City Bakery already had its lights on and I almost stopped for a scone.

Instead, I drove a few miles north and left Highway 1 at Davenport Road, the entrance to Davenport Beach. I'd chosen this beach because it wasn't that isolated: there were a few houses along the road, and I knew that at least one or two surfers would already be plying the waters in search of the perfect wave.

The beach was bathed in soft yellow light and startlingly quiet after the loud music and the rumble of the car. I grabbed my backpack, slung it over my shoulder, and ran to the sand, stopping to take in the view. The sky was clear, with a few stray jet trails catching the last pearly pink of the sunrise. Bright blue water spread in front of me and an even white hem of surf bordered the sand. The swell was large and I inhaled the salty tang of the ocean as the waves crashed on the shore.

I pulled off my shoes and socks, stuffed the socks into my pack, and held my shoes by the laces as I ran to the water, caught up in the roar of the waves. The sun glinted off the rumpled surface, fracturing into shards of light that zinged right into my eyes and made me squint. A line of pelicans flew along the surf break inches from the water, their silhouettes like prehistoric dinosaurs in flight. They skimmed the surface, dipping down, rising up, flapping their wings infrequently, as if the breeze created by the breaking waves was enough to propel them forward.

A wave broke and I got caught in its remnants, my hot pink toenails buried under the wet sand. Though I would never paint my toenails on my own, I loved that pink. I blamed it all on Ashley. Last weekend, she and I had a beauty afternoon. We'd gone to the drugstore, where she'd picked out the most outrageous colors of fingernail and toenail polish: Pink Paradise, Plum Shock, Magenta Moments, Teal Teaser, Silver Shimmer, Gold Gotcha, and Lemon Burst. I'd insisted on monochrome — one color for all my toes and another for all my fingers. Ashley had opted for the full court press, with each of her tiny teardrop nails a different color.

I wondered if Lisa had ever painted Justine's toenails. Though a set of flaming red toenails along with reading glasses on a chain around her neck would have matched the child's demeanor, I doubted that she would stand for such nonsense. I could not understand her. I could not figure out why she was the way she was. There had to be an explanation. I just couldn't see it. Yet.

Finding Justin was key. Not only to get him back, to make sure he was safe. And not only because I said I would, but to figure out why he'd been taken in the first place. So far, there was no ransom demand. No communication at all from the kidnappers. No one had heard or seen anything. No reports of strange cars in the neighborhood. No shouts, screams, or yells. No doors left open or unlocked. The child had just vanished, swept out of his life as if he never existed. I thought back to my conversation with Justine. She hadn't actually said what had happened. She'd told me that they'd both climbed into bed and that Justine had climbed back out to turn off the light. She'd gone to the bathroom and when she'd returned, Justin was gone, with the only clue a chloroform-soaked rag. At that point, our conversation had veered into new territory: the bear.

The beach was bordered on the north and south by sheer cliffs rising from the sand. With the tide on its way in, I moseyed along and didn't venture past the narrow margin of rock shelf and beach on either end. I kicked my feet through the cool sand, and occasionally bent over to examine a shell fragment or pick up a piece of sea glass that I dropped into my pocket. At the far end of the beach, near one of the rock shelves jutting out into the water, I could see a silhouetted figure standing in the surf. His arms were crossed and his body flexed and swayed as waves buffeted his legs. Three fishing poles were stuck in the sand, angled out toward the water. The almost-invisible nylon fishing line, strung tight, thrummed against the pale sky.

A dark-haired woman approached him, a small baby on her hip. I stopped and watched, like a voyeur. The woman cupped her hand around her mouth and called; the man turned and slogged out of the surf. They met above the surf line and hugged, and then turned toward the waves, shoulders touching, and faced the ocean.

I lifted my head, surprised to find a tear track. But the wind whipped it away and I wondered if I'd imagined it.

14

I DROVE BACK SOUTH ON HIGHWAY 1 toward Bonny Doon Road where I would turn inland, thinking about the last time I'd been to the property on Ice Cream Grade. I'd borrowed Dexter's car to check out a hunch. The car, in serious need of a tune up, had died as I sat at the side of the road by the gate, engine idling, trying to decide what to do. I'd tried repeatedly to start the car so I could escape and leave the hunch for later, but it wouldn't turn over.

So, I'd walked in. At that time, the property felt abandoned. The driveway had been littered with a carpet of leaves and pine needles. Weeds poked up through the gravel surface. The landscaping was overgrown, with more than half the plants dead or dying. And the buildings had been destroyed. The door on the main house hung on its hinges, wooden slats on the porch had been chopped out, and windows had been broken. The cottage was gutted. Graffiti covered the walls. Trash was strewn across the floor — empty beer bottles, greasy fast food bags, tattered blankets, newspapers, magazines, containers of rotting food, rat and mouse poop. I remembered trying not to look, knowing I'd see more evidence of ruin: needles, bloodstains, and crumpled wads of singed aluminum foil.

Now, I could feel my heart race as I made the turn on Ice Cream Grade. Who knew what was in that envelope? It might prove everything once and for all. It might contain the name and address of The Stork. A complete list of where all the kidnapped babies had ended up. Or even a list of all the bogus intended parents in central and northern California. Anything would help. Anything.

Exactly at eight, I found myself sitting in the car, staring at a low iron fence. The fence was now only a few feet tall, designed to keep pets or children in, rather than an imposing fortress that had been created to hide something and keep people out.

I took a deep breath and pressed the accelerator. The motion-activated gate slowly slid open. The driveway had been resurfaced recently and was now black and shiny, a smooth pavement that a skateboarder would die for. The bushes and trees had been cut back and the wildness I remembered had been tamed and manicured. I couldn't even identify the tree where I'd hidden the baby quilt, the one item I'd grabbed as proof of the crimes the Entwistles had committed. But I could remember that quilt precisely. Created by a loving birth mother, as a gift to the baby she was giving up, it was composed of nine separate panels. Each panel told a story, chronicling the life of a Peter Rabbit-like creature, from birth to old age. The card I'd found pinned to the bottom right corner read:

To Zachary,

I'll think of you all my life, and know that you're happy.

Love, Auntie Carol

I rounded the last curve in the driveway and slowed, trying to make sense of what I was seeing. The cottage was gone. Vanished, as if it had never even existed. In its place stood a flower garden: a riot of giant sunflowers, gaudy mauve and red dahlias, brilliant orange California poppies, white and yellow daisies, feathery purple and pink cosmos.

The main house had been repaired and painted a cheery blue with white trim. A few rocking chairs sat on the varnished porch. One of them still rocked, as if the woman who stood, waiting, had just risen from it. I stopped the car, turned it off, and got out.

The woman walked down the stairs and strode over to greet me, stepping past a big wheel trike and an umbrella stroller. She held the envelope in her left hand. "I'm Michelle," she said. She caught me staring at the flowers and asked, "You like it?"

"Very much," I replied. "It's beautiful."

She was thin and strong and held herself in an erect, exacting posture. "The first thing we did when we bought the place was tear down the cottage," she said. "Living here gave me the creeps at first, but my husband saw the potential. And, as you can imagine, the price was right." She gave a small laugh. "We built a new cottage, out past the garage, where the storage shed was. My in-laws live there. They help with the kids."

I nodded. She continued to talk as if she'd been itching to tell this story to someone who knew.

"We also tore down that shed by the creek. It's a lovely spot, and someday we might build a new structure there, but for now, it's all cleared out. And we're letting the trail grow over."

Michelle's voice faded as I remembered —

Following Jackson to the shed, hiding below the window, peeking in. Seeing the shiny chain link. And my realization that the chain link was actually a cage, with a top, bottom, four sides, and a gate with a lock on it, all sparkly, like it had just been polished. I was looking at a cage. A cage holding a panicked, pregnant woman. Megan.

I shook my head to clear the memory. Michelle was still talking and I hoped she hadn't noticed.

"We gutted the inside before we moved in," she was saying, "starting with the office. We removed the soundproofing and opened the room up to the house. When we did that, we found this tucked into the wall behind the insulation." She waved the envelope in the air. "We kept thinking we should call the police, but just never got around to it." She shivered. "This place had so much evil when we moved here. It took so long to expel it; the idea of bringing it all back down scared me."

I wished I could have felt that evil on the day I'd moved in here.

"I didn't know how to find you, so I just held on to it. It's been sitting in my to-do pile for so long now. When I read that article in the paper, my prayers were answered." She stared off into the distance. "And here you are. Funny how things work out."

She handed me the envelope, a five-by-seven inch manila rectangle. "Take it. It's yours. When we pulled it out of the wall, it was wrapped in a few layers of plastic. To keep it dry, I expect. I pulled off the plastic to see what was inside, but I never opened it. Never wanted to know what was in it.

"You can keep it or give it to the police. You can tell them where you got it. I don't care."

The envelope was an ordinary manila rectangle. I held it by the corner. Even though I had no intention of taking it to the police, my training kicked in. Keep the evidence intact.

I jiggled it; paper slid inside. A still shiny clasp held it shut. All I had to do was lift the two metal hasps, open the flap, and turn the envelope upside down.

I glanced away, hoping to compose myself, thank her, and scurry off to the privacy of the car where I could give in to my almost overwhelming urge to rip the thing open. But the scene across the driveway stopped me — the scrubby bushes that once dominated that spot had been replaced by a field of lavender. The purple spikes waving in the slight breeze took my breath away.

"That's beautiful," I said.

She turned to me, a smile on her face. "Lavender has healing properties. Did you know that? Not only the fragrance, but also the oil. I make soap, essence, and lotion. My shop's in the garage. Wait here."

I watched her walk away. Her blue linen skirt fluttered in the breeze and the brilliant multicolored scarf wrapped around her neck streamed behind like a rainbow. When she opened the door to the garage and disappeared inside, I lifted the envelope again and reached for the flap holding it closed. But I stopped myself and slid the envelope into my backpack. I realized that I couldn't even hold it without it commanding my full attention, as alive as a crying baby.

A buzzing noise caught my attention; at this early hour, a few bees were already at work. The flowers bobbed and swayed under the weight of the tiny insects. An intense sweet smell overcame me, and I felt like Dorothy in her field of poppies. I just wanted to lie down and nap.

"It's mesmerizing, isn't it?" Michelle had returned holding a small paper bag. "Here's some soap, a vial of lavender essential oil, and lavender salve," she said, handing it to me. "Whenever you're feeling overwhelmed, put one drop of the oil in a bowl of boiling water and sit with it in a small room. The bowl should be ceramic, the essence releases more completely than it does in glass, metal, or plastic. It will calm you and help clear your head. And the salve will take care of a cut or scrape in no time. Good for aching muscles, too."

"Thank you," I said. "That's very kind."

She smiled. As she reached over to give me a hug, she said, "Nice meeting you. I hope that envelope doesn't bring back too many bad memories."

15

I STOPPED THE CAR IN THE ANGLE OF THE DRIVEWAY next to the road and turned off the engine. With shaking hands, I gently lifted the envelope out of my backpack, picking it up by the corner. I turned it over. It was slightly darker than a standard envelope of that type, as if being wrapped in plastic and hidden in a wall for years had aged it, like fine wine. And, it was light, almost insubstantial, perhaps holding only a few sheets of paper.

Diane would have been the last person to touch the contents of this envelope. I was sure of it. She thought these items were important enough to squirrel away, to hide.

I knew that I should hand it over to the police, have it dusted for fingerprints, but I also knew that this case was closed, shoved to the backmost back burner. The envelope would be given a cursory once over and bounced to the evidence room. If I wanted to know what was in it, I'd have to open it. What was the saying? Ask for forgiveness, not permission. Though I knew that law enforcement didn't exactly abide by those rules.

Using a tissue to preserve any possible fingerprints, I unfastened the clasp. The two hasps broke off at the join and I wedged them in the cup holder next to my go cup. I held the envelope upside down and shook it.

Two pieces of yellow lined paper, folded in half, fell into my lap, along with two four-by-six photographs. The photos were turned over, and a date and time were stamped on the back of each. The ink had faded, but I could still make out the October 7, 2002, 2:32 p.m. timestamp.

Long before I'd met Diane or the thought of being a surrogate had even crossed my mind.

I reached into the glove box, grabbed a pen, and gently turned one of the photos over.

It was a picture of Diane holding a baby. Or what I assumed was a baby. She held a bundle wrapped in a pale blanket. A pink cap, similar to the one the nurses had put on my baby girl, covered the infant's head. Diane was not cradling the baby in a tight embrace, as you'd expect a happy new mom would do. She held the infant at arm's length, as if she were worried the baby might mess up her blouse. Her hair was shorter, but her expression was the same: bottom jaw set, lips compressed, eyes shadowed. I'd seen that look before.

A young woman stood behind her, off to the right, cautiously watching, arms folded across her chest. The birth mother? Was she already having second thoughts? The setting was odd. There were no identifying characteristics. The backdrop was as blank as a set in a photographer's studio. Just a plain off-white wall. No doors or windows. Not even a shadow.

Again, using the tissue, I picked up the photo by the edge and slipped it back into the envelope. With the pen, I flipped over the second photo. Another picture of Diane. Here, she was standing with an older woman on the front porch of a small bungalow. Their arms were around each other's waists.

The plain features of the woman standing next to her struck me. Her gray hair was short, parted in the middle, blunt cut to her ears.

She wore a dark blue skirt with a V-pleat in front and a white blouse with three-quarter length sleeves. I couldn't see any jewelry, not even a watch. Black, round-toed walking shoes adorned her feet. Her cat-eye glasses reminded me of glasses I'd seen my mom wearing in photos taken during the early years of her marriage. There was nothing remarkable about this woman. In a crowd, she'd vanish.

I carefully placed the second photo back in the envelope with the first and unfolded the yellow lined paper, holding it in the corner with the tissue. The top sheet was blank. But the bottom sheet held pay dirt. A list of addresses, written in Diane's careful script, took up four lines at the top of the page. 15890 Highlands Terrace South, 250 Canyon Road, 90 Blue Heron Drive, 789 PCCR.

Just a list of house numbers and streets, with the last one abbreviated. No city, town, county, or state.

These addresses could be anywhere: from right here, in the Santa Cruz Mountains, to as far away as New Zealand or Australia.

But for some reason, my gut was telling me California.

Somewhere close by.

·　　·　　·

Kathleen's car, a gold Lexus, was parked in the lot when I arrived, and I stopped by her office on my way in. But instead of handing me the laptop, she held out a heavy tome titled *The Pro's Guide to Surveillance*. My wrist bent as I took it.

"Change of plans," she said with excitement. "Computer work this afternoon. This morning I want you to read this excellent book. I pulled it off my bookshelf last night. It's got everything you could possibly want to know. I used the first edition of this book way back when. Start with the vehicle surveillance section," she ordered, adding, "Quiz tomorrow!"

I couldn't tell if she was joking.

I lugged the book to my office and dropped it on the desk where it landed with a loud crack. Sitting down, I fished my phone out of my backpack and set the alarm for ten-thirty. Break time. My rendezvous with Cody.

But before that, I needed to do a little research on my own. Ten minutes, I thought. Enough time for a quick search.

First, I decided to photograph the packet. I snapped on a pair of latex gloves, removed each item from the envelope, and took a picture of the front and back of each photo. I then zoomed in on the sheet of addresses, making sure I'd recorded each one. After returning the items to the envelope, I pulled a Ziploc bag out of the box Kathleen had given me, placed the envelope inside it, and put it into one of the drawers in my desk that I could lock.

From now on, I'd leave that envelope here, safe. I'd use the images on my phone for backup and for reference.

I entered the house number and street name of the first address on the list into my phone. No exact matches. I tried street names alone. Highlands Terrace South gave me a match in Oroville, out in California's central valley. There was a Canyon Drive in just about every county in California. And any community remotely near a body of water seemed to include a Blue Heron Drive somewhere in its master plan. A search for "PCCR" returned nothing. Thinking I might be looking at an error, I tried "PCR", which returned dozens of business locations. "789 PCR" took me to "Perryville, Missouri".

I changed the "R" to "road", trying both "PC Road" and "PCC Road". I was rewarded with a few more results, but nothing local, ending up with addresses in New Jersey, Minnesota, Michigan, and Illinois. I inserted periods after "P" and "C" and ended up with the same locations, adding Pennsylvania and Kansas to the mix. I thought of logical combinations for the two letters: Pacific Crest, for example. With this, I was getting closer, landing in Covelo, California, smack dab in the middle of the Mendocino National Forest. Adding Santa Cruz, Watsonville, Aromas, or any other local town or incorporated area gave me the friendly Did you mean ...? message with a far-flung address appended. I was out of luck.

I swiped into the gallery on my phone and opened the photos. In both photographs, Diane stared directly at the camera. This surprised me; she was always camera shy. At the time, I thought she was being coy, but now of course, I knew that she didn't want to leave any incriminating evidence in her wake. I sharpened my gaze on the photo where Diane stood with the older woman. Even though their arms were linked, it still seemed as if they were separated, as if the photographer had cajoled them into touching. Neither of the women smiled.

Something was off. Usually a photo of two people meant they knew each other. Someone wanted to capture the moment. But Diane didn't do moments. Moments were not in her lexicon. The more I stared at the picture, the more I noticed how stiff the two women were, rigid as broomsticks, as if they barely knew each other. Or, as if they knew each other well enough to harbor deep seated resentments and long felt mistrusts.

I looked at the other photo, the image of Diane holding the baby. Again, she stared directly at the camera. She cradled the infant in her forearms, but held the bundle out in front of her, obviously uncomfortable. The young woman standing behind Diane wore an expression of concern and was leaning in slightly, as if poised to take back what was hers.

Diane and the baby were the focus of the photo. Had the young woman strayed into the frame just as the shutter clicked? Her hair was frizzy, pulled back from her face with a headband. Her round face matched her round body, and I wondered if the baby was so brand new that the woman's belly had not yet shrunk to its after baby normal.

•   •   •

An entire section of the book Kathleen had given me was devoted to vehicle surveillance, with chapters on daytime tailing, nighttime tailing, tailing in traffic, in rural areas, alone, with a partner. The first thing I learned was that my car wouldn't do. The bumper stickers, from the fading "God loves everyone — even you" blue and white saying, to the hot pink Santa Cruz mermaid decal and the De Anza parking pass were too memorable. The vintage of my car would also stick out: the neighborhood where Randy Vinson lived was one of two story houses evenly spaced on well-manicured large lots, with newer model SUVs and active neighborhood watch groups.

Just as I was reading about how to keep the target car in sight while navigating heavy traffic, Kathleen knocked on my door.

"Hi," I said.

She nodded in return, waving her phone at me. "There's an app you need to get," she said.

I picked up my phone and asked, "What's that?"

"SnapApp. It's much more comprehensive than the free real estate apps. You enter an address, along with a photo of the house, and you get the square footage, when it was built, when it sold, the price, and the current value. But the best thing is that you get a 3D rendering of the house and the property. It's a virtual reality thing. I've used it a few times. You might find out something useful about Randy's house.

"It's not free, so use the company account when you install it," she added.

"Thanks," I said. "I'll get it today."

Kathleen pointed toward the book. "How's the reading going?"

"Good. I never knew there was so much to think about."

"I remember my first surveillance job," Kathleen replied, as she glanced at her watch, a substantial black wristband with a large face and a glowing digital display. "It wasn't pretty." She looked up, saying, "It's almost ten. Claire should be getting me the data I requested by lunchtime. I'll forward it as soon as I get it. Let's meet again, say around four, and see where we are. Sound good?"

"Yes." I added, "I have to go back to the Boyd's around noon. I promised them."

"Have you found anything?"

"No," I replied, shaking my head and spreading my hands in a gesture of resignation. "Nothing. I don't have anything to tell them. I don't even know where to start. Or how to start. I'll show Justine the bear and see if that rings a bell, but I don't have anything more to go on."

Kathleen put her hand on my shoulder. "The police are doing everything they can," she said. "You're limited in what you can do. Maybe they just need moral support."

I looked at her, feeling despair. "But they called me for a reason. They think I can find him." I shook my head. "I don't know where to start," I repeated. "And you know what they say about a kidnapping. The first twenty-four hours …"

Kathleen interrupted. "Shelby, they didn't even call you until after those hours were up. Just start at the beginning," she advised. "At the beginning."

She turned around and walked back across the hall, closing the door to her office. The hallway immediately darkened and I felt like my office had been plunged into shadow. I stood, turned on both overhead lights and levered the blinds to the open position.

I sat back down and tried to immerse myself in the book, her words echoing in my mind. At the beginning, I thought. The beginning.

16

S URVEILLANCE WAS NOT AS SIMPLE as the cop shows on TV made it seem: pick your spot, watch, follow at a safe distance, and peel off before you get caught. I was learning about all kinds of issues I'd never even thought about. How do you use the bathroom? How do you remain undetected in the middle of the night when the road is deserted? Where do you set up to wait and watch? And what do you do once your target reaches their destination?

I'd need a heavy-duty gym bag to cart all the recommended equipment. Change of clothes to confuse the target. Blanket. Pee bottle. Binoculars, video camera, still camera. Notepad, pens, map, flashlight, night scope, binoculars, cell phone, digital recorder. Water bottle and snacks.

There were the complications of watching before Randy left his house. And once he'd left the house, I had to gauge exactly when to turn the car on and start driving. Too soon and he'd be suspicious. Too late, and I'd lose him. And finally, the difficulties of trailing at night, with few cars on the road. I was starting to wonder exactly what Kathleen meant when she said that her first surveillance wasn't pretty.

The best advice I found was on the internet. Keep mentally ahead of your target. Imagine what he will do. Light coming up? Speed up. Target turning? Speed up. On the highway? Keep a few car lengths behind and track every lane change, every acceleration, and every deceleration. Anticipate his next move.

And if you think you've been discovered, exit. Try again another day.

By the time my alarm rang, my eyes had glazed over and I couldn't take in another word. I slammed the book shut, stood, stretched, and glanced out the window at my parking lot view. Cody's green-and-white was just pulling in.

I picked up my phone, badge, and keys and stuffed some cash in my pocket. Outside, as I walked toward the coffee kiosk, I searched for Cody. Never one to take advantage of a cop's privileges by parking in an undesignated spot, he'd parked the Sheriff's car across the lot. He called it his unspoken motto: the more he followed the law, the more other people might be persuaded to do the same.

He strode toward me, smiling, and I wished we were at that point in our relationship where I could reach out and hug him.

"Hi, Shelby. Did you get your coffee yet?" he asked.

"Nope, just got here myself," I replied.

He gestured for me to go first, and when the barista rung me up, I added, "I'm getting his, too." Cody nudged me and said, "You don't have to do that."

"You bought mine yesterday, remember?" I replied, handing over a five.

He smiled, saying, "Thanks."

Once we picked up our drinks — black coffees for both of us — we walked to a bench facing the water. A small Boston whaler putted through the harbor toward the open ocean, passing a sailboat with sails furled, motoring in. The water was still, glassy, and below us, next to the dock, a sheen of oil slicked the surface.

"So what's new today?" he asked.

I hesitated. If I told Cody about Justin now, he'd wonder why I hadn't mentioned it yesterday. I was sure he'd been briefed; it was all over the news. The tip line, manned by the Watsonville police department, was in full swing. The Polly Klaas Foundation was organizing search volunteers.

And besides, if I told him about Justin, I'd have to tell him everything.

"Not much," I said lightly. "Dexter and I saw our friend, Megan, and her daughter, Annie, last night. They came over for dinner." That was a safe topic. He knew Dexter was my brother. "You?" I asked, sipping my coffee.

"Not much for me either," he answered. "I went to the gym after work. Thought about going to a movie but fell asleep on the sofa instead." He chuckled. "Pretty exciting."

Staring into my coffee cup, as if the liquid were my salvation, I took a breath and asked, "What are you doing tonight?"

I turned toward him and could see him gazing into his coffee, as if he were thinking. Was he trying to figure out how to ward off my inevitable next question? How to wiggle out of it before I could voice it? A hot flush rose from my toes and I wished I could crawl under the bench.

But to my relief, he said, "Nothing much. Got something in mind?"

Hoping I didn't look too much like a love-struck fool, I grinned and said, "I'm going to the beach for a picnic with Dexter and Megan. Can you join us?"

Cody turned toward me and looked at me with his warm brown eyes. Delicious, warm brown eyes that flamed my insides. He smiled, revealing perfect teeth and those perfect dimples.

"I'd love to," he said. "Where?"

"Seabright Beach. Six," I said.

He started to reply, but the radio on his belt squawked to life and he held up a finger. I heard, "Ten-fifty or ten-fifty-one, 1625 Silvia Lane."

Lifting the radio to his mouth, he pressed a button and spoke into it: "Three-Wilson-B. On my way." He repeated himself, and then turned to me. "I'll see you tonight."

I smiled, waved, but he was already sprinting to the cruiser. I wondered what a ten-fifty was.

•   •   •

The Boyd's house was deserted, looking closed up and abandoned, as if the occupants had met a rough patch and moved out months ago. A tree limb lay across the front yard, the branch jagged and shredded. The lawn sported muddy patches where the grass had been trampled. Dirt covered the porch steps and a few roof shingles were scattered in the driveway. The newspaper lay on the sidewalk, its edges curling in the sun. And the police officer had disappeared from the porch.

What had happened?

Feeling exposed, I ran up the steps and knocked quietly on the door. There was no answer. I turned around just in time to glimpse a white lacy curtain fall back into place in the house across the street. I knocked again, this time louder. "Anyone there?" I called.

Within seconds, the front door swung open. The hallway behind was dark and close. And empty.

"Hello?" I whispered.

"Here," a small voice chirped.

I looked down. Justine stood with her hand reaching up to the doorknob. She still wore her pink bathrobe, but today wore matching fuzzy pink slippers instead of yesterday's sheepskin pair. Her hair frizzed into a cloud around her head and down her back.

I crouched, placing the paper bag with the teddy bear next to me. "You shouldn't have opened the door," I said, hoping I didn't sound like I was scolding.

"I knew it was you," she answered, matter-of-fact. "I could tell by your footsteps and how you walked."

"Seriously?"

"Yes," she answered. She squinted as she tried to explain. "You walk on the balls of your feet, and you kind of skip up stairs. The ball of your foot hits the riser and you spring up, the tiniest bit. I can hear it and hear the vibration. You probably don't even notice."

It took me a minute, but I realized that what she said was true. I did walk on the balls of my feet. A springing step, my mom called it. I did skip up steps. After a beat, I asked, "Where is everyone?"

She gestured up the stairs behind her. "Ryan's resting. The police went out to get some lunch. The undercover cops are still here, somewhere." She peered around me looking out the door, and then added, "Lisa isn't here." Justine still hadn't changed her tune on her parents. They were on a first name basis.

"Where's your mom?"

"She's not my mom, you know," Justine said, putting her hands on her hips and throwing me a sour look. Her eyes glinted like a cat's. "She's still in the hospital." The child left the door open and started up the stairs. "You can come in. I don't know when Ryan will get up."

"Justine," I said, "Wait." The child turned toward me. "What do you mean, 'she's still in the hospital'?"

She pointed up, toward the ceiling. "Yesterday after lunch, Lisa got out on the roof. She said she was going to jump."

"Jump?" I asked, dumbfounded.

"Yes. As in leap off the structure and land on the lawn." The girl's voice was flat, empty of any emotion. "A fire truck, ambulance, and two police cars came. They took her away."

I shook my head. Disaster had fallen on the Boyd's house like a plague.

"Can you go get your dad up?"

"Ryan? Yes."

I closed the front door, threw the deadbolt, and watched Justine walk up the stairs, not in any kind of hurry. Her head was only a bit taller than the banister and I kept suffering from the illusion that my perspective was somehow stunted. A few minutes later, I heard a door at the top of the stairs open followed by footsteps. Ryan called down, "I'll be there in a minute. Can you make a pot of coffee?"

"Sure," I answered. I navigated through the overstuffed living room to the kitchen, placing the bag holding the bear and my backpack on the kitchen table. This room was just as cluttered as the living room. Appliances covered most of the limited counter space: a toaster, blender, food processor, mixer, George Foreman grill, crock pot, electric kettle, coffee pot, popcorn popper.

The refrigerator was a minefield as well. Plastic containers were filled with pasta, a meaty red sauce, salad fixings, enchiladas, and a macaroni and cheese casserole. A whole drawer gleamed with meat, still shiny in the plastic wrap. The top shelf sagged with a gallon of milk, three containers of juice, two boxes of almond milk, a container of chicken broth, and a quart of half and half, while the shelf space inside the door was crowded with condiments. I found the brown bag of Peet's coffee, a California favorite, on the bottom shelf and lost track as I doled out tablespoons of coffee into the coffee maker.

17

A S SOON AS THE HEADY AROMA OF BREWING COFFEE filled the kitchen, Ryan appeared, dressed in a pair of gray sweats, a black t-shirt, and black socks with a hole in the toe on the right foot. His face was shadowed with gray-black stubble.

"You okay?" I asked, dispensing with the niceties.

He shook his head. "I don't think so. First my son, now my wife." His voice had a catch and he had to prop himself against the wall as he spoke. "I can't get it out of my mind. After lunch, she said she was going to take a nap. When I went upstairs, she wasn't in the bedroom. The window in the hall was open. Justine mentioned she'd heard her crying outside and had tried to get her to come in." He shivered. "I can still see Lisa sitting up there. Weeping.

"We all ran outside. The two police officers, Justine, me. Lisa was on the roof hollering that she was going to jump. By the time we got out there, she was about halfway down the roof. And she wouldn't stop. She just kept repeating, 'I'm going to jump. My life is over.'"

His head was down and his arms were crossed. I pulled two coffee cups out of the dish drainer. They happened to be the ones Lisa had used yesterday: the mug with the happy, cavorting snowman and the one decorated with the repeating pattern of sleighs and holly berries.

Ryan said, "I was yelling at her to come down. But she kept scooting closer and closer to the edge, and wouldn't stop. The officer called the fire department. They in turn called the ambulance. And more police."

I glanced at him as I poured the coffee. "Why did she go up there in the first place?"

"After you left yesterday, the detectives, along with an FBI officer, came back. Snooping. Asking questions. Insinuating that somehow, Lisa was involved. That she'd hired someone to take him because she couldn't cope."

Not quite sure what to say, I pointed to the mugs and asked, "You take anything?"

"No, thanks. Straight up." Ryan yanked a chair out from the kitchen table and slumped into it.

I moved my bags to the chair, pushed a pile of papers out of the way, and set the mug down in front of him. "Did you complain?"

"No." He took a sip and grimaced. "I didn't even think you could do that."

"You can," I said. "If he was out of line, you can definitely complain."

"Maybe later." He shook his head. "They want to keep Lisa for forty-eight hours." His voice was shaky and I could tell he was trying not to cry. "She was admitted last night around five, so I won't see her again until tomorrow at five."

"How's Justine?" I asked.

Ryan shrugged. "What do you expect? She watched the whole damn thing. She followed me out to the street. She didn't say anything, let alone seem upset, or god forbid, cry. Justine never cries." He sipped his coffee again. "She just stared at her mother like she was a ..." his voice broke, "a bug in a jar. Then she ran inside."

Ryan sighed, a long groan. He rubbed his eyes with one hand and cradled his mug with the other. "I can't even go see Lisa. They won't let me in. We've been married for almost nine years and I can't even go see her."

"Do you have anyone to help you?"

"The neighbors brought over a ton of food. And Lisa's sister, Allie, is flying in from Oklahoma this afternoon. She'll be here when Lisa comes home and will stay with Justine when I go to work tomorrow. I have to go to work; if I don't, I'll lose my job."

I didn't want to point out that he was in no mental state to work. Hopefully, when he got there, the boss would send him home.

"How's your sister-in-law with Justine?"

Ryan shrugged. "How's anyone with Justine?"

After a beat, I asked, "Can I go talk to her? I brought the bear."

Ryan waved his hand. "Sure, that's fine. You'll learn about her latest dictionary word, but you won't learn much about anything else."

I left Ryan staring into the black maw of his thick coffee, eyes bloodshot and puffy.

Upstairs, I knocked lightly on Justine's door and opened it. "Hey," I said. "Can I talk to you for a sec?"

Justine sat in her tiny armchair and waved her arm toward the adult-sized chair. "Be my guest."

I opted for the floor instead and lay back across the plush carpet, propping myself up on my elbows. Justine eyed the paper bag containing the bear as I asked, "What letter are you on?"

"W," she said. "But this is my second time through."

"Second time? Since yesterday?"

She nodded. "Yup."

"Are you tired?"

"No," she said. "I don't get tired."

"So, your mom was on the roof yesterday?"

"You mean Lisa?" I nodded and she said, "Yes, she was."

"What was she doing up there?"

Justine shrugged, her eyes fixed on the dictionary. "I don't know. Ryan says she was going to jump, but I disagree. All for show. He was trying to get her to come down, so I came in."

"I heard you found her."

The child gave a small irritated sigh. "I heard her. She was crying."

"Oh?" I collapsed on to the carpet and stared at the flat white ceiling.

"I heard someone walking around above me and went to look."

I sat back up and looked at Justine, totally absorbed in the dictionary. With any other child on the planet, you'd know they were just looking at it because they liked the rustle of the thin pages or were intrigued by the gold embossed letter indents running along the side of the book. But with Justine, it was all about the contents, about the words printed on the page.

"I brought you something to look at," I said. I pulled the bear out of the paper bag and held it up. "Does this look like the bear that was on the shelf?"

Keeping her finger on the dictionary, she lifted her chin for a split second, said, "Yes," and then put her chin down. Back to her words.

"Do you want to look at it?" I asked.

Eyes on the page, she shook her head. "No. It looks like the bear that was on my shelf. That's what you asked and that is the question I answered."

"Okay." I had no idea what to say next and hugged the bear in my lap. "You can't even tell there's a camera in there, can you?"

No reply.

"Or a microphone."

Nothing.

After five minutes, I scooped up the bear and stood to leave. She wasn't going to cooperate and pushing her wouldn't get me anywhere. But Justine surprised me, carefully placing a bookmark in the dictionary and closing it.

She then lifted her ringed eyes to me. "Wait," she said. "I have to tell you something."

I paused and lowered myself back to the floor. "What is it?"

"I talked to Justin yesterday," she announced.

I tried to hide my disbelief. "How did you do that?"

"On the phone, silly. How else would I do that? Ryan's cell rang while everyone was outside trying to rescue Lisa. I heard it; that's why I came in. I had to run. Justin said he was fine. More than fine. He said he was playing a lot of games with someone."

"Games?" I was confused.

She nodded. "Games." She smiled, a wistful, certain expression on her face. "And he said they were coming for me. Soon."

•   •   •

Downstairs, I asked Ryan if I could look at the phone. I scrolled through the caller ID list, noting the names, times, and phone numbers for every call that had come in yesterday, and for good measure, the two days before. There were calls from the police department, the Toyota dealership, news organizations, a variety of cell phones that showed up as California call with no number, and a few from named individuals. Friends, neighbors?

Then, I asked for his cell phone. He trudged upstairs and returned with an old-style flip phone. The log showed only a few calls in the last week. The two calls to me, the string of calls from me in return, and one more, logged as Unknown, arriving yesterday afternoon at 2:53, right when Lisa would have been on the roof.

Even though I knew it wouldn't matter, I grabbed a pen and piece of paper from the counter and wrote it all down: numbers, callers, and times from both phones.

When I finished, I explained what had happened. Ryan continued to stare right into his coffee cup, now empty.

"Ryan," I urged, "you have to show the officers this phone when they come back. They'll talk to Justine and see if they can trace anything with the cell phone. This is evidence." I left out the part where Justine said they were coming for her. No need to spook the man into a heart attack. Besides, it might not even be true.

He threw me an exhausted, defeated stare. "Can you wait and tell them? I can't handle anything else today."

I shook my head. "No," I said firmly. "This is something you need to do." I placed the small black flip phone next to his coffee mug, picked up the bear and my backpack, and let myself out.

18

I TOOK A CIRCULAR ROUTE BACK TO WORK, heading north on the highway. I exited at Larkin Valley Road, a country lane that paralleled the highway for a mile before cutting to the east. No music on this trip. I needed the quiet to sort through my information overload.

As I drove, I thought back to when I'd first met intended parents Jackson and Diane Entwistle. They'd been so kind, so professional, as they'd laid it all out for me. My eggs, his sperm. The fertility treatments. The egg retrieval, the in vitro fertilization, and the embryo transfer to my uterus. The pregnancy reduction if needed. How they wanted to help me through it and support me, both financially and emotionally. I was so flattered, so astonished, that they'd chosen me. Me, above all the rest.

Of course, now I knew better. They'd chosen me because I was young and naïve. Trusting. Accommodating. Because I'd never carried a baby to term and had no idea what I was getting into.

Because I was so fixated on the dollar signs that I couldn't see anything else.

And now that I'd met Justine, something else was stirring in the back of my mind. A shimmering feeling, that an answer was just within reach, if only I could pick it out of all the random pieces dangling in front of me. But another thought occurred to me. Maybe I'd just been looking at it all wrong. Maybe the pieces I was looking at weren't the right ones.

Something about my pregnancy had required Diane's vigilance. At the time, I'd thought Diane was fixated, a bit overboard, a tiger mom right from the get-go. But once I'd discovered the baby-brokering scheme, it made more sense. I'd assumed it was because the couple paying for Justin and Justine had also given Diane a hefty sum to keep me close. After all, I'd learned from her that one of the babies was slated to be a medical donor for a third sibling. But what if there was something else? Something that Diane didn't even know?

The night Diane had held Megan and me at gunpoint, when she'd been so sure that Megan and I were done for, she'd told me that Jackson was not the biological father. Sometime after the egg retrieval and sperm production appointment, before the in vitro fertilization, there'd been a switch.

There'd had to have been at least one accomplice.

And then, a new thought popped into my head.

Something that had never occurred to me in six-plus years. I put on the blinker, jammed on the brakes, and veered to the shoulder. As soon as the car stopped, I turned off the ignition, and curled into myself, pulling my arms to my chest, trying to get warm. Trying to dismiss the icy feeling that had crawled up my back and now sat around my neck like a scarf.

Had the eggs also been switched? Had another woman's eggs been inserted into me?

But that was impossible. Except for those eyes, Justine looked just like me, down to the spray of freckles that dotted her nose and upper cheeks.

Or did she? Did she just look like anyone on the planet who had brownish-red hair and freckles? Was I seeing things that weren't there? And why had this thought never, ever crossed my mind?

Tonight, I'd have to spend some time researching The Reproductive Health Center of Los Gatos.

Once I collected myself enough to drive, I pointed the car in the direction of Corralitos and the market, a small grocery store that was famous for its handcrafted sausages. Dexter cycled out here every month just to buy a few pounds of the fresh meat.

I wandered around the store in a daze and ended up with a fudge ice cream bar. Instead of getting right back in the car, I walked across the street to the park. At this time of year, with no rain for months, the grass was as brown as dirt. I plopped down at a half-shaded picnic table and scarfed the ice cream before it melted, relishing the sugar that zinged through my body like an adrenaline shot.

Across the park, a family piled out of a minivan and crossed the park to the playground. The mother held the hand of a toddler, while the father and an older child, a boy, jogged alongside each other. They both wore baseball gloves. The dad gestured for his son to stop and then backed away from him. He gestured again and his son lobbed a straight fast ball right into his father's glove.

What kind of games would a five-year-old play? I thought about Annie. At the park, she went on the swings. She climbed on the jungle gym and slid down the slide. She threw soft round rubber balls big enough to hold on to. She liked Crazy Eights and Slapjack and she loved her doll, Tiffany.

Even though I'd never met him, I knew that Justin wouldn't be caught dead playing those kinds of games.

•   •   •

Forty-five minutes later, I knocked on Kathleen's office door. "I'm back," I said. "Sorry I'm late. My visit to the Boyd's took longer than I thought." I plopped into the chair by her desk, dropping my pack on the floor beside me and hugging the bear to my chest. Kathleen angled down her laptop screen and stared. "Lisa, the mom, is in the psych ward," I explained.

Kathleen shook her head and drew in a breath. "That poor family," she said.

"It gets worse," I added, placing the bear on her desk. "Just before I left, Justine told me that she'd answered Ryan's cell phone yesterday afternoon when Ryan was outside. Justin, of all people, was on the other end. Not the kidnapper with a ransom demand. Just Justin. They talked. He said he was fine and that he was playing games."

"Games?" Kathleen asked, clearly surprised.

"Yes, games."

"Did she say what kind of games?"

I shook my head. "No. I didn't think to ask her." I paused. "And she said they were coming for her. Soon."

Kathleen's eyebrows rose. "Coming for her?" she repeated.

I nodded. "That's what she said. I went right downstairs and told Ryan to talk to the detectives."

"Did you tell Ryan what she said?"

I shook my head. "No, I didn't. I couldn't tell him. He's so fragile. And, for all I know, she could have been making it up. Wishful thinking and all that."

Kathleen nodded and tapped her pen to her lips. "So strange. No ransom demands."

I shook my head. "None that I know of."

"No ransom, and the first communication happens when all the adults are preoccupied. Almost as if they were watching." Kathleen continued on her train of thought. "Or maybe she made it up? Would she?"

"Anything's possible," I allowed. "But there was a call recorded on the cell phone in the afternoon. Came in as Unknown."

"Do you have a next step?"

"No," I answered. "The bear didn't lead anywhere. I checked the house phone for all the incoming calls. I'll track them down and see if I can learn anything. But I can't actually call and talk to anyone, since the detectives are doing that. I guess I'll go back tomorrow or Friday to check in.

"I'm stuck," I admitted. "Completely stuck."

"Something will give," Kathleen said. "It always does. Start by taking your mind off Justin." She handed me a slim folder. "Work on this. Dig up some dirt on Randy Vinson. See what you can find on

Claire. Maybe by not thinking about Justin, you'll think of something."

I opened the folder. The first item I saw was a photo of Randy and Melanie. Randy was tall, with a sultry smile that would charm anyone and everyone. A buzz cut. Strong features, with a chiseled jaw and a dimple on the left cheek. He leaned toward the photographer, smiling. A brown beer bottle was raised in one hand. His other hand was on his wife's elbow, as if he were pulling her close. Melanie had been a beautiful woman, with cascades of black hair, and striking, well-proportioned features. She wore a black sleeveless sheath and held a glass of red wine. She was smiling, a small, cautious smile.

The next page in the folder was a print out of an email with all the particulars on Randy. Address, place of employment, vehicles, social security number, Facebook account, children's names, their ages, and schools.

The third page was another photo. This one showed Randy and Melanie on a terrace, at a patio table, underneath an umbrella. Melanie was sitting and held a small bundle pressed to her chest. Randy stood behind her with one hand on her shoulder. With the other, he seemed to be reaching for his daughter, Sarah, who stood off to the side in the direct sunlight, squinting. Randy — dressed in pleated trousers, topsiders, a pressed, long-sleeved shirt, and a sport coat — seemed to lord over the two females. Home for lunch? Or did he always dress like that? He wore that same smile. As if he loved life and life loved him back.

When I raised my head, Kathleen said, "Go see what you can find."

19

WITHIN TWO HOURS, I'D FOUND OUT PLENTY about Randy Vinson and his mother-in-law, Claire Rutherford. The Vinson house was in a well to do neighborhood in upper Monterey, along the contours of the ridge top that connected Pebble Beach and Pacific Grove to the outside world. After purchasing the home, before moving in, they'd completely gutted it. Now, the house was owned outright by Randy, no mortgage. It had been paid off in full two years ago. Randy drove a new Honda Civic, purchased with cash two years ago.

A quick check showed that when their son was born, Randy had purchased a million dollar life insurance policy for each of them. Melanie's policy had paid out in full. And like Claire, he'd also received a substantial settlement from the charter jet company. The ratty van Claire had mentioned was a 1989 Ford Econoline. Randy was thirty-eight, just as Claire had said. Everything else checked out: employment, salary, taxes, social security number, marriage certificate, Melanie's death certificate, his children's birth certificates, their socials, even their immunization records. He hadn't used Facebook in at least three years, and Melanie's account, if she ever had one, was gone. No other social media.

In addition, two guns were registered to him, a Sig Sauer P229 and a Glock 26. Both semi-automatic pistols. Both specifically designed for concealed carry purposes. And, no surprise, he had the concealed carry permit for both.

The Sig Sauer could chamber twelve to fifteen rounds, depending on the ammunition used. The Glock could chamber up to thirty-three rounds, if you switched out the magazine. Twelve, fifteen, thirty-three. Didn't matter. That was too many bullets to try to count, and if either of those guns were pointed at me, I'd be trying to get away, as fast as possible.

Claire lived in Pebble Beach in a three thousand square foot home with a view of the ocean. While her husband spent his career in banking, she'd raised Melanie and volunteered. Not as the typical parent volunteer in the classroom. She'd started in the PTA at her daughter's public elementary school in Carmel and had become PTA president when Melanie was a high school student at the Stevenson School, a private school in Pebble Beach. When Melanie left for college, Claire started serving on the boards of various high-powered philanthropic and cultural non-profits: the Carmel Bach Festival, the Robinson Jeffers Tor House Foundation, the local hospital, the Carmel Women's Foundation, and the Sunset Center. She and her husband took golf vacations, cruises, and cultural trips. They made the round of fundraisers and charity auctions. But since her husband and child died, she'd been a recluse.

I knocked on Kathleen's door; she motioned me in as she finished up a phone call. "What did you find?" she asked.

As I filled Kathleen in, she sat back in her chair and picked up her gold pen. It clicked against her wedding ring as she rolled it between her fingers, a comforting, relaxing sound.

"What's your take?" she asked. "Is Claire fishing? Trying to get us to find something so she can have more access to, or even custody of, her grandchildren? Or do you think there's nothing there?"

I shook my head. "It's not the first time one member in a family wanted something the other didn't." I thought of my mother and her grandchildren, two children unknown to her, living their lives as Justin and Justine Boyd.

"It is strange," Kathleen said, "that she would drive all the way up here to us when there are at least a dozen P.I. firms in her area. What is she not telling us?

"This thing with Randy might be nothing. Or it might be a new relationship. Or even something illegal. I do wonder if Randy is a man with an anger management problem."

"Why?" I wondered.

"What Claire said about the broken arm. Melanie's bruising. The crying she heard.

"The guns have me concerned," Kathleen continued. "He has two permits to carry concealed weapons. It's hard enough to get one concealed carry license in California. But two? He doesn't get any special compensation for being military. You still need the license.

"To get it, you have to prove you're of good moral character." She raised an eyebrow in response to my expression. "Yes, that's right. Good moral character. My cynical side says that this means you're part of the good old boy system, the NRA, or you know somebody who knows somebody. Randy might fit all of the above. But, in truth, you're interviewed.

"You have to show good cause. You have to get fingerprinted and you can't have any outstanding restraining orders or warrants, of course. In California, CCWs are issued on a municipality basis. You apply locally. In addition to proving your moral fiber, you also have to pass a firearms and gun safety test."

Kathleen stood and walked over to the windows, staring out to the beach and the blue ocean beyond. With her back to me, she said, "In my experience, I find that people with CCWs are very strident about their gun rights — and their personal protection. They tend to see the world as a fearful place." She turned toward me, and hesitated in front of the window before she walked back toward me, her silhouette backlit, as if she were on stage.

"Anyway," she said, as she walked back to her desk, "you should just assume he's carrying one, if not both, of those weapons all the time. So no foot surveillance." She stared at me, hard. "Got that? You are not to trail that man on foot until we know more about him. Okay?"

"Got it," I said, shaking my head to get rid of the image of a gun being pointed at me. Where would he stash them? In his waistband? The small of his back? A shoulder holster? A pocket?

Kathleen added, "I wonder if Claire knew that and just forgot to tell us." She shuffled a stack of papers on her desk, sighed, and seemed to settle herself. "How did that surveillance book go?" she asked. "You're ready for this?"

"Yes," I replied. "Absolutely. I will be able to manage it." I paused. "But I'm worried about blending in. My car is too noticeable. Those bumper stickers."

"Good point," Kathleen said. "I've been thinking about that. We'll rent you a car. A white one. We can pick it up tomorrow afternoon."

I nodded in surprise.

She laughed. "We charge it to the client, Shelby. You're sure you're ready?" she continued. Without giving me a chance to reply, she said, "Surveillance is not easy. You'd be surprised. You think you're just sitting there, watching, but there are a ton of things to think about. Parking, potty breaks, neighbors. And how do you follow Randy in the middle of the night without him noticing?"

"Some of them I've got figured out," I replied. "Others, I'm not so sure about."

Kathleen glanced at her watch. "I've got to head out in a few minutes." Addressing me, she said, "You need to get a good night's sleep. You probably won't get much tomorrow night. Come in late tomorrow. Say around noon? We'll go over it. Do a few test runs. Then, we'll head out for dinner and get you set up."

"Great." I hoped I sounded more confident than I felt.

20

W^{HEN I ARRIVED AT SEABRIGHT BEACH,} Cody was waiting for me by the path that led from the street to the sand. I almost walked past him. I'd never seen him in street clothes, just his uniform. His voice, a smooth, "Hey, Shelby," caught me off guard, and for a second, I didn't know who was talking to me.

I stopped and Cody walked over, wearing jeans and a Santa Cruz t-shirt, with a black sweatshirt slung over his shoulder. He pulled me into a familiar strong hug, as if we'd known each other for years. I liked that. I held his hand as we hit the sand.

The hot edges of the day had cooled, and the fog lurked off the coast like a threat, ready to pounce on the beachgoers and put an end to everyone's evening. But for now, the beach was packed. I located Dexter's blanket, a patchwork of logos from pro football teams, long before I spied Dexter and Megan down by the water. Still holding hands, Cody and I sprinted toward them, stopping suddenly and kicking up sand in a rooster tail.

Before I could even say hello, Dexter stuck out his hand and said, "Hi. I'm Dexter, Shelby's brother."

"Cody," Cody replied, as he dropped my hand and reached for Dexter's. Turning to Megan, he said, "You're Megan?"

She nodded. Introductions over, we stood awkwardly for a few minutes. A small voice called, "Auntie Shelby, come here."

Ashley sat with Annie in the damp sand. The girls were in full on battle gear to combat UV rays: Ashley in a wide-brimmed pink sunhat, Annie with a bland olive-green hat with brim, ear flaps, and neck guard. Their faces were white with sunscreen. I wondered how long it would be before I developed skin cancer, due to my former life as a softball pitcher in high school.

"Want to make a castle?" I asked, flopping down next to them. Both girls nodded enthusiastically, as if building a sand castle with me was a dream come true. I waved off Dexter and Megan, saying, "We'll take over. You guys take a walk."

"Who do we have here?" Cody asked, lowering himself on to the sand next to me.

I introduced him to the girls, and we started in earnest to push sand into a pile. I smiled at him and he smiled in return. Our hands brushed as we sculpted and molded sand. Each time we touched it was as if an electric shock coursed through me.

Within thirty minutes, we'd constructed a fortress, complete with moat, turrets, and roads, patted smooth with tiny hands. Feathers served as flags, and shells and stones decorated the moat's towers. When we ran up to the blanket to tell Dexter and Megan, we found Megan asleep, with her head on Dexter's belly.

Dexter put his finger to his lips on our approach, but it was too late. Annie jumped on her mother's torso in a fit of excitement: "Come see our castle, Mama. Come see our castle."

"Sure baby." Megan shook her head as she pulled herself up. She was wearing long pants. Lightweight linen, but long pants all the same. I remembered her withered leg, the skin pale and wrinkled.

Ashley took Annie's hand and the two children trotted in front of us. My niece, Ashley, was a solid child, sturdy and firm, and already a head taller than most of her classmates. By contrast, Annie was a petite dynamo. She never walked; she skipped, leapt, ran, hopped. For every one of Ashley's steps, Annie took two.

But in the few minutes we'd been away from the castle, a rogue wave had come up and destroyed it. The moat was filled with water. The turrets we'd painstakingly shaped and molded had collapsed, the decorative touches scattered. The feathers used for our heraldic flags had washed out to sea. While we stood there, disbelieving, a dog ran over and jumped on what was left, his front paws a blur as he dug. Ashley screamed. Then Annie screamed too, her mouth wide open, arms down, elbows locked, her body rigid with disappointment. I knelt next to them, extended my arms, and folded them in, saying, "We'll have to come back and build another one, okay? Another time?"

Cody, Dexter, and Megan stood behind us. As we watched the turrets and walls of the ruined castle crumple, wisps of fog covered the sun. I glanced up. The fog bank had grown and was now a dense wall of white, touching the steel-gray water below and the blue sky above. The air cooled and we shivered. It was time to put on our sweatshirts, take a few photos, eat our sandwiches, and head for home.

•   •   •

"Watcha doing?" Dexter asked, sliding onto the sofa next to me. With a beer in his right hand, he picked up the remote with his left.

"Surfing," I replied, angling the screen of the laptop down. I didn't want Dexter to see what I was doing. "How's Jessica?" I asked.

Dexter shrugged. "Fine. The same. Barely polite. I can ignore it." Dexter had just returned from dropping Ashley at her mother's house.

"Cody seems nice," Dexter offered. "But I didn't get to talk to him much. You kind of hogged his attention."

"Hey, what do you expect? It was our first date, if you can call it that," I answered lightly.

"What does he do and how did you meet him?"

I elbowed Dexter. "What is this, the inquisition?"

"Just interested," Dexter said.

"He's a cop. Sheriff's deputy, actually. He patrols South County, and I met him in line at the coffee kiosk in the parking lot by work."

"Wow."

"We just started talking and hit it off."

"Anything else to add?"

"Nope," I said. "Not a thing. What about you and Megan?"

"Nothing to add," Dexter replied. "Yet."

He turned on the TV and flipped through the channels, landing on a *Daily Show* rerun. Like usual, Jon Stewart was on a rant about Fox News. Dexter chuckled.

Tuning it out, I returned to my computer, lifting the top and watching it spring back to life. My search for The Reproductive Health Center of Los Gatos had returned pages of hits. Most of them were newspaper articles related to the closure of the clinic three years ago — another victim of the recession. But I wondered if something more was buried in one of these articles: misconduct, suspicion, allegations, legal problems.

I clicked a link on the first page of search results, and started reading an article in the *San Jose Mercury News.*

> A long-time Los Gatos business, The Reproductive Health Center, will close its doors at the end of next month. Office manager Ruth Janowski says, "We're working with our few remaining clients to place them with other clinics. Our doors will close at 5 p.m. on March 31st."

When I glanced up, Dexter had muted the TV and was staring at me with an intensity that made me uncomfortable. "Earth to Shelby," he was saying. "Earth to Shelby," he repeated, dropping the remote and circling his hands around his mouth like a microphone. "Are you there?"

I paused, hands hovering over the keyboard, and reluctantly tore my gaze from the article I was reading. "I'm here," I replied. "What's up?"

Dexter's eyes registered concern, but his mouth was pulled down in annoyance. I knew that if I didn't answer him, I'd never hear the end of it. "You're rather preoccupied," he pointed out.

"Just reading something," I replied.

"What's up?" I repeated.

He leaned over and tried to look at my screen. I pushed the cover of my laptop down a notch. But he was my brother, after all, and I'd already told Megan. For all I knew, Megan had already told him.

"Actually," I said, "there is something I need to tell you. Maybe a few things." I took a deep breath, pushed the laptop closed and heard it click. I spread my palms across the smooth surface and took a breath of air. "I saw my babies," I said. "I mean, one of them," I corrected.

"Holy shit." Dexter picked up his beer. "Why would you do that?"

"Their parents called me."

"What?" Dexter asked, holding his beer midair.

"In the middle of the night. Night before last. Around two in the morning." Now I had his attention. His hand was stock still, with the edge of the brown beer bottle touching his bottom lip. "One of them was kidnapped. The boy, Justin."

Dexter took a swig, sank back into the sofa, and ran his left hand through his hair, scratching his head. His worried gesture. "And you had to help."

"Yes. Absolutely. Lisa, the mother, was hysterical."

"How did they find you?"

"The article in the paper. The one you set up." As an aside, I added, "I also heard from someone else because of that article. The woman who now lives in the house on Ice Cream Grade."

"What?"

"I went up there this morning, and she gave me something. An envelope, with some photos and a list of addresses. She found it when they remodeled the property."

Dexter's forehead furrowed. "Not a good idea, Shel."

I shook my head and countered, "That article was not my idea."

"I didn't think the nut cases would come out of the woodwork," Dexter protested.

Seriously? I almost asked. But in order to maintain a healthy sibling relationship, I bit my lip.

Instead, I said, "There's more." Just as I started to tell him about the twins, their genius-plus IQ, the nanny cam, the family dynamics, the phone call Justine claimed she'd received, and my suspicions about the fertility clinic, Dexter's phone rang; a shrill trill that caused us both to jump.

He pulled it out of his pocket, glanced at the display, smiled, and as he tapped it, said, "Hi, Megan." Waving at me, he stood and walked into his bedroom.

I grinned and settled back in to my research, clicking links to articles on The Reproductive Center of Los Gatos, news stories about Justin, ads for surrogate mothers, articles on bogus intended parents. I also searched the four addresses again, hoping I'd find something new, something different. But nothing had changed and the addresses still made no sense to me.

I stayed up way too late, fixated. Searching. Looking for anything that might take me one step closer: to Justin, to The Stork.

DAY THREE

THURSDAY, JULY 19

21

After my morning coffee/email ritual, I walked outside, cell in hand. I was standing in front of our duplex, dressed in sweatpants and sweatshirt, as Dexter wheeled his bicycle out of the apartment. He caught me with my phone held up in front of my face, ready to take a photo and try out SnapApp.

"What are you doing, Shelby?" he asked. "Why are you taking a picture of that?" He gestured behind him at the concrete block we called home. "And don't you have to go to work?"

Just as I started to explain, his phone chirped. "Oops," he said as he wiggled it out of his pocket, "gotta get this. Work."

With the phone to his ear, he gracefully swung one leg over the bicycle bar, slid on to the seat, and started to pedal. A heavy backpack weighed him down and for a second, I thought he was going to lose his balance. But he rode away quickly, picking up speed, navigating the sidewalk to the parking lot with ease, as comfortable on his bike as a yellow jersey winner in the Tour de France.

I walked through the apartment complex, snapping different buildings, including the office building and the front entrance. Though the app couldn't locate our building, it did provide a 3D rendering of the entire complex. It spit out the date the complex last sold, the number of units, and the selling price. Very helpful.

As I wandered down the street and snapped a few photos of houses, trying for stealth, no one noticed me. The app did even better with photos and addresses of individual homes, returning the most recent selling price and date of sale. In addition, I found the square footage, the number of bedrooms and bathrooms, the property taxes, what school district the house was in, a link to a floor plan that existed somewhere on a server in the county coffers, as well as a 3D walkthrough of the structure.

Back at home, I left Dexter a note, and then texted Cody, telling him I wouldn't be at the kiosk this morning and explaining why. He texted back: "I'll miss you. Good luck!" A second text followed: "I'm heading to Fresno tomorrow to see my parents. Quick trip. I'll be back Saturday for work at three. Nights for the next two weeks, maybe in a different part of the county. See you soon." He closed it with a heart. I texted him one in return and stared at my phone, giddy.

Although I had plenty of time, I decided not to stop at the Boyd's on my way south. I didn't want to be reminded of my complete and total failure. With next to nothing to go on, no way to find out where the police were in their investigation, and no new information, I couldn't stop by. I couldn't bear Ryan's pain, and the disappointment that would flit across his face when I told him that I had zip, nada — a handful of nothing. And I until I could understand Justine, it was too difficult to be near her. All I could think of was the fantasy I'd harbored for five and a half long years.

•   •   •

Around four in the afternoon, I parked the rental car a block away from Randy Vinson's house. The trip had taken me over an hour. I spent most of it wondering why Claire Rutherford had driven all the way to Santa Cruz for a P.I.

I picked up my backpack from the passenger's seat, jammed a Giants baseball cap on my head, and pulled out a pair of oversized sunglasses. As I walked toward the house, I fished out my phone and opened the app. I'd get one chance — I knew that I couldn't stand in front of the Vinson's house and snap away, taking my time to frame the best shot. At the corner, I paused to take in the view. I could see much of Monterey Bay, from the long open stretches of beach near Seaside to the power plant towers in Moss Landing and the hills north of Watsonville that rose above the haze.

The Vinson's house — an enormous stucco — was the second house from the corner at the top of a steep hill. The back of the house faced the view. The tidy front yard contained a small oval lawn, dwarf citrus trees in oversized blue ceramic pots, trimmed bushes, and recently planted annuals. A driveway along the left side of the house led to the detached two car open bay garage. An outdoor patio, with an ornate three level fountain and a compliment of teak furniture, was tucked between the garage and the house.

I walked past the driveway, stopped and said, "Oh, shoot," as I fumbled in my pockets, pretending to look for something. Then, I held up my phone, aimed, took the photo, and hurried away.

Back in the car, I opened the app. As I already knew, the house was purchased in May, 2005 for eight hundred thousand and was extensively remodeled. It had lost value in the recession of 2007, but the value had roared back and the house was now worth well over a million. A million dollars for a twenty-five hundred square foot, three-bedroom, two-bath, house.

The 3D tour showed three entrances on the bottom floor. The front door opened to the small front yard. French doors in the living room opened on to a deck that ran along the backside of the house and overlooked the view. The third door led from a small utility room off the kitchen to the side patio and the detached garage.

That's what I would watch tonight.

•　　　•　　　•

The light was fading as I slammed the brakes and watched the tail end of Kathleen's Lexus disappear into traffic. The rental, with brakes much more receptive than those on my aging Honda, screeched to a halt just as the light turned red. For the third time in our practice session, Kathleen had managed to skip through a yellow light and leave me in the dust.

She had the courtesy to wait for me, pulling back into traffic as soon as the light turned green. We hadn't tried the freeway yet. Kathleen said that if someone knew they were being tailed, they wouldn't even use the freeway. Too obvious. And the freeway was capricious — it was easy to get stuck in traffic. The best way to lose someone was on a busy street at a yellow light. As she'd proven three times now.

Several blocks ahead, Kathleen turned right. By the time I made the turn, she'd vanished. Keeping just below the speed limit, I cruised the Monterey neighborhood of small stucco homes, glancing up and down cross streets. Two blocks down, I was rewarded by the sight of Kathleen's gold Lexus a half block ahead. I followed her, keeping well behind. She turned right at a stop sign, onto a main street. A car pulled in between us, but I managed to keep up, easily navigating all the choke points.

Then, I lost her. The gold Lexus was gone. A sign for the Del Monte Mall pointed to the left. I gambled, turned toward the mall, noticing the parking garage ahead. Kathleen had warned me against parking garages. Death traps, she called them. Too easy to drive around a corner and find a car blocking your access. If you were lucky, the driver would have disappeared on foot. If you weren't quite as lucky, the driver would be waiting for you, squatting behind the open car door, gun at the ready.

I gave the parking garage a pass and was rewarded by the sight of Kathleen's car parked in the outer reaches of the uncovered lot. I pulled in next to her and got out.

Kathleen exited at the same time as me. "Good job, Shelby," she said. "You didn't take the bait."

"Always avoid parking garages," I said.

"Always," she repeated, glancing at her watch. "Almost seven," she said. "We should find a place to eat, then do one more drive through the neighborhood."

"Sounds good," I answered. A sudden fatigue hit me, starting at the backs of my knees and rising upward, making me feel shaky, nervous, and tired. Not a good combination.

22

H OURS LATER, MY FATIGUE had been replaced by surges of adrenaline. I was out with a dog leash, walking, half-running, calling, "Skipper, Skipper," over and over. My voice held a frantic edge. The ruse Kathleen and I had come up with was simple: after dark, I'd prowl the neighborhood, pretending to look for my lost dog. I'd drive the car from block to block, hop out, and look around. At nine-thirty, I planned to end up close to the Vinson's, where I'd sink low in the driver's seat, wait, watch, and hope no one would report me.

By the time my voice and legs had given out, sheets of thick fog shrouded the car in a dense mist. Though the fog cut down on visibility, it also shielded me from prying eyes. I pulled the blanket up around my chin, thankful Kathleen had checked my list and made sure I had everything I might possibly need.

I picked up the night scope, focusing on the garage. Both of the cars were there: the practical Honda and the old Econoline van. The plan had sounded simple enough when Kathleen and I reviewed it over dinner. Follow Randy, see where he ends up. Watch from the car, get a video if possible.

And don't get out of the car. Kathleen repeated this, several times: "This is only vehicle surveillance, Shelby. This is not foot surveillance. Watch only from your car. We know he carries. For your safety, you need to be in the car when you're following him. If we need to be on the ground, we can do that another night. Together. Got it?"

I'd nodded in agreement.

We'd also discussed what merited a phone call. If I found Randy having sex with a minor or engaged with child pornography, I was supposed to call Kathleen, no matter what time. If he was running guns or drugs, I should call. Discovering a girlfriend, alcohol, adult entertainment, recreational drugs, a poker game, or all five, did not warrant a call.

The light gathering scope allowed me to see the entire property clearly. The house was closed up tight. The entryway, living room, and den on the first floor were completely dark. A soft glow came from one of the upstairs windows. The hall maybe or a bathroom. I glanced at my watch, barely nine forty-five. I sank back down in the driver's seat and pulled the blanket closer.

My phone buzzed. I picked it up and smiled. A text from Cody: "How's it going?"

"Slow," I texted back. "Cold. Boooring."

"Haha," was the response. "I've been thinking about you. Can I take you to brunch on Sunday?"

"Absolutely," I texted back.

I received a smiley face in return, along with the message: "See you then." All I could think of was Cody's smile, his touch, his eyes.

And now, I was stuck. I should have told him my history. That morning I came from Ryan and Lisa's, I should have told him about Justin and Justine. The surrogacy. The baby-brokering. My research. About all of it.

I could tell him on Sunday. I could give him the article to read.

Or I could wait until Justin was found.

I sighed, defeated. Kathleen had told me to go back to the beginning. What was the beginning? The night Justin was taken? Or was the beginning further back — that night when Diane held a gun on Megan and me? Or was it when I'd moved to the cottage on Jackson and Diane's property? Or when I got pregnant? Or even before that, when I'd interviewed for the position of surrogate?

I had no way of knowing. I hadn't even kept a journal. But Diane had. She'd religiously recorded every finding at every doctor visit, from my blood pressure to my weight, my iron levels, the doctor's comments, the uterus measurement. I remembered that book as clearly as if I'd seen it yesterday: a five-by-seven red leather journal, the size of a paperback, just the right size to slip into a purse. Once, when I'd tried to pick it up, Diane had yanked it away from me, giving me one of those chilling looks that froze my insides and made me back off.

As far as I knew the journal had not turned up in the police sweep of the property on Ice Cream Grade. What had happened to it?

•　　　•　　　•

At five past ten, a security light flicked on, and I could see the vague outline of a tall man pushing his way through the fog, head down. Another light popped on when he reached the perimeter of the garage. Randy Vinson — dressed for trouble in jeans, a dark sweatshirt, and dark tennis shoes.

A car door slammed and the van started up, noisy and rough. Randy backed the dark blue Econoline out of the garage and swung the van toward the street. Foot steady on the accelerator, he turned right, heading away from me, and then left, up the hill to the two-lane road that connected to Highway 1, where he'd have to choose: north toward Santa Cruz or south toward Carmel. Before starting my car, I forced myself to count to five. I remembered what the book had said. If you left too soon, your target would see you. Too late, and you'd lose him.

By the time I turned the second corner, Randy had already reached the stop sign at the junction. He turned left. I followed, my eyes glued to the van's taillights, keeping my foot on the gas, slowing down, edging past the speed limit in fits. Randy pulled ahead, doing fifty-five in the forty-five mile zone. I stayed just above the speed limit, hoping he wouldn't get too far ahead. I almost lost him at the traffic light by the hospital. The light was turning yellow as Randy zipped through; I had to step on the gas to follow him, streaking through just as it turned red. To my surprise, Randy went north on Highway 1, toward Monterey, Seaside, Marina, Watsonville, Santa Cruz. For some reason, I assumed that he'd be turning south, to Carmel, where the money was.

Once on the freeway, he veered into the left lane, immediately taking the car up to seventy. I stayed to the right, keeping a healthy distance between us. There weren't too many drivers on the road and I knew I'd be able to see him when he cut across to exit. Ten minutes later, Randy pulled into the right lane, taking the exit for Marina, one of the lowest income cities in the area. It used to be the hub for Fort Ord, but after the base was decommissioned, the local economy had crashed. Now, there was a Walmart, a few strip malls and gas stations; and neighborhood after neighborhood of sixties style ranchettes. The wind and fog whipped through Marina constantly, making the town always cold, always winter.

I followed Randy through three traffic lights, luckily all green, passing an entrance to the Walmart on the left. We were the only cars on the road, and I slowed at a stop sign, pretending to fiddle with my phone. But as soon as the van's taillights disappeared into the fog, I continued. The road narrowed and the road surface disintegrated into potholes and ruts. Randy blew through the next stop sign. I stopped. To my right was a sagging four square apartment building. To my left, a row of mobile homes lined the street. A block down, the van turned left on to a dark, narrow, unlit street. I wouldn't be able to follow. It'd be too obvious. I drove past the turn, trying to see where he'd gone, but it was too dark. I turned around and pulled into the parking lot in front of the apartment building, driving to the far end where I hoped I wasn't taking anyone's spot.

And I waited.

Thirty minutes later, Randy hadn't returned, and I wondered how long I should watch, grateful that Kathleen had insisted I stay in the car. I pulled my jacket close around me, huddled under the blanket, and thought about Randy's guns, the Sig Sauer and the Glock, wondering if he was carrying them now.

By midnight, there was no sign of Randy. One in the morning came and went. At one-thirty, I gave up, assuming that Randy had driven home another way. I wondered if he knew he'd been followed.

DAY FOUR

FRIDAY, JULY 20

23

IT WAS ALMOST HALF-PAST TWO WHEN I ARRIVED HOME. The futon sofa in the living room was pulled out and someone had unrolled my sleeping bag and carefully placed my pillow at the head of the bed. A note lay on the pillow:

> Megan and Annie are in your room. Megan wasn't feeling well, and I offered them your bed. I thought it'd be easier for you to be out here. I hope that's okay. Sleep well!
> Dexter.

A smiley face softened the fact that he'd given my bed away without asking.

It didn't matter — I fell into a deep sleep as soon as my head hit the pillow.

Sunlight refracting through the sliding glass doors woke me a few hours later. I got up, pulled the sleeping bag around me like a robe, and cautiously pushed open the door to my room. Just like a princess, Annie had commandeered most of the bed, pushing Megan into the small inside corner. The child lay on her back with her pink nightgown twisted around her body. Her dark hair curled against her rosy cheek, just like a child in a Mary Cassatt painting.

Megan stirred and I grabbed my workout clothes from the hook behind the door, found my walking shoes, and slipped out. I dressed and left the apartment, key in my pocket. The complex was quiet at this time of day. I started at a slow pace and by the time I reached the street, I was at a brisk walk. I followed my customary route, out 14th street, right on East Cliff Drive to the harbor, with the lagoon on my right and the beach on my left.

I walked along the beach to the mouth of the harbor, passing my office building. Mesmerized by the shifting gray waves rolling in through the jetty, I sat for a moment on one of the wide, flat stones. A lone kayaker in a bright yellow kayak punched through the breakers, the waves frothing over the bow of the boat like whipped cream. A dense curtain of fog sat out in the bay, its boundary pushing toward shore, then being sucked back out. A sailboat motored into it, the blue hull and white sail melting into the fog bank, with the top of the mast glinting in the sunlight for a few seconds before being swallowed up, whole.

I broke into a slow jog, following the road that circled the harbor, passing the slips with deep clearance where the mega-yachts were berthed. Farther on, I passed a storage yard, reeking of epoxy, and then the dock where rental kayaks and paddleboards were stored. I looked up when I heard a shout: a man standing on the deck of his small motorboat was hollering to someone a few slips over. An engine sputtered. A slight breeze rocked the boats — ropes thwacked hollow aluminum masts and metal stays thrummed.

Suddenly fatigued, I stopped, put my hands on my thighs, and paused to catch my breath. I decided to turn around and head home. I was just too tired. Instead of exercise, I needed a bath and a cup of coffee.

I retraced my steps. Once I left the safety of the harbor and was back on the road, cars whizzed by at a constant, steady clip. A truck passed too close and I flinched. A motorcycle roared by, the throbbing of its engine echoing in my ears.

I followed the street as it angled up a hill, away from the water. At the top of the hill, just before my turn, it curved sharply to the right into a blind curve bordered by a tangle of ivy, blackberries, and poison oak. There was no sidewalk and only a sliver of a shoulder. Miraculously, drivers always managed to avoid me and I was able to squeeze by the thorns without getting poked.

But today, my good luck was about to run out.

Just as I reached that curve, I heard the screech of tires. I turned around to look. Down by the water, a large dark pickup was slowing traffic, with the driver gunning the engine and then slamming the brakes to squeal to a bouncing, shuddering halt. The pickup continued its slow progress up the hill and the line of cars behind him increased. A few drivers started to honk in irritation. One driver in a convertible pulled over and I could see her pulling out her phone, presumably calling 911.

The guy looked like a loose cannon and I wondered if I should try to cross the street. But cars kept coming down the hill in the opposite direction, and for now, at least, I was trapped. I turned and started to jog, sure I'd have time to slip around the curve and make it to safety before the truck reached me.

Then I heard the hum of tires on the road behind me. My jog turned into a sprint and I glanced over my shoulder as I ran. The pickup was bearing down on me like a heat-seeking missile — straight, true, and unwavering.

I leapt and landed head-first in the bushes, falling through the brambles to the asphalt beneath. The pickup driver slowed and honked at me, a reproaching rat-tat-tat that reminded me of a machine gun. I rolled over just in time to give him the finger. The truck squealed around the curve and was gone.

As I slowly climbed out of the brambles, thorns scratched and tore my skin. Blood beaded on my palms, knees, and elbows.

A silver minivan pulled over, blocking traffic. The driver, a middle-aged woman, opened the passenger window and called out, gesturing, "Honey, are you okay? That guy tried to mow you down."

Panting, I lifted my hands in the air and eyed them. "I'm okay. I think." I gestured across the street. "I live over there."

"You need a lift?"

I pointed to my cuts and scratches. "I'm all bloody," I said.

"Even more reason you need a ride," she replied. "Hop in."

Wiping my oozing palms on my shirt, I opened the door with my fingertips, and sank gratefully into the seat.

"I got the first three numbers off the guy's license plate. California plates. I think you should report it," the woman said as she navigated back into traffic. "Open the box there, okay?" She pointed to the glove compartment and I pulled it open, trying not to leave bloody fingerprints. The contents were clean and organized. The owner's manual, two maps, an envelope, and a notebook with a pencil stuck in the spine. "Write this down," she said. "4XZ. That might be enough to find him.

"And here's my number, in case you need a witness." She rattled off a phone number.

"Thanks," I said, scribbling down the information.

I tore out the paper, stuck it in my pocket, and returned the notebook to the glove box.

She pulled into the left lane, put on her signal, turned, and drove to the end of the street.

"In here?" She pointed to the entrance of the apartment complex and I nodded.

The woman stopped the car and I opened the door. "Call the cops," she advised. "They'd want to know there's a homicidal driver on the loose."

24

WHEN I LIMPED INTO THE APARTMENT, Dexter, already dressed for work, was sitting at the small table reading the newspaper. The aroma of freshly brewed coffee filled the air.

"Hey," he said, eyes fixed to the paper. He looked up as I walked across the room. "What have you been …? Jesus, Shel, what happened to you?"

I hobbled past him into the kitchen and said, "Someone tried to mow me down." I grabbed a wad of paper towels to staunch the blood seeping from scrapes on my palms and then pulled a mug out of the dishwasher.

Dexter followed me into the kitchen. "You're a mess." He took the mug out of my hand and filled it with coffee.

A scrape ran up my right shin. My left knee was bloody. Leaning over, I could see that in addition to harboring dirt and leaf debris, I'd picked up a few small stones. I examined my hands. My palms were red and oozing, pockmarked with small grains of dirt.

"I was walking up the hill, around the curve," I said, and Dexter nodded in recognition of the spot. "I turned around, for one last look at the beach, and saw a pickup way down by the water. The guy was stepping on the gas, then jamming on the brakes, like he was trying to get the car to bounce." I shook my head and cupped my hands around the mug, wincing as the heat radiated into my palms. "I kept walking, not really paying attention. Next thing I knew, I heard tires on the road behind me. I swear he was aiming right at me.

"So I dove. The pickup roared past me. A woman stopped and offered me a ride here. She got the license. Some of it, anyway. California plates."

"You recognize the car?"

I shook my head. "Never seen it. It was dark. Maybe old? The paint was kind of dull."

Dexter glanced at my knee. "You better call the cops, Shelby."

I shook my head. "I don't want to."

"Shelby," Dexter said. "You have to. You're studying criminal justice. Just think how you'd feel if he actually hit someone." He marched across the room, picked his cell up from the kitchen counter, and handed it to me.

"Dexter, I don't want to," I heard myself whine. It was like we were kids again. That, or shock was setting in.

"Just imagine if Annie, or Ashley, had been out there, walking to school." A shudder ran through him and he thrust the phone at me again.

I took his phone and held it with my fingertips. Dispatch, a woman with a serious, efficient voice, picked up on the first ring. "Do you have an emergency?"

"Sort of," I shook my head even though she couldn't see me. "I was just out on a walk and someone tried to run me down."

"Where?"

I gave her the location. "Any identifying features?"

"Black pickup. It was squarish, an older model. California plates. I have the first three letters of the plate: 4XZ."

"Are you hurt?" she asked.

"I have gravel in my knee and hands." I gingerly bent my leg; my kneecap was starting to throb. "My leg is scraped up from diving head first into the bushes. But I don't need to go to the hospital."

"Name?"

I gave her my name and contact information. "Thank you for your report," the woman said. "I'll pass this along to the Sheriff's department and they'll forward it to the CHP. We may be calling you back for more information."

Dexter heard me thank the dispatcher and called, "All done?"

I limped back into the living room, my left leg throbbing. "Done," I replied.

"Sorry I gave away your bed without asking. Megan was having a hard time last night. Panic attack. I thought that asking the two of them to stay here would be easier than me sleeping on the sofa over there."

"It's okay," I said. "Is she alright?"

"I think so," he said. "We didn't talk about it much. We ate and I played with Annie while she studied. Annie went to sleep early and I quizzed Megan." He stood and stretched, downing the last of his coffee. "I'm outta here," he said. "See you tonight and tell Megan I'll call her at lunch."

•   •   •

Fifteen minutes later I was sunk deep in the bathtub, immersed in warm water up to my neck. I lifted my left leg and propped it on the side of the tub. Taking a washcloth, I delicately scrubbed, wincing as I flicked out the small fragments of gravel. When I'd finished with my knee, I dabbed it one last time and turned my attention to my hands.

Upon examination, I could see a thorn embedded in the flesh of my right palm, picked up when I'd plunged into the brambles. Had that driver really been heading right for me? The woman in the minivan had seen it from behind; she sure thought he had been. I closed my eyes and put my hands back in the water, wondering if I'd have to go to a doc in the box to extricate the thorn. Maybe if I soaked it for a while, and kept it covered overnight, it would work its way to the surface.

I saw the pickup in my mind's eye, the driver gunning the engine, slamming on the brakes, forcing the truck into a bounce. I was sure I'd never seen him before, a bulky man with a maniacal frenzied look, wearing a battered cowboy hat.

Even though the water in the tub was still warm, a shiver ran up my back and goose bumps rose on my legs. Did this have something to do with Justin? Randy Vinson? It did seem like that driver had been aiming for me, slowing the car, and speeding up when he knew he'd catch me on that curve where I had no way out. I looked around in alarm, as if some evil had just surfaced right there, in the bathroom.

A knock on the door interrupted my thoughts. "Anybody in there?"

"Hey, Megan, I am. But come on in." I reached up and pulled the shower curtain across the tub.

"Thanks." The door opened. Megan padded across the bathroom and plopped down on the toilet. The toilet seat shifted. We needed to call the property manager before the thing fell off.

"How are you?" I asked. "And how did you sleep?"

"I'm okay. Your bed is so comfortable. Thank you for letting us use it, even though you didn't have a say." Megan yawned. "How did your thing go last night?"

"Okay."

Megan reached out and yanked on the shower curtain, rattling it. "What do you mean, okay? It had to have been more exciting than just an okay. Did you catch him doing anything?"

"No, nothing. He drove to Marina and turned down a small road that looked like a driveway. I couldn't follow him. And that was it."

"That was it? No girlfriend? No drugs? No parties?" The toilet paper rattled in the holder, followed by the sound of flushing.

"Nothing. At least I didn't see anyone else drive down that road."

Water ran in the sink.

I sat up and turned on the bath water. "I'll be out in a sec."

"Okay," Megan said. "We have to scoot. I want to get home and ..."

"Wait," I interrupted. "I have to give my sweet pea a hug. There's coffee out there."

When I exited the bathroom, one towel wrapped around me and another around my head, Annie let loose an excited shriek and ran over to me. She was still dressed in her princess nightgown and her small tummy pushed against the shiny fabric.

"Guess what?" she asked.

I knelt down next to her, one hand at my throat, holding the towel in place, the other on top of my head, steadying the turban. "What?"

"I slept in there." She pointed toward my bedroom and bounced up and down in excitement.

"How was it?" I asked.

But the child didn't answer. Her eyes were looking upward, and she appeared fixated on the towel covering my wet hair.

"What's that?" she asked, pointing.

Megan came out of the bedroom, dressed. "What's up?" she asked. I could see her eyes move from her daughter to me, and back to her daughter. Confusion, followed by alarm. "Shelby," she said, "something's bleeding. There's blood all over the towel."

I yanked my hand off the towel on my head and it tumbled to the floor. A dark red splotch on the white terrycloth caught my attention.

"Oh," I said. "That. I was out for a walk this morning and I fell."

"Ouch," Megan said, "that looks bad." She threw her daughter a worried look and held out her hand. "Come here, pumpkin. Let's get Auntie Shelby some Band-aids."

"Thanks," I said. I stood, picked up the bloodied towel and tossed it toward my bedroom. Then, I grabbed a handful of paper towels and pressed them against my palm, while, at the same time, made sure the other towel stayed wrapped around me.

"Your leg, too?" Megan gestured when they returned.

"Yeah," I said. "Elbows too. I took a nosedive."

Megan peeled the Band-aids open while Annie watched, carefully accepting the wrapping her mom handed her. I held out my right hand, blotted my still-oozing palm, and Megan applied the strips. We repeated the process for my left.

"Thanks," I said.

"You're welcome," she replied. Megan gestured to the child. "Give your auntie a kiss," she said.

Annie came over and I knelt down. "I'm sorry you have a boo-boo," she whispered. Tenderly, she inspected the clean Band-aid on my palm and kissed it, her lips as light as butterfly wings.

Blinking away my sudden, unexpected tears, I stood, saying, "Thanks. I better get changed. Please, help yourself to whatever you can find."

I went into my room, pushing away the soiled towel with my foot, deciding I'd just cut it up for the rag bag. That bloodstain would never come out.

25

LATER THAT MORNING, after I pulled myself together, I returned the rental car and called Kathleen for a ride. Fifteen minutes later when I hopped into her car, she did a double-take, noticing the bandages on my hands. "What happened to you?" she asked. "Are you okay? Is that from last night?"

"No," I replied. "I tripped when I was out on my walk this morning."

"Looks bad," she said. Then, as she maneuvered out of the lot and turned right onto Ocean Street, she asked, "So what happened with Randy?"

I talked quickly, giving Kathleen an overview, ending with, "It was a bust. A complete bust."

"Not at all," Kathleen replied. "You found out where he went. And that he drove there alone. We'll do this again next week, say Monday night? We'll work out a plan ahead of time, and figure out how we can follow him down that driveway. We can scope it out during the day to see if there are private property signs. If not, we can walk down the road and see what's there."

"Ready to hear the blow-by-blow?"

"Not yet," Kathleen replied. "Once I'm in the office and settled in, I'll let you know."

Thirty minutes later, she was sitting at her desk, pen in hand, poised over a yellow pad. "Go," she said.

"He left his house right after ten, just like Claire said. He drove to Highway 1 and went north."

"Start earlier," Kathleen ordered.

I paused and began with my drive to Randy Vinson's neighborhood, and then wandering the streets looking for my pretend lost dog. When I reached the part about counting to five before turning on the car and following him out of his driveway, Kathleen leaned in. "You don't think he saw you?"

"I don't think so," I replied. "At least, if he knew I was there, he didn't try to shake me. He stopped at all the lights on Del Monte in Marina, and even put on his signal when he disappeared down that driveway.

"And that was it. I waited, and waited, and waited. At one-thirty, I gave up."

Kathleen nodded and said, "Get a map and see if we can approach from the other side." Her voice lifted in excitement. "Maybe we'll need two cars. Type up your report and I'll send it to Claire."

And to my surprise, she added, "Good work, Shelby."

A slight tingle ran up my spine as I exited the room. A compliment from Kathleen was like an A++ from professor David McGuire, who taught one of the most difficult criminal justice classes at De Anza, Crime and Criminology. That class was on my schedule next semester.

•   •   •

The first thing I did was find the property in a mapping program. I opened Google satellite view. The road led to a structure that looked like a double-wide trailer. When I switched to street view, I could locate the turn, but couldn't navigate down the road. I switched back to satellite view and captured the image, and then used a drawing program to circle the road and the trailer. I saved the image for the report. Without an address, I couldn't do a title search.

My written report was two pages long; I hoped it was enough information, without too much embellishment. I read it over several times and after a few edits, I was satisfied. What I said was true. Accurate. I emailed the report to Kathleen and continued with the background check I'd been working on.

At four, I closed the laptop and packed up. I knocked on Kathleen's door. "What are you doing this weekend?" I asked as I stowed the laptop.

"Not much. Watching the grandkids. You?" Kathleen asked, looking up from her computer screen.

"Not sure yet," I answered. "Laying low."

"Anything more on Justin?" she asked.

"Nothing," I replied. "I'm going over there now. Lisa should be back from the hospital. Maybe the police will have made some progress."

"I'll make some calls for you this weekend," Kathleen offered. "See if I can find out anything."

"Thanks," I replied.

"See you Monday, Shelby," she said. "Have a good weekend."

Four words. Four everyday words that millions of Americans toss out on a Friday afternoon. I should have savored them when I had the chance.

•　　　•　　　•

The police officer was absent from the Boyd's porch, and when I knocked, I heard an immediate brisk footfall, the sound of someone light on their feet. The door was pulled open by a petite woman about Lisa's age. Without giving me a chance to say anything, she shot, "You're not a reporter, are you? If you are, you can get off this porch right now. Vultures, the whole lot of you."

"No, no. I'm not a reporter." I was trying to interject my response, but she would have none of it until she'd finished. "No," I repeated. "I'm not. I'm Shelby. Family friend."

Without pulling the door open, she called over her shoulder. "Ryan. Someone named Shelby says she's a family friend. Should I let her in?"

A faint, "Yes," came from the direction of the living room and kitchen.

The woman offered her hand. "I'm Allie, Lisa's sister."

I shook her hand saying, "Pleased to meet you."

I followed her back to the kitchen, weaving my way through the cluttered living room. The table with the Christmas train had been moved off to the side, giving the illusion of additional space. Ryan sat at the kitchen table, sipping a cup of coffee. "Want some?" He gestured wearily toward the pot. "You two met?"

We both nodded.

"Well, I'll leave you alone," Allie said, as soon as she confirmed that Ryan really did know who I was. "I'll check on Lisa." With that, Allie left the room and I could hear her feet hit each step on the way up the staircase.

"How are things?" I asked as I grabbed a glass from the cupboard and helped myself to water.

I turned around in time to see Ryan shrug. "As good as can be expected, I guess. Lisa is home, but she won't get out of bed. Justine hides in her room all the time. Thank goodness for Allie. We'd all starve otherwise. I tried to go back to work, but they told me to go home, with pay."

"Anything from the police?"

"No, not really." He lifted his mug, stamped with the Toyota logo, and took a long sip. "They were here this morning, but they're not telling us anything. They say they're working on it. That they have leads."

I raised my eyebrow. "Leads?"

"They set up a tip hotline. With a reward we're posting. Ten grand."

I nodded. "And no one's called for a ransom?"

Ryan shook his head and glanced up, saying, "Apparently, no one credible." His eyes were huge in his gaunt face and dark circles shaded his cheeks. The man had aged since I last saw him.

"Anything on the phone call from Justin?"

"No, no, no. They questioned Justine, over and over. I don't think they believed her."

I winced. I never thought to doubt her.

"How's Lisa?" I asked.

He rubbed his temples and said, "She came home yesterday, heavily sedated. She's still out of it. I took her to her appointment this morning, and the doctor said it was just a normal reaction to all the meds. When I asked him when she'd return to her old self, he stared at me like I was an idiot.

"I can't sleep. My doctor won't give me any sleeping pills, says I'll get addicted to the stuff." He cradled his head in his hands. "Fine I say. Fine."

"Can I go see Justine?"

"Sure." He waved his hand toward the stairs. "Just knock. She's now into this privacy thing."

She's barely a kid, I wanted to remind him, but I kept my mouth shut.

•   •   •

"Who is it?" Justine's high-pitched voice filtered through the closed door.

"Shelby. I was here a couple of days ago. You told me about the phone call from Justin."

"I remember you. You can enter." The queen granting her subject an audience.

Justine sat in her tiny red armchair, her bearing like royalty. She glanced up, and then returned to her book, finishing the sentence or paragraph or page, however fast she read, before looking back at me.

"Hello." She stated this as a fact, apparently not expecting me to reply.

"Hey," I replied. "What are you reading now?"

"It's a collection of Greek classics. Aristotle, Euripides, Herodotus, Homer, Plato …" Her voice trailed off.

"Oh," I said, wrestling with the image, trying to imagine Annie saying those words, let alone knowing what they meant. "Where did you get it?"

"Mail order. Ryan got it for me. Amazon probably." Today, she was dressed like an Ivy Leaguer. Or what an Ivy Leaguer might wear in a college catalog. Dockers. Khakis. A cream-colored turtleneck, with only the collar and cuffs showing from underneath a lime-green cable knit sweater.

"Anything else from your brother?"

She shook her head, keeping her eyes on the book. "Nothing." She turned the page and then the next one and the next. It was as if she was skimming the material, but I knew if I asked, she'd be able to recite every word, give the historical and cultural context, and provide an analysis.

I stared out her window. It faced the backyard and I could see directly across into the neighbor's property. The lawn in the Boyd's backyard was overgrown and surrounded by a six-foot tall plywood fence. The ornamental hedge bordering the fence was browning, the branches sparse, and the leaves sagging. A faded plastic pink and green Fisher-Price dollhouse sat by the hedge, next to a small turtle-shaped blue plastic sandbox, empty of sand. The window wasn't locked and rose smoothly and silently on its track. I stuck my head out. It was a twenty-foot drop, straight down. No scuffs on the window frame. No nearby roof dormers for easy access. Whoever had snatched Justin hadn't come in this way.

I closed the window and locked it, saying, "Let me know if you hear anything else from him, okay?"

She didn't answer, but just continued to turn pages.

Ryan was still sitting in the kitchen, head in his hands, staring into his coffee cup. He held the cup to his mouth, sipped, and grimaced. "This stuff is terrible."

I gently pried the mug from his hands. "It's probably cold. Do you want another cup?"

"No," he shook his head. "No thanks. I'm going to try to take a nap."

"Call me. I'll be back sometime this weekend, okay?"

He nodded and looked at the tabletop. Not at me. "Okay," he said. "I will."

Had he lost all confidence in me? I wanted to remind him that I was trying. But I had nothing to go on. A missing child, taken in the middle of the night. A ghost bear. And a phantom phone call. More than anyone, I wanted to find Justin. But wanting to wasn't enough.

26

I HIT AFTERNOON TRAFFIC on my way back to Santa Cruz, a steady stream of stop-and-go that lengthened my drive by three-quarters of an hour. By the time I reached the apartment, I was ready for a quiet house, a long nap, and a beer. But my immediate needs weren't met. Dexter was home and he'd already commandeered the TV. The blare of a sports announcer filled the room.

"Can you turn that down?" I yelled as I walked in. "Can't hear myself think." Dexter complied, aiming the remote toward the screen. As soon as the volume diminished, I commented, "I didn't think you liked baseball."

"It's all that's on right now that I can stomach. Something to take my mind off a long week."

"That bad?" I asked, dropping my pack on the kitchen counter and filling a glass with water.

"Yes. That bad." He turned to look at me as I flopped onto the sofa next to him. "You must be exhausted," he said. "Was that just last night you did your surveillance thing?"

I nodded. "Yes. Seems like years ago."

"How're your injuries?"

I held up my palm to show the two Band-aids covering the scrapes and the thorn. "Fine. I'll heal."

"Did you hear back from the cops?"

Shaking my head, I said, "Nothing."

Dexter shrugged. "I'm glad you're okay." He aimed the remote at the TV and flipped channels. "So what are you up to this weekend?"

"Trying to find Justin. And I have to chase down a couple of addresses, but otherwise, not much. Hanging around. Seeing Cody on Sunday morning."

Dexter gave me a poke in the ribs and chortled, saying, "Sounds good. I have Ashley Sunday afternoon. Maybe we could all do something — you, me, Ashley, Megan, and Annie. Cody?"

I elbowed Dexter in the ribs in return. "I think he's working, but that sounds like fun. Do you want me to call Megan or do you want to?"

"I already did," he said, turning to me with a broad smile. "Taken care of."

"Great," I said, trying to hide the grin I felt creeping across my face.

I stood up and walked back to the kitchen, where I filled up my glass again and drained it. I placed the glass on the counter, grabbed my phone, and swiped to the photo I'd taken of the sheet of addresses. As I sat back down next to Dexter, I handed him my phone and pointed to the last address on the list: 789 PCCR.

"Kathleen wants me to see if I can figure out where this is." The lie slipped out effortlessly.

Dexter stared at it. "You're sure? This is not one of the addresses in that list you were telling me about?" Dexter stared at me, eyes searching for anything that would give me away.

I shook my head, staring at my phone, sure Dexter would see right through me. "No, of course not," I said. "I'm not stupid."

He sighed, obviously doubtful. But he didn't press. "No city?" he asked.

"Nope," I said. I glanced at him. "Does PCCR mean anything to you?"

"Not PCCR," he said slowly as he handed my phone back to me. "But PCR does. Pescadero Creek Road," he said. "It's up the coast, off Highway 84. I see it all the time on one of the bicycle forums I check. Crazy people are always riding that road. It's narrow, steep, and slippery. It's always shaded. In the winter, it can be icy. I've never done it."

"Pescadero Creek Road," I muttered, staring at the piece of paper. "Maybe she added in an extra 'C' by mistake. I wonder if there's a '789'."

"Check it out online," Dexter said as he flipped through the channels.

Within five minutes, I found a "Pescadero Creek Road", forty miles north of Santa Cruz. Numerous spurs shot off the main road and squirreled across the landscape in random loops and whorls. When I overlaid the satellite view, I could see that the squiggly road pattern actually made sense. The twists followed the contours of the mountain range, switching back and forth up a steep grade and swooping down the backside. It didn't take much longer to locate a "Pescadero Creek Canyon Road", a narrow windy track that curved along a canyon bottom into a dead end.

It would be the perfect place to hide babies. Off the beaten track, no other houses nearby. In fact, it might have been the last place Frankie had driven me to, when I was tied up in the back seat of his truck.

I couldn't find any house numbers, but I knew it was definitely worth a visit.

An idea formed in the back of my mind. As much as I wanted to ask Megan along, I knew I shouldn't. She'd have to bring Annie and the excursion might prove risky. But I could meet up with Megan after. A kind of insurance policy. If I didn't show up, she might think to call Dexter. Or someone.

I escaped to my bedroom, closed the door, picked up my phone, and swiped and tapped. "Hey," I said when Megan answered. "What are you doing tomorrow afternoon?" Even as I asked the question, I remembered. Her mom and her mom's partner were in town until Sunday morning.

But Megan's answer surprised me. "Trying to figure out how to study for my midterm. Mom and Tracy are here, but they're in Capitola all day tomorrow with their friend Betsy. They're helping her with her booth at the Capitola art show. At the end of the day, they're going out to eat. They asked me if I wanted to join them, but I have to study."

"Great," I replied, hoping the enthusiasm in my voice filtered through. "I am your salvation. Meet me at Waddell Creek, at the beach, tomorrow afternoon. Say around one? We can have a picnic. I'll watch Annie and you can study."

Megan replied immediately, excited. "Wonderful. But what are you doing before that?"

"I'm checking out an address up in the mountains. It's north of here, off 84. On a side road."

"For work?"

I hedged, not wanting to lie to my best friend. "Not really," I said.

"Shelby?"

I sighed and gave her an abbreviated version of my visit to Ice Cream Grade, ending with the photos and the list of random addresses.

"Shelby, you are crazy." Megan's voice had taken on a sharp tone and her emphasis on the word "crazy" didn't escape me. Though, just as I started to protest, Megan surprised me, "Look," she said. "I know there is no grand scheme. No Stork. No baby selling. It's just a wild goose chase, Shelby. Why waste your time?

"But let us join you. I know you'll do it with or without me. Annie and I can be your protection. We'll strong arm the bad guys."

"What about studying? Are you sure? It's at least an hour up there. It's way up in the mountains. Isolated."

Megan laughed. "I'll get up at five and study until eight. I'll put on the *Harry Potter and the Sorcerer's Stone* audiobook for Annie to listen to while we drive. She loves it, even though she's probably a little young for it. That narrator's voice is like a liquid tranquilizer. I'll be able to study and you can quiz me when we get to the beach."

"You sure?" I asked again, hardly believing it. "I have no idea what's there. There's no Google street view to let me get a look at it."

"That's because there's nothing there. And for that reason alone, I can't let you go by yourself. Pick us up around nine?"

"Don't tell Dexter, please? He already thinks I'm crazy."

"Of course not," Megan replied. "I'll tell him after, when we're laughing about it."

A warm feeling flooded through me. Besties. "Thanks," I said, softly. "See you at nine."

DAY FIVE

SATURDAY, JULY 21

27

I ARRIVED AT MEGAN'S APARTMENT a few minutes before nine, enjoying the sleepy feel that cocooned the housing complex. Megan's mother, Anne, answered the door and enveloped me in a hug. Releasing me, she put her hands on my shoulders, sizing me up. "How are you doing, Shelby? It's so nice to see you."

"I'm good. It's nice to see you too," I replied.

Her brown eyes searched my face and I was able to return her direct gaze with one of my own. At one point, I suspected that Anne had blamed me for Megan's injury. I'd been there, yes, but I had not aimed the gun or pulled the trigger, firing that bullet into her shin. I'd been trying to save us both.

I hadn't seen Anne in a year or more, and today, she looked youthful, rejuvenated. Her eyes were bright as she smiled at me. Her skin glowed and her thick silver hair fell to her shoulders. Turquoise earrings complimented her muted makeup. She wore a shawl of deep blue, the draped cloth accentuating her height and her tall, lithe lines.

Her hands slid off my shoulders as she turned and gestured toward the woman sitting on the sofa. "This is Tracy."

Tracy smiled as she stood and offered her hand, saying, "Good morning." She was a tiny woman, with graying hair that curled around her ears. Her sparkling blue eyes sized me up as she pumped my hand. She dressed simply, for function, not style, wearing a light green nylon jacket, a pair of jeans, and tennis shoes. No makeup, dangly earrings, scarves, shawls, flowing skirts, or earth shoes. I immediately liked her and wondered how she meshed with Anne's connection to all things ethereal and new age: shamans, fairies, colonic cleanses, juice diets.

"Hi," I said extending my hand to grasp hers. "Nice to meet you." Anne excused herself and hurried back down the hall toward the bedroom.

"It's nice to finally meet the famous Shelby I've heard so much about," Tracy said. Her voice was quiet and strong. Steady.

"I'm Shelby, yes," I replied, "though I'm not so sure about the famous part."

Tracy grinned and her whole face, from chin to forehead, crinkled in genuine joy. "I read about you in the news when it all happened and I remember thinking, 'Wow, that girl can kick it.'" The grin faded and she leaned over to me, raising her hand to her mouth and speaking as if we were sharing a secret. "Besides Anne here can't say enough good things about you."

I laughed and shrugged, trying to hide my pride. Tracy glanced at her watch and hollered, "Annie, we need to go. Don't want to be late." The name Annie didn't get by me. Like grandmother, like granddaughter.

"Coming," Anne shouted. Her voice floated from down the hall.

"You're here for the art festival?" I asked.

"Yes. Our friend, Betsy, is one of the artists. We helped her set up yesterday. They leave those paintings out there on the wharf in the fog and damp all night long. Not good for the canvases, but Betsy covers them with towels and tarps. Says this is one of her best festivals every year."

"What kind of artist is she?" I asked.

"Water colors. Landscapes. She does a lot of commissioned work for wineries in our area. They'll pay her to paint a view of the winery from the vineyard, or a view of the vineyard from the winery. Don't tell, but for one of them, a generic California winery, a huge commercial enterprise, she painted it from a postcard she bought in the gift shop. She couldn't have done a nicer job if she tried."

Now, it was my turn to laugh.

"Annie, we gotta go," Tracy called again, stepping over to the door.

Anne hurried back down the hall, calling, "Ready."

"Let's go then." Tracy held the door open and gestured for Anne to walk through. "Nice to meet you," she said.

"You too," I replied. "Bye, Anne. Nice to see you."

Anne waved. "Have a great day, Shelby. I hear you're off to the north coast?"

I nodded. "For a day of fun and sun. Annie loves the beach."

"That she does." Anne paused. "Keep an eye on that child," she said. "Don't let anything happen to her."

"I won't," I replied. "Don't worry. She'll be fine."

•　　　•　　　•

The sun sparkled off the hood of the car as I turned out of the family student housing parking lot. We were lucky, it was one of those bright, clear mornings with no fog or wind. The day would be warm, but not boiling. Megan slouched in the passenger seat, eyes closed. Her car, a Subaru wagon, was the easy choice. Comfy, good gas mileage, and to move all the kid stuff into my car — booster seat, CDs, the scattered toys and books, the extra bag of clothes — would be way too much work.

"How's the studying going?" I asked as we drove down the hill to the traffic light at the intersection that led out of campus. An unobstructed view of the bay opened before us. The Monterey peninsula looked like an island, floating in the blue waters to the south.

"The textbook is in my bag." She grimaced. "I think I know everything about DNA, base pairs, alleles, nucleotides, adenine, cytosine, guanine, and thymine. I still need to nail replication. So many terms." She sighed. "You'll watch Annie later while I review? And then quiz me?"

"Yup," I nodded, glancing at her. "Hey, those earrings look great." She was wearing the silver hoops I'd given her for her birthday last year. Shiny silver wire to accent her short dark hair.

"I love them," she said, as she touched them gently. "I wear them all the time.

"So when does your semester start?" she asked.

"Not for another month or so," I replied.

"What are you taking?"

"I've got a couple of required courses and one elective. Writing for Administration of Justice. That's a required class. Crime and Criminology. It's also required, hardest class from the hardest professor. My elective is Federal Courts and Constitutional Law, so I'll have a total of twelve units. I will be busy."

I turned right onto Western Drive, the street that would drop us on Highway 1 at the north edge of Santa Cruz.

"And what's the latest on Justin?"

As Megan reached down and pulled out her heavy textbook, I filled her in on Lisa's unscheduled visit to the psych ward, the phone call, and Justine's belief that she would soon see her brother.

For a few seconds, Megan was quiet. "That poor family," she said. "But that phone call doesn't make sense," she continued. "That it would come just at the exact time that no one else was in the house? And that she heard it? Maybe she just wants Justin to come home so much that she's making it up."

"I don't know," I said dubiously. "A call marked as 'Unknown' did come through on the cell that afternoon."

"Of course it did, Shelby," Megan said. "Justine looked at the phone, saw the call, and made the whole thing up. Even I could do that, and I don't have a genius IQ." Megan laughed. "Besides, she could probably figure out how to set it up."

I shrugged, not at all convinced.

"Anyway, I'm not that smart. You need to quiz me later," she said.

"Sure," I nodded, leaning back into the driver's seat and stretching my arms out straight, stifling a yawn. "Just tell me what to ask you about."

"Hey," she said, "it's not that boring. Anyway, it's time," she announced. "I better get to work."

She reached down and picked up the CD case, extracted a CD and put it into the player. Wiggling her hand into her pocket, she pulled out a pair of earplugs and rolled the small pink oblong foam between her fingers.

"Mama, start it," Annie demanded from the back seat.

"Hang on a sec," Megan said, twisting to look at me. "Hey, Cody was nice," she said. "Nice looking, too."

I glanced at her; she was smiling.

"Mama," Annie hollered.

Megan ignored her and added, "I knew he was going to be there. Dexter spilled the beans."

"Brat," I said. We reached the intersection with Highway 1 and I turned right on red, slowly accelerating.

She poked me in the ribs and I glanced at her. She was laughing. "Tell me about him," she demanded.

"Mama," Annie raised her voice to a shriek.

"Hang on, baby. Shelby's going to tell me about her new boyfriend."

A tingly feeling came over me and everything I knew about Cody came out in a rush. But there was so little to tell. When I faltered, she said, "That's it? Nothing else?"

"I don't know him that well," I protested. "Yet," I added.

We both laughed as Megan pushed the Play button and the strains of the introductory music filled the car. Megan began to work the pink foam earplug again.

I turned my attention to the road. Fields of Brussels sprouts stretched in long, tidy rows from the side of the highway to the edge of the cliffs over the Pacific, at least a half-mile away. Parked cars jammed every possible pullout. I glimpsed a minivan with all its doors open, two kids spilling out, followed by a dog, and then a smaller child. They took off running down a dirt road that cut through the fields across the bluff, with the dad behind, hands cupped around his mouth, yelling. The mom reached to the back seat of the minivan for something: a picnic basket, a blanket, a baby? I'd never know.

Another rutted pullout, another microcosm of beach life. A wet-suited surfer hefted his surfboard under one arm and took off for the water at a jog. A group of twenty-somethings wearing UCSC Banana Slug sweatshirts hovered around two cars laughing and snapping photos, while pulling coolers and towels out of back seats. A woman held on to the leashes of two straining dogs — a black lab and a golden retriever.

Ten minutes later, when we reached the small town of Davenport, I poked Megan and pointed. "Coffee?" I mouthed.

She shook her head, replying in a loud voice, "No thanks. I'm okay. You want one?"

"Nope," I said.

Later, I'd wonder. If we had stopped, would that have changed anything?

I glanced in the rearview mirror. Annie clutched her doll to her chest and stared out the window, almost in a trance, as if Harry Potter and the passing landscape were bewitching her.

Eight miles north of Davenport, the road swooped down a small grade to Waddell Creek Beach, famous for the steady wind, pounding surf, and dozens of kite surfers. As we drove down the slope, I could see a huge tipi-like structure constructed from driftwood sitting on the beach, well up from the surf line. Farther up the beach, a few kite surfers were assembling their gear, stopping to gauge the wind and study the trajectory of the boards already on the waves. The wind lifted the kites into the air off the large swells and the red, yellow, and green sails splashed against the blue sky like dabs of color in a Jackson Pollock painting.

Ahead, the sun glinted off the water like broken glass. Whitecaps dotted the surface of the blue ocean. When I turned to look at Megan again, she'd fallen asleep, her head leaning back against the headrest and her mouth open.

We followed the sweep of the road from one magnificent vista to the next. Steep tawny hills rose sharply to the right, on the inland side. On the left, always the ocean, a rumpled deep blue hemmed by white surf and rocky shores. When we passed the lighthouse at Pigeon Point, I wanted to elbow Megan and wake her, to revel in the unexpected magnificence. The white lighthouse rose pencil thin from a scrap of land that poked into the sea and I wondered how many lives that light had saved over the years.

Twenty minutes later, I put on my blinker and turned right, leaving the highway.

Megan stirred. "Where are we?" she asked.

"Just turning inland. About twenty more minutes," I said, wiggling my hand into my pocket and pulling out the map I'd printed earlier. I wasn't going to depend on my phone up here.

We followed Highway 84, a two-lane road, along Pescadero Creek for about ten miles until the road split, where we veered to the right. A few miles farther on, a small green reflective sign read Pescadero Creek Road. We turned left, deeper into the mountains. A mile past that, another sign marked the intersection with Pescadero Creek Canyon Road. Now, we turned right. The two lanes shrunk to one and one-half lanes and the pavement disappeared into rutted potholes.

I slowed as we approached a cluster of houses that seemed to be as old and crumbling as the road surface. A sprawling house, the patchwork turquoise and yellow paint now peeling, butted the shoulder of the road. A rusting, sagging trailer sat next to it, flanked by a smaller cottage leaning on its foundation. Half of the road was blocked by an ancient white pickup. I cringed as the passenger's side of the Subaru scraped the scrubby brush on the roadside.

Megan glimpsed a house number. "157," she said as we passed.

"We're looking for 789," I replied. "Keep your eyes peeled."

28

TWO MILES FARTHER ON, we found ourselves in a fairyland canyon. The road, shaded by redwoods, meandered along a creek. A small cabin, having seen better days, sat on the side of the road just before it dead ended at a locked gate. The cabin was run down, with boarded windows and a sagging porch. Slats were missing from the steps. Curling black roof shingles lay scattered on the ground. There was no identifying number on the building to indicate if this was the place I was looking for.

I stopped in the road, in front of the house. Megan elbowed me. "You going to get out?"

A small voice piped up from the back seat, "Mama, I have to pee."

"See you in a minute, Shelby." Megan hopped out and slammed the door behind her.

After I turned off the car, I put my phone in my pocket and climbed out, keeping my eye on the house as I walked up the steep dirt driveway. The driveway ended at a brand new aluminum-sided garage. The retractable garage door slid into the roof, but was now closed and locked with a shiny monster padlock. A narrow dirt road meandered into the redwood forest behind it. As I walked to the garage, I noticed crisscrossing tire tracks in the dirt. Wide tracks, as if from a truck. They disappeared up the road behind the garage and I decided to explore.

Even though it was almost ten-thirty, the first rays of the sun were just hitting this road cut, drawing back the long shadows of the morning. The cool air hit my face and I breathed in, smelling the sharp piney scent of the woods, refreshing after the long drive. Beneath my feet, the dirt was loose and sandy, twisted with tire tracks, footprints, imprints of deer hooves, a few delicate oblong impressions from a rabbit, and the s-shaped groove of a snake. Small puffs of dust rose with each step. The sharp rap of a woodpecker broke the silence and I looked up, hoping I'd catch a glimpse of it. But the forest was thick and shadowed, and although the tops of the redwoods glowed in the sun, I couldn't see through the shaggy branches to pick out the bird.

The road was steep, and after a few minutes, I decided that it was just a fire road, leading nowhere. There was nothing here.

Later, I'd wish I'd taken just five more minutes.

Just another five measly minutes to explore.

Instead, I turned around and walked back. The cabin was a small structure, a basic rectangle with a small porch and a front door flanked by two windows covered with plywood. I circled the building. All the windows were boarded up. The paint was peeling and flaking, the wood was rotting, and the entire structure looked like it was about to sag into the ground. I took a few photos. When I was back online, I'd run them through SnapApp and see if I could learn anything.

But without a number on the building, this whole trip had been a waste of time. I didn't even know if this was the right place. Besides, the house could have been sold multiple times over the past few years. I shook my head; I didn't even think to do a simple title search before driving all the way here. Basic P.I. 101.

If Dexter were here, he'd chide me about being on a wild goose chase. Even though this would be the perfect place to hide babies. I shivered, thinking back to the drive I'd taken with Frankie. What he'd called my last drive. I'd been tied up in the back seat, a gag smothering my mouth. Frankie had driven for hours on small mountain roads, winding up and down over rough terrain. Just like this. He'd parked out in the forest, where I could see the moon through the redwoods.

Back at the car, I slid into the driver's seat and angled my head back, keeping the door open for fresh air. After a few minutes, I grew restless and decided to look for Megan and Annie.

I slid down the embankment. The springy redwood duff gave way to a small sandy beach and I was surprised that Megan and Annie weren't right there, throwing stones. I stood for a minute at the stream bed, listening to the quiet dribble of water and the chatter of birds. I turned to follow the creek down the road, away from the car, past the house. The dense undergrowth forced me to hop from one bank of the narrow creek to the other. I doubted that they'd have come this way — too many obstacles.

Retracing my footsteps, I passed the car. A few yards farther on, I heard the sound of Annie laughing. I clambered over a downed tree, its roots jutting straight up from the ground like a wall. When I poked my head around the end of the root ball, I saw Megan and Annie. Annie wore a pink swimsuit and stood in the creek, scooping up water and letting it trickle through her open fingers. Megan stood next to her, pants rolled up, flip-flops off. The contents of Megan's blue backpack were strewn across the sandy beach behind them. The water bottle had rolled into the stream and bobbed in an eddy like a buoy. Annie's extra clothes — a purple fleece jacket, yellow t-shirt, jeans, and a pair of tennis shoes — had been dumped out on the sand. Megan's wallet and camera lay on top of the backpack.

A jay screeched in a redwood, its squawk sharp, angry.

"Hey, Shelby," Megan looked at me and smiled. "We came down the road. Much easier." Annie took a few steps and Megan lightly grabbed her elbow to steady her. The dappled sun glinted off the child's hair, her skin glowed a rosy pink. "Did you find anything at the house?" She turned back to watch Annie, who was now hitting the surface of the water with her hands. The water sprayed up, like a force shot from a hose, dousing the child, who screamed in delight. Megan leaned away, but not before her shirt got soaked.

"No," I replied. "Nothing."

"Get our picture?" she asked, gesturing toward the small point-and-shoot.

I picked it up, turned it on, and called, "Annie," as I held it up to my eyes.

The child turned to look at me and raised her hands in the air, ecstatic, like a pilgrim in the Ganges. I snapped and gestured for Megan to wade in. She crouched and put her arm around her daughter's shoulder. I took another one, and then reviewed the two photos. The first captured Annie's excitement and exuberance. In the second, mother and daughter smiled, their features as sharp and certain as if I'd taken it with a full on professional camera on a studio setting. I gave Megan a thumbs up. She stood and smiled. "Can you grab a towel from the car? It's going to be hell dragging her away from here, but maybe promises of the beach will do it."

"Okay." I turned away from them, as Megan said, "Five minutes, Annie. We need to leave in five minutes."

As far as I could tell, the child completely ignored her and kept splashing. I admired that single minded focus.

29

ALMOST AN HOUR LATER, we pulled off Highway 1 into the parking lot at Waddell Creek Beach. We slipped into the last empty slot and were rewarded with a view of the sand, now packed with kite surfers, at least a dozen unleashed dogs, kids playing in the water, beach walkers, and sun worshippers.

"I'm tired," I said, leaning back against the headrest and stretching my arms out, pushing against the steering wheel. I still hadn't recovered from my lost hours of sleep the night before last.

"Me too," Megan replied. Even so, she plucked her textbook off the floor by her feet, grabbed her backpack, hopped out of the car, circled it, and opened the rear door.

In the mirror, I could see her collecting the beach gear — sand toys, towels, and a blanket — and placing them in a striped canvas bag.

I pulled the keys from the ignition, opened my door, and swung my legs out. Spying the map I'd used to navigate to Pescadero Creek

Canyon Road, I picked it up and crumpled it. Then, I stuck the keys in my pocket, saying, "Hang on. I'll be back in a sec." I jogged across the parking lot and tossed the wadded paper into the trash can. By the time I returned, Annie was out of the car, standing by the hood, staring out at the beach. She held her doll, Tiffany, to her chest with one hand and gripped Tiffany's horse, Rainbow, by a hoof.

Megan wiggled the straps of her pack over her shoulders, picked up the canvas bag, slammed the rear door, walked over to Annie, and crouched down. "You should leave Tiffany and Rainbow in the car and let them rest," she said. "They'll get all sandy."

Reluctantly, Annie let Megan take the doll and horse out of her hands and put them in the back seat. Annie held her hand up to Megan, who took it and smiled down at her daughter. As they slid down the small berm that separated the parking lot from the beach, I said, "I'll be right there." I grabbed my pack from the back seat, slipped my phone into the side pocket, and picked up the bag of food. I pulled the keys out of my pocket, locked the car with the key fob, and attached the key ring to the hook sewn in the front compartment of my pack.

We wandered away from the crowds clustered by the parking lot, passing a group of teens playing Frisbee. A terrier ran frantically between them, barking, chasing the disc as it flew from one person to the next. Waves foamed across the wide shore, depositing bite-sized pieces of plastic, broken shells, and tiny rocks. The gentle, steady breeze felt like a fan on my face and the sound of the pounding waves formed a soothing backdrop.

The creek the beach was named for, Waddell Creek, ended in a small brackish eddy. The algae floating on the surface reminded me of the small lagoon behind our apartment building, and I hoped we'd get days and days of rain this winter. The driftwood tipi, the structure I'd glimpsed as we'd driven north, stood a few yards beyond this briny backwater. Up close, it loomed even larger, at least fifteen feet high, and I realized that not all the wood had been scavenged from the beach. Some of the poles looked like they'd been recently cut — they lacked the polished sheen of wood that had been rolling around in the ocean for months.

We dumped our bags outside the structure and crawled in through the small opening. Light filtered through the frame, creating bright ribbons of sun in the otherwise dim interior. The air was cool. Annie walked the circumference, touching each pole in turn. Then she stilled and sank down next to her mother. The thunder of waves receded into the background and we sat, mesmerized, as if in a Gothic cathedral.

Annie was the first to crawl out, followed by Megan, and then me. We picked up our bags and moseyed a bit farther down the beach, chose a random spot, and plopped down. While I arranged the blanket and set out our lunch, Megan slathered Annie with sunscreen and pulled on her long-sleeved top and floppy hat. I watched as they walked to the water's edge, with Megan holding Annie's hand firmly, keeping the child well away from the waves. Annie started to tug her mother's arm, urging her closer to the surf. And instead of keeping an eye on the incoming waves, Megan was looking down at her daughter.

An enormous wave was approaching, the first of a new set, and I could tell it was going to be a monster. The crest of the wave rose from the swell, tall, powerful, crushing. I cupped my heads around my mouth and yelled. Megan didn't turn, but something alerted her, for she swung Annie to her hip, turned, and ran. Seconds later, the wave broke, pushing tons of water onto the shore, sliding across the beach in a foamy white sheen.

From my vantage point, yards up the beach, the water now looked lazy, bewitching, inviting. But I knew how quickly the ocean could snatch someone. At least once a year, an unsuspecting beachgoer was swept out to sea.

Megan continued to carry Annie, who was now arching her back and flinging her feet in protest. I could see that Megan was limping. The sand must be hard enough for her to negotiate, let alone ferrying a protesting five-year-old.

I ran over to help her. "You okay?" I asked as Megan handed over her charge.

"Yes. Annie here, though, is eager to get back down to the water." She shot me a wry smile. "I guess you could tell." When we reached the blanket, I set Annie down, then handed her a cracker. She accepted it, solemnly.

"I'll take her," I offered. "You study." I said to Annie, "Eat up. We'll build a sand castle after lunch. But we can't get too close to the water, okay?"

I gestured to Megan and then to the food. "Help yourself."

Megan took a carrot and carefully scooped it into the tub of hummus. "I love this stuff," she said as she tore a chunk of bread off the baguette and handed it to me, smiling. "Want some?"

As I accepted the baguette, I returned her smile, studying her. Her short hair was pushed off her face by the wind, and she looked young and carefree.

Later on, I'd remember this minute and yearn for a time machine. I'd ache for a magic trick, for the impossible ability to travel back in time and return to this minute, to this second.

I'd warn Megan, hold her back. Stop her.

30

AFTER WE FINISHED OUR PICNIC, I placed the remaining food back into the bag. As I set it on the corner of the blanket, Megan dropped her biochemistry textbook next to me, where it sank down, forming a deep divot. It was a thick hardback that probably weighed more than the bag of food I'd carried across the sand.

"Wow," I said. "You have to know all of that?"

Megan sighed. "He gave us a list of what to study." She slapped her hand to her forehead. "Darn it. I left my notebook in the car. You got her?" She nodded at Annie who sat in the sand, already holding a bucket in one hand and a shovel in the other.

"Sure," I nodded, yawning. "We'll be here." I curled on my side, body on the blanket, feet in the sand, and tucked my arm under my head. Megan grabbed her phone and held it in her left hand, the hot pink case covered in red heart stickers. Her flip-flops dangled from her right hand and her linen pants were rolled up. A blue UCSC sweatshirt was draped around her shoulders, hiding her red short-sleeved shirt. She walked slowly, limping slightly, and I hoped she'd take as much time as she needed.

I worked my toes into the warm sand, glad that I was wearing shorts. Annie filled her bucket, dumped sand over her bare legs, and then repeated the process. Her face was shadowed by the brim of her hat, and her cheeks were flushed. As she struggled to lift the heavy pail, I couldn't help compare her with Justine, a mystery I hadn't yet solved. I yawned again, my eyes closing. Suddenly, I snapped them open, rubbed them, and sat up, relieved to see Annie right next to me, still absorbed in burying her legs. The child pointed to the water.

"Sand castle?" I asked, extending my hand.

With only one bucket and one shovel, our sand castle took shape slowly. While I mounded the sand into giant hills, Annie pounded it flat with the shovel. Every few minutes, I'd walk to the water's edge and use the bucket to scoop up heavy, wet sand. In one bucketful, Annie found a sand crab, a gray hard-shelled creature about the size of her thumb. It crawled on her palm for a few minutes. When she offered it to me, I took it, but dropped it in surprise. The crab was light and its touch feathery, nothing like the scabby presence I was expecting.

It burrowed quickly into the sand and disappeared. Annie turned to me, annoyed. "Why did you do that?" she asked.

Just as I borrowed the shovel to try to find it, or another one, I heard a shout. Someone down the beach was waving at me and pointing to the ocean. Without looking, I dropped the shovel and leapt up, grabbed Annie and sprinted. Seconds later a wave obliterated our sand castle and chased us up the beach. The bucket and shovel were swept away.

Annie started to cry, pointing toward the water that had stolen her toys. I put her down, murmuring soothing platitudes as we walked back to our blanket. Maybe it was time to call it a day. We could head back to town and I could take Annie to the playground for a few hours, leaving Megan to study at home.

I gazed toward the parking lot. The droplets of haze from the waves rolling into the beach misted to a sheen that obscured my view. Clusters of people down the beach blurred into pointillist muted blobs. We were, at most, ten minutes from the car. And Megan had been gone for at least thirty minutes. I cupped my hands over my eyes, binocular-style, staring, willing Megan to emerge from the hazy backdrop. Maybe she'd run into a friend or a classmate and was talking. Maybe she decided it was easier to sit in the car and study. Maybe she'd decided to take a walk. But to the north, past the parking lot, the sandy beach disappeared into a cliff, leaving little or no room for beachcombing. She might have crossed the road and walked into the state park, but why? She hadn't said anything and I couldn't see her just leaving us. There was no good explanation.

Back at the blanket, I offered Annie more food and she calmed down. After fifteen more minutes of fighting sleep, resisting the roar of the waves that faded in and out of the background like a relaxation CD, I began to imagine other things that might have happened. Maybe Megan had fallen. Maybe she was unconscious, with a crowd gathered around her. Maybe someone was calling 911 right now.

Even though I was sure my phone wouldn't work, I decided to check. Maybe she'd sent a text, and by some unlikely twist of technology, I'd received it. I lifted the pack to reach for my phone in the side pocket. Something jingled. The keys. I'd attached the keys to the ring inside my pack so they wouldn't get lost. The keys were here all the time. Megan couldn't even open the car.

I threw my pack on my back, shoved the biochemistry book into Megan's pack and picked it up, and then held out my hand, saying, "Let's go find your mom, okay?"

Annie jumped up eagerly.

We trudged up the beach, walking at a snail's pace. As we passed the driftwood tipi, I glanced in — empty. When we reached the parking lot, I picked up my gait again, jogging to the car, pulling Annie along. I peeked inside the car. Megan's notebook was on the floor of the car, where she'd left it.

It was well into the afternoon now and cars were still circling the small lot, looking for parking. A family climbed out of a nearby SUV. The father carried the picnic basket and sported a backpack, while the boy tossed a football in his hands. The mother, hauling a blanket and umbrella, cajoled along the young girl, who held a Barbie in each hand. A few seconds later, a herd of children pushed past them, whooping and screaming. They were followed by a woman carrying a beach towel in one hand and a book in the other. She gave me a tired smile.

Not knowing what else to do, I popped the locks and helped Annie climb in. I gestured for her to move to the passenger seat. Annie looked at me, as if she knew something wasn't quite right.

I slung both packs into the back seat and reached down into the well between the seats for the water bottle I'd left there. Megan's walking stick was still lying between the seats. I took a long sip of water and offered the water bottle to Annie, but she shook her head.

She asked, "Where's Mama?"

"I think she went on a walk, pumpkin. She'll come back," I said, hoping I sounded reassuring. But I couldn't sit in the car and wait; the time was passing impossibly slowly and I needed to move. Do something.

"Let's get your clothes on. Then we better go back to the beach and get the food and the blanket," I said, reaching to the back seat for my light blue hooded sweatshirt, emblazoned with De Anza in large block letters.

Five minutes later, Annie wore her jeans, t-shirt, purple fleece jacket, and tennis shoes. I pulled on my sweatshirt and deposited my phone and the car keys in the front pocket, leaving my pack in the car, tucked on the floor in the back seat. We marched across the parking lot. A gust of wind blasted sand against my legs and Annie squealed, turning away, lifting her arm to protect her eyes. I picked her up and she burrowed her head into my shoulder, her curls as soft as a bunny's fur against my cheek.

I pushed into the wind, the sand now blowing across the beach in horizontal waves. Every few steps, I lifted my head and could see the blanket, anchored by the bag of food, whipping in the wind like a cornered snake. We trudged toward it, my back aching from the weight of the child. When I stopped, Annie wiggled down and burst into tears when she realized that there was no magic here. Her mother wasn't hiding underneath the blanket or going to miraculously appear from the bag of food.

Gesturing for Annie to stand behind me, I picked up the blanket and shook it, then stuffed it into the bag, where every last morsel was already coated with a layer of sand.

We began the slow trudge back to the car.

31

WHEN WE REACHED THE CAR twenty minutes later, the parking lot was almost deserted and strewn with trash that skittered across the dirt lot in the wind. I was at a loss. It was after three in the afternoon and it had been almost two hours since I'd seen Megan.

I put Annie in the back seat and she climbed into her booster seat, picking up her doll and cradling her. I sat beside her, pulling the door shut. The wind shook the car. I checked my phone again. No service. I could drive back to town, thirty minutes away, and see if something had possessed Megan to hitchhike home. That seemed unlikely. I knew there was a visitor center across the highway, about half a mile from the road, past a locked gate and only accessible on foot or by bicycle. Surely, they'd have a phone. I could try Megan from there. I could also call Kathleen. She'd know what to do.

Once Annie and I crossed the highway and walked past a stand of trees, the stiff wind abated somewhat. To our right, the creek meandered through a small marsh. A small viewing platform overlooked the wetland. The grasses nearby were bent, as if someone had ignored the "Sensitive Habitat: Keep Out" sign. A jay squawked and another bird trilled from across the marsh. Behind the wetland, the forested hillside rose into a shadowed ridge of tall pines and a dense understory.

The road was steeper than it looked. We paused multiple times on the way up, both to rest and to check for a signal. At the crest, I stopped again, looking back toward the wide sweep of the beach, wondering if Megan was down there now, looking for us. I wished I'd left a note on the car.

The visitor center at the top of the hill was a small building, no larger than a double-wide trailer. Inside, a counter with a cash register, a rack of earrings, a box of state park stickers, and a stack of maps ran along the far side of the room. Bookshelves lined the opposite wall and a map of the park and an interpretive display covered the other. A small table in the middle of the room held a variety of nature-related items: a coyote pelt, a snakeskin, a pinecone, and the delicate skull of a mouse.

The docent, an older woman wearing jeans topped with a tan shirt that sported a State Parks patch, looked up from her perch behind the counter, where she sat reading. She smiled and stood. "Can I help you?" she asked.

I nodded, trying to keep relief from my voice. "Yes. I need help."

"With what?"

"My friend is missing."

"Missing?" she repeated. Annie pulled away from my hand and skipped over to the table, where she stood, looking.

The docent glanced at her and said, "It's okay, honey. Pick up whatever you want." She turned back to me and mouthed, "Missing?"

"Yes. We were over at the beach," I said, pointing toward the ocean. "My friend, her mom," I gestured toward Annie, "went to the car to get something. She never came back." I tried to keep my voice under control. "I realized later that I had the keys all the time, so she couldn't have even gotten into the car. It was about three hours ago. She's gone."

The docent leaned toward me, her face registering concern. She whispered, "Could she have gone missing in the water?"

I shook my head. "No, I don't think so. I watched her walk down the beach. She wasn't anywhere near the water."

"And she never came back?"

"No, she just vanished."

"Okay, hang on." The docent picked up a handset on the counter, pressed a button, and said, "Visitor Center to ranger on call."

The radio squawked. "Ranger on call here." The voice was fuzzy; it was impossible to distinguish gender or age.

"I have a situation here that needs a ranger," the docent said.

I heard a staticky response: "I'll be there in ten minutes."

The docent looked at me and smiled. "Ranger Sanchez will be here. She's a good one." The woman lifted a hinged section of the counter and ducked out. "You want some water?" She gestured toward the small food display next to one of the bookshelves.

"I'm okay," I replied. "Annie," I asked, "do you want a snack?"

Annie looked at me and followed my eyes to the food rack. Knowing how closely Megan monitored the child's sugar intake, I reached the display first and pointed to the cracker and peanut butter pack. "How about this?" I asked. "And a juice?"

The child nodded and grabbed the offered treats. As I reached in my pocket for my wallet, I remembered I didn't have it. It was back in the car.

"I'll have to pay you later," I said, my face reddening. "No money."

The docent waved her hand. "On the house," she said.

"Could I borrow your phone?" I asked.

Shaking her head, the docent said, "Sorry, my cell doesn't work here. And there's no phone. Just the radio."

Trying to conceal my disappointment, I thanked her, and then reached for Annie's hand. We walked outside and sat on a bench. Annie ate and drank methodically, savoring the treat. I gathered her into my lap and within two minutes, her breathing slowed and her head fell back against my chest. Her fingers loosened and I placed the juice box on the bench next to us.

To my right, at the end of the porch, a three-paneled oversized bulletin board sported faded posters. All seemed hell bent on warning people away from the wilderness. One poster depicted a cartoon-like figure, outlined in blue, cartwheeling off a cliff, with an international "NO" symbol plastered over the cliff edge. Another poster sported an oversized photograph of a tick, crossed out with a giant red "X". Small text below warned of Lyme disease. A third poster showed a furry squirrel on the right, with a hand reaching in from the left. Another giant "X" loomed in the space between the two. The small text on this poster warned of bubonic plague.

Bits of paper, torn up napkins, back sides of envelopes, book tear sheets, and corners of maps were tacked up on a second bulletin board. I had to squint, but I could make out some of the notes from where I sat.

Amy, Meet us at the first campground.

read one, written in large letters on a piece of yellow lined paper. Another, on the back of a candy bar wrapper, bemoaned:

Bob, What happened? We waited all afternoon.

And,

Fred, Waited as long as we could, but had to get going. We have your food.

One of the notes promised a reward for the return of a lost phone. Another, a camera. At least half of the notes were in foreign languages. French, German, and Spanish I recognized, but some of the notes were written in alphabets unknown to me.

I wondered if the notes were removed periodically or if they remained indefinitely, left up until the sun faded them to faint traces of what they once had been.

32

A WHITE TRUCK, EMBLAZONED with the California State Parks emblem, drove into the lot and a young woman, dressed in a khaki uniform, climbed out from behind the wheel and swung to the ground. She was so short that her duty belt seemed to ride from her hips to right below her breasts. Her blunt cut dark hair bounced as she pulled a small notepad and pen from her chest pocket.

She clomped up to the porch, saying, "Ranger Yvonne Sanchez. Did you report something?"

I nodded, saying, "Yes, that was me."

"What happened?" she asked.

As I told her the story, gently rocking the still sleeping child in my lap, I could see that she was not taking any notes. Her eyes wandered to the building behind me. When I finished, she took a deep breath, "Look," she said, "I know you're not going to like my answer, but here goes. Your friend probably just wandered off.

Maybe she ran into someone she knew and left with them. Maybe she took something, you know what I mean?"

I stared at her, my eyes flat. I knew what she was trying to say and I wasn't going for it. "She wouldn't do that. This is her daughter." I gently patted Annie's back. "She wouldn't up and leave her."

"I'm sorry," Yvonne peered at me. "What did you say your name was?"

"Shelby," I replied. "Shelby McDougall."

"I'm sorry, Shelby," she repeated. "We can't take a missing persons report for twenty-four hours. I'm sure she'll turn up."

As a P.I., I knew that, but I also knew that pushing might work. "She's been gone for over three hours now," I replied, my voice rising. Annie stirred in her sleep.

The ranger threw me an *I'm-really-sorry-it's-out-of-my-hands* gesture.

"Can we at least try her phone? She took it with her. I can't call. I don't have any service."

"Sure, hang on." Yvonne clomped back to the truck and returned a few minutes later with a phone as long as a tablet and as thick as *War and Peace*. "Satellite phone," she said, as if reading my mind. "Number?"

I recited it and watched her dial. Suddenly, I heard a faint stutter coming from behind me. The Sesame Street song. I knew that ringtone by heart — Megan and I had installed it on our phones one night after watching the show with Annie. The child had been in a fit of giggles over Elmo, Kermit, and Big Bird. We started looking for Sesame Street jingles, and the next thing I heard when Megan called me was the refrain about how to get to Sesame Street.

"Megan," I shouted, relief in my voice. Annie startled awake. My cries of "Megan" were interspersed with Annie's joyful shrieks.

"That's Megan's phone," I said to the ranger with excitement, in answer to her bewildered expression. "That's our ringtone."

I heard the door to the visitor center creak open behind me, the jingle drawing closer. I turned around, fully expecting to see Megan on the porch, willing to sort out my confusion later.

Instead, the docent stood there, holding an iPhone in a pink case covered with heart stickers.

Megan's phone.

"Where did you get that?" I asked, trying, for Annie's sake, to keep the panic out of my voice.

"Someone turned it in a couple of hours ago," the woman said.

"That's Megan's phone. My friend's," I said. My voice was quiet from shock.

Annie started to cry and I bounced her in my lap trying to calm her.

"Where was it found?" Yvonne asked.

"Down by the viewing platform, next to the marsh," the docent said.

My eyes blurred. "That's Megan's," I repeated, taking it from the docent and swiping the glass. Megan might have left a message, buried in an email message or a text.

The ranger looked at me. "Maybe she dropped it."

"But we weren't on this side of the highway," I replied. "We were at the beach. The car was parked in the lot by the beach. Not on this side of the highway."

"She'll turn up," Yvonne said. "I'm sure of it. In most cases, ninety-nine point nine percent of people turn up. They just wander off, go to a bar, or forget to call. Maybe she ran into a friend. Or made a new one."

I nodded forlornly, unable to keep the tears from dribbling down my cheeks. I knew something was wrong. Terribly wrong. Megan was not part of that ninety-nine point nine percent. She wouldn't wander off, go a bar, or forget to call. She didn't even go to bars. She had a midterm this week. And if she had run into a friend, she wouldn't just take off.

"So, good luck." Offering nothing more, Ranger Yvonne Sanchez returned to her truck, opened the door, climbed in, slammed the door behind her, and turned on the engine. She backed out and circled the lot as if looking for something. Her brake lights flared as she started down the hill.

Suddenly, something leapt into my consciousness. The bent grasses by the platform. Her phone found right there. Could she have dropped the phone on purpose? A marker?

I picked up Annie and stood. The child started to whimper, calling for her mother. I jiggled her on my hip. "I have an idea," I started to tell the docent.

But I was interrupted. The ranger was backing up the truck. Dust under the tires billowed into a plume. She stopped the car, rear tires squared perfectly at the one parking space next to the building. I stood, watching, continuing to bounce Annie on my hip, hoping she would stop crying.

"You're right," Yvonne said as she climbed out of the driver's seat. "If she'd taken off, there would have been signs. Drugs. Alcohol. Men. Gambling."

I shook my head. "There's nothing," I said quickly. "Nothing like that. Megan doesn't do that kind of stuff."

Yvonne continued, "Why don't we go look around? Let's check out the platform where the phone was found."

We piled into her truck and were silent as we drove down the hill. Yvonne parked by the small viewing platform, hopped out, and crouched by the bent and broken grasses. She pulled her mega-flashlight off her belt and shone the light underneath the platform. Nothing. Even though it was broad daylight, she kept the flashlight on as she crouched, turning her neck to angle her head sideways. She pointed the flashlight at the grasses. I didn't see a thing, but she must have, for she leaned in slowly.

"Look." She gestured at a muddy depression a few feet away from where we stood. Then, extracting a pen from her breast pocket, she leaned over and carefully pried a shiny object out of the muck. She dangled it on the pencil and held it up.

A delicate silver hoop.

One of the earrings I'd given Megan for her birthday. One of the earrings she'd been wearing earlier today.

"You recognize that?" the ranger asked.

I nodded. "Yes. It's Megan's."

"That's enough for me, then."

33

THE SMALL TRAIL CONTINUED FOR A FEW YARDS and seemed to end at a barrier formed by a stand of scotch broom. Yvonne must have known what I was about to do, for she said, "Don't go down there. It's a crime scene now. She might be down there alone, or with someone. Who has a weapon." She mouthed that last word, pointing to Annie.

Yvonne reached for her duty belt and pulled out her radio. She pressed a button, held the device up to her mouth, and then released it, saying, "It's going to get very busy here in about thirty minutes. Do you have somewhere to take the child?"

"I can make a call, but my phone doesn't work. Megan's probably won't work either." I held up Megan's phone.

The ranger shook her head. "Can't use that one anyway. It's evidence. We'll need it for later." She held out her hand. "Let me take it." She took it and held it by the corner, even though my fingerprints were all over it, as were the docent's, and the people who'd found it in the first place. The ranger delicately set it in the truck bed, asking, "Do you have a photo?"

"I do," I said, thinking of Megan's camera and the picture I'd taken earlier. "In the car, in Megan's pack. I'll run and get it. Can you watch her for a second?" I asked, as I glanced at Annie now standing by the platform. I called, "Annie, sweetie, I'll be right back. I have to get something from the car. Stay here."

Without listening for Yvonne's refusal or the child's protest, I sprinted across the road, dropping the keys two times before I managed to open the car door. I fumbled in Megan's backpack and pulled out her camera. I turned it on, set the dial on preview mode, and flipped back through the pictures. The last picture was the one of Megan and Annie at the creek. The perfect shot.

I cycled back through the photos and located the images from our evening at the beach earlier in the week. Dexter had picked up the camera and posed us. There were two of Ashley and Annie; one of Cody, Megan, and me; one of Megan and me with the girls; and another of Cody and me. Then one of all of us that he'd asked a passerby to take, and bless him, one of just me and Megan. We were smiling. Our arms were thrown around each other, carefree and happy, passing an evening at the beach.

I rubbed the inch square screen with my thumb, stroking it, as if I could reach through the glass into the pixels, pull her out, and hang on to her. I ran to the road, impatient as a line of cars led by a rubber-necked tourist slowly drove past. Then, I sprinted across the highway, shouting and holding up the camera when I reached the ranger. "I found a few pictures. Here." I handed the camera to Yvonne, suddenly grateful I hadn't used it to take any pictures of the house at the end of the road, and at the same time ashamed that such a thought had even crossed my mind.

She took the camera and walked over to the truck. I followed her. "Can I make one call on your phone? If I can reach this one person, she can call Megan's mom to come get Annie."

"Number?"

Yvonne dialed the phone number for the office and handed me the phone. I took a few steps away. Thankfully, Kathleen answered on the first ring. The backup phone meant that the P.I. agency was always in.

"Hello. Kathleen Bennett, P.I.," she said. Her voice was strong, friendly, professional, yet harboring a hint of caution.

"Kathleen, it's Shelby. I need your help." I launched into my story. Before I'd even finished, she promised to be here within two hours. She said she'd call Dexter as well as Megan's mom, though once I'd hung up, I had no idea how she'd find either number. But Kathleen would be able to do it, I was sure.

I thought about calling her back, asking her to call Cody, but would I be calling him as a friend, a hopeful romantic interest, or a hysterical citizen? I decided it was easier not to, and returned the phone to Yvonne.

"You two can wait in my truck," she offered. "Do you need anything to eat?"

Though I wasn't hungry, I knew that Annie would be ravenous soon. That snack had been more sugar than anything else, and lunch had been hours ago. "Any kid food?"

She smiled and said, "Yes, I have plenty of that. I'll ask my husband to bring some down. We live just up the hill, by the visitor center."

Annie climbed into the driver's side of the truck and scooted over, and I pulled myself up after her. Every few minutes, Annie would ask, "Where's Mama? Where's Mama?" I repeated, until the words sounded hollow and shallow even to me, "She'll be back, sweet pea. She'll be back." Each of my reassurances seemed to escalate her hysteria, so eventually I stopped talking, pulled her into my lap, and held her close.

Fifteen minutes later, a burly bear of a man, pushing a stroller ferrying a sleepy toddler, rapped on the window. With a smile, he handed me two juice boxes, four string cheeses, a sliced hot dog, and a box of animal crackers.

As Annie slowly ate her food and played with the animal crackers, I took stock of the cars pulling in next to the truck. Two more state park law enforcement officers, two California Highway Patrol officers, and three Santa Cruz County Sheriff units. I wished, hoped, prayed, that Cody would climb out of one of those Crown Vics. But he didn't. The docent, who'd stayed well past the time her shift ended, had set up a refreshment station on the platform.

Searchers were starting to leave the lot in pairs. Two sheriff's officers followed the bent and broken grasses to the barrier of bushes and shoved their way through. So much for the crime scene. Even though it was not yet dusk, they turned on their flashlights and the beams shone in splintered slivers of light through the scotch broom and cattails. I opened the door a crack; the wind had finally died. It was now almost seven, with about an hour and a half of daylight left.

I shifted in the seat, wiggling my butt to the left, trying to lay Annie down beside me. Maybe the docent could stay with her while I searched. But what if the docent was … I sighed, not wanting my thoughts to drift down that path. I owed it to Megan to stay here with Annie. I understood now, in a way I hadn't just twenty-four hours ago, how big the world is. And how powerless we truly are. No wonder Justin's mom, Lisa, had ended up in the psych ward. No wonder Ryan wore that bewildered, exhausted look. The look of a man who'd just had the rug of life pulled out from under him. This had happened to me before, and I remembered it now, with a sudden, startling clarity that terrified me.

Bad things happen.

I knew that. Oh, how well I knew that. That fact was drummed into my cells, my being. But I'd become complacent and had forgotten, glossing over the sharp edges of that particular terror with the joys of daily living.

Did misery just happen to follow me? Was I being punished for something karmic that I was completely unaware of? Or was this just a random, unpredictable coincidence?

Shaking my head, I knew I couldn't waste time now going down that rat hole.

My first priority was to find Megan.

And then, I would find out who had done this to her.

And why.

34

A SHARP RAP ON THE WINDOW, accompanied by a high-pitched voice startled me. "Did they find her?"

Anne pulled the truck door open, and Annie woke up, her face red. Her fine hair, now sweaty and tousled, stuck to her forehead.

"Hey, baby," Anne said.

On seeing her grandmother, the child began to cry again. Shuddering, wrenching sobs twisted her body. Anne leaned into the truck to pick her up and Annie burrowed into her grandmother, throwing her arms around her neck and cinching her legs to her waist. Anne bounced Annie, rubbed her back, and began to sing, her voice a surprising high soprano that cut through the background noise and escaped like a fluttering bird into the cool evening air.

The child quieted. I wondered if the tune was a comforting memory for Annie, a lullaby that had been sung to her when she was an infant.

As I climbed out of the truck, Tracy hurried toward me. "Any news?" she asked.

I shook my head, saying, "Nothing recent. The phone was found over there," I gestured to the platform. "And we found one of her earrings there also.

"The search is already under way. I know that State Parks doesn't want me to search, but I told them I was going to, either on my own, or with them."

Anne announced, "I'm searching too. Same as you, Shelby." She continued to sway as she held Annie, and I had the momentary illusion that she was dancing. "Tracy here is going to take Megan's car and head back to the house. That's best."

I nodded as Tracy said, "It will be good to have someone there in case," she paused, "in case ..." Her voice trailed off and she didn't have to say any more. Tracy caught Anne and her granddaughter in a hug. Then, she whispered in the other woman's ear. Anne squeezed the child again and then handed her over to Tracy. Annie started to cry, but Tracy jiggled her and Anne rubbed her back. "Auntie Tracy is going to take you home, okay baby?"

"Where's Mama?" the child asked.

Anne said, "We're going to find her. She'll be back home later."

I winced. I didn't know if that was true. I didn't know what was true anymore.

Tracy shifted Annie to her left side, reached in her pocket and pulled out a set of keys that she handed to Anne. "Here," she said. Turning to me, she asked, "Can I have the keys to Megan's car?"

I extracted them from my pocket and handed them to her. "I'll walk over there with you. I need my pack."

The gate that had been locked earlier in the day was now wide open. As we crossed the deserted highway, Tracy said, "Call me as soon as you know anything, okay?"

I nodded, saying, "My phone doesn't work out here. But we'll make sure someone gets hold of you." I gestured back across the road toward the clump of cars. "I used the ranger's satellite phone to call Kathleen, my boss, so I know we can get in touch with you later. Seems like she reached you in record time."

"She did," Tracy said. "We were just sitting down to dinner at a place in Capitola when we got the call. Kathleen said she would be along as soon as possible, but she was coming from way out in Carmel Valley."

We reached the car and I unlocked the door, yanked my pack off the back seat floor, and then handed Tracy the keys. Leaning over, I gave Annie a peck on the back of her head and a quick squeeze.

Tracy deposited Annie in her booster seat. As she buckled the straps, she said, "Take care of Anne. She's a wreck, as you can imagine. And think positive."

"I will, on both counts."

·   ·   ·

Anne stood by the truck, mesmerized by what was unfolding in front of her. A spotlight was set up next to the platform, where Megan's phone had been discovered. Ranger Sanchez sat behind a folding table, head bent over a map. Three burly state troopers stood off to the side, watching. A group of late-returning hikers stood on the periphery, waiting while one of them approached the table, presumably to ask how they could help. Radios crackled constantly.

I put my hand on Anne's shoulder and she turned toward me, her face drawn. She wore the outfit I'd seen her in this morning. Chic clothes, not clothes for searching. Mine weren't much better for a backcountry search — I was still dressed in the shorts, t-shirt, and sandals from this morning, but luckily, had the bulky, warm sweatshirt I'd put on earlier.

We side-stepped around the hikers and walked up to the table. I said, "Yvonne, this is Anne, Megan's mother." Yvonne glanced up at us.

"What can we do?" Anne asked, her voice clear and firm, indicating that she wouldn't take no for an answer.

"Hang on. I need to coordinate these guys." Yvonne nodded to the state troopers. "I'll be with you in about twenty minutes."

But twenty minutes became thirty, forty-five, an hour. Each time we went up to the table, Ranger Sanchez was on the phone, or talking to someone, or on the radio. Finally, long after the sun had set, at the edge of night, she gestured to us. I dropped my pack on the ground and shoved it under the table. If we didn't find Megan, a lost wallet would be the least of my worries. But I kept my phone securely in the front pocket of my sweatshirt. Just in case.

Yvonne handed us two flashlights and a radio to share, and pointed to the map. "Go down the highway, here," she traced the route with her pencil, "and follow the signs for the nature center. The turn is about a half-mile south. Then, take the marsh trial.

"In some places, the trail vanishes, so you'll be on the edge of the muck. You can angle up the slope a bit to avoid it. When you hit the forest again at the top of the marsh, just follow the trail back to the visitor center where I met you this afternoon." She looked at me and I nodded. "You'll see the spotlights. It shouldn't take more than an hour. If you're out longer than two, we'll have to send out a search party to find you." She wasn't joking. "It's nine-fifteen now, so we expect you by ten-thirty."

I followed Anne south on the shoulder of the highway, across the bridge that spanned Waddell Creek as it meandered out of the marsh. The moon was a small pinprick of light close to the horizon. We found the road Yvonne had pointed to on the map and turned inland, plunging into the almost pitch-dark night. Our flashlights lit the trail that cut off from the road, turning toward the marsh through a dense, claustrophobic stand of willows. We followed it across a boardwalk, toward the middle of the wetland. The boardwalk deposited us on the far edge, where we located a narrow muddy path that ran along the edge of the shallows.

Our flashlights were as bright as spotlights, and we could pick out cattails, clumps of reeds, logs, and tall feathery grasses. A loamy odor, one of mud and algae and decay, as pungent as gas, surrounded us. I imagined dead creatures floating, belly up, their carcasses festering in the putrid water.

Everything was still, so still. Nothing moved, either behind us or in front of us. It was as if the forest were holding its breath, keeping still; an alive, malevolent thing, colluding to keep Megan hidden, captive.

Anne led the way, lifting her feet high as she walked along the edge of the sucking mud. I followed, keeping a few yards off-trail on more solid ground, knowing how easy it would be for one of my sandals to be suctioned off my foot, lost forever in the muck. We began to yell, reciting Megan's name over and over, until our voices grew hoarse. Our calls were echoed by other searchers, but the chorus simply vanished into the night.

I spotted a pair of eyes gleaming behind a tussock of marsh grass. A raccoon or a possum.

Anne kept her light angled toward the ground as she continued to slog through the muck. Something caused me to look to my right — the crack of a branch or the tread of a footfall — and I angled my light up the steep slope. Above me, in the beam from the flashlight, I could see tree trunks, boulders, brush.

I stopped. Anne paused too, a few yards farther on.

She turned toward me. "Shelby?" she asked.

Leaning in toward the hillside, craning my neck, cupping my hand around my ear, I was positive I heard something. I aimed my light up the hill; a slender hoofed leg slashed through the beam. Then another. Deer.

"Yvonne told us to stay down here," Anne said. She waved her flashlight in the direction of the marsh. Tendrils of mist hung in the air, swaying like ghosts.

In the distance, we could hear other voices calling, their chant a two-tone plea, rising on the first syllable, falling on the second, like a mantra. Or a prayer. "Me-gan, Me-gan."

Again, I zigzagged my light up the steep slope and picked out a narrow trail, no wider than a foot. The ground was packed down, but I swear I saw a scuff mark.

I shivered.

Megan was somewhere up there. I knew it.

Whoever had forced Megan back here would not have slogged through the heavy, wet mud. It would be too much work and too easy for a misstep. They'd stick to solid ground, where they could keep a firm grip on her.

A few minutes of exploration wouldn't cost anyone. I'd be back before Anne reached the top of the marsh. I took a few tentative steps up the trail and stopped. Anne was still moving forward, calling Megan's name, her voice cracking, thick.

"Anne," I called, "Anne. Wait."

She stopped and played her flashlight back toward me. "Where are you going?"

"Up. Just for a second. I'm sure she's up here."

"Shelby, stop," she returned. "We're supposed to search this grid. They have a system."

"I won't be gone long," I countered. "I'll catch up."

I pointed the light up. Above, I could see the trail as it switched back a few times before vanishing. I started walking.

"Shelby, stop," Anne repeated.

I ignored her.

Something was calling me upward. Likely it was a delusion, based on the belief that I had the singular, cosmic connection that would lead me to Megan.

But I wouldn't know unless I checked.

35

I LOCATED THE TRAIL and started climbing. When I paused to catch my breath, I could see Anne's flashlight below, a bright dot in the darkness. I heard her yell, "Damn it, Shelby." I kept going, hurrying now, as if my life depended on it.

At the first switchback, I pointed the light down, and then up, surprised at the steepness of the slope looming above me. My foot slipped and a few rocks skittered downhill. Two turns later, I stopped to catch my breath. A small breeze lifted my hair and I shivered.

"Megan," I yelled. "Megan, are you there?"

The trail cut across the slope and the hill angled up, making it impossible to figure out where it went. I hoped I hadn't made a serious tactical error. Anne had the radio, so I was out of communication. I'd have to be extra careful. If I fell, or got lost, they'd have to mount a search party for me too.

After repeated short rests, I reached the top, an open meadow crisscrossed with small trails. Above, a few stars dotted the darkness. A forest of stunted trees bounded the meadow to my left, on the inland side. In the gloom, the dwarfed, gnarled, and twisted trees looked like those in a fairy tale forest, where nothing came to a good end. To my right, the meadow ended at the edge of a sharp cliff, reminding me of the poster I'd seen earlier while waiting at the visitor center.

My flashlight threw rounded shadows that altered my perspective, making the ground seem soft where it was hard, or causing a rock jutting from the ground to look like a mound of loose dirt. "Megan," I yelled as I walked across the meadow. "Megan. Megan? Megan." The breeze had picked up again and my voice was lost to the wind.

I stopped well away from the cliff edge, acutely aware that if I fell, no one would find me. Ever. Even though I couldn't see it, I knew that the black ribbon of the highway threaded far below me and that the beach lay at least a quarter-mile beyond that. I imagined how the ocean might look from up here in the sunlight; smooth and burnished, like the surface of an old oil painting whose ridges of paint had softened over the years. The sound of the waves slamming the beach was muffled, as if I were inside a house, looking out the window.

Something cracked behind me; I whirled around.

Blackness.

As I continued to shuffle along the path, I tried to keep my panic under wraps, while darting my flashlight back and forth and yelling, "Megan, Megan," over and over.

My instinct had told me to climb up here. But why? Was that scuff mark real or imagined? Was it because I was feeling claustrophobic, hemmed in by the stink of the marsh? Was I too uncomfortable with Anne? Or was there actually something up here to find?

My route was taking me across the meadow toward the boundary of tangled trees. The flashlight couldn't penetrate far into that murky labyrinth. I thought of the steady diet of horror movies Dexter and I had watched while growing up. Movies that made me swear off hiking and camping. Movies where people vanished in the night, in horrifying fashion, snatched by a vampire, a supernatural creature, an alien, a ghoul. Here one minute, gone the next.

But I knew that those kinds of evil forces, devilish monsters out to get you, weren't real.

The only monsters I knew were human.

In the light of day, this forest was probably a welcoming stand of weathered cypress, their size and bizarre shapes a result of the constant winds. It was likely a friendly place, a respite from the sun, a perfect hide-and-go-seek forest, a place for a picnic.

Squaring my shoulders, just like all those determined actresses I'd watched, I gripped my flashlight and plunged forward.

A few yards in, it was as if nothing else existed. The darkness snapped down like a curtain across a stage. It didn't seem friendly at all. Tree limbs seemed out to get me; their sharp and spiky boughs clawed at me as I pushed them out of my way. A low hanging branch scraped my arm; another poked my leg, scratching me from mid-thigh to knee, as if the tree wanted to leave a reminder. Cursing, I shoved my way through. My foot rammed an exposed root and I could feel warm blood seep from a cut in my big toe.

I stopped and angled my flashlight downward to get a closer look.

Then, my skin prickled. Every cell of my body was on full alert.

There was something, someone, in here with me. I could feel it.

I played the flashlight along the ground. The light bounced off trees, bushes, and logs, forming a crazy kaleidoscope of darkness and light. Shadows flit at the margin of the flashlight's reach. I tried not to give in to panic; I tried to suppress the images that crowded my mind — dangling bodies, severed heads, limbs scattered across the forest floor like felled trees.

And, at the eleven o'clock point to where I'd started, there was ... someone.

A body lay on the ground, curled in a fetal position. The person's back was to me. I slowly moved the flashlight up the body to the head. Dark hair was pressed flat to the skull. The neck curved forward above a red shirt. A sweatshirt was tied around the waist, and the skin on the backside of the calves gleamed soft and pale in the beam of my flashlight. The bare feet were as small and delicate as a child's.

Megan.

I dropped the flashlight and sprinted, falling to my knees when I reached her. I rolled her over. Her arm flopped as it hit the ground, limp, arcing rakishly through the beam of light. Her leg thumped lifelessly into the soft duff of the forest floor. I touched her arm. Her skin was cool and clammy, and for one swift, horrifying second, I thought she was dead.

I pinched her cheek, trying to rouse her. But instead of feeling smooth skin, my fingers came away sticky.

I ran back for the light and trained it on her as I stumbled forward. The right side of her face was covered with blood. Thick, viscous blood matted her hair and pooled in her ear. Her nose had been flattened and a large purple bruise bloomed on her left cheek, from jawbone to eye socket.

"Megan," I muttered as I shook her.

She was unresponsive. No flicker in her eyelids, no soft moan.

I shook harder, harder, desperately wanting her to wake up, to struggle to a sitting position, to smile at me with her sweet, goofy grin, and say, "Hey, Shelby."

But she didn't respond.

My heart raced and my pulse thrummed in my ears. I tried to call for help, but my voice squawked, small and useless.

I placed my fingers on her neck and could feel her pulse, faint, but steady. Her chest rose and fell, slowly, as if she were under anesthesia.

"Megan," I put my hands on her shoulders and jiggled. Her head bounced against the ground but her eyes remained closed, as if she were keeping them shut on purpose, blotting out the world. To forget what had happened, to forget what she'd seen.

"Megan," I repeated, keeping my hands on her shoulders, "wake up. You need to wake up." My efforts were pointless. She was out cold.

I jogged away from her, turning around every few steps to aim my light at her. But when my light no longer reached her, I ran back, terrified that in my absence, she'd disappear. Vanish.

My experience with unconscious people went as far as television shows. I knew you weren't supposed to move people with suspected spinal injuries, but I doubted Megan had one of those. She just seemed to have had the life beaten out of her. People could die from an attack like this. Or suffer such a traumatic brain injury they would never recover.

I had to get help. Either find help and bring it here, or take her to it.

36

I KNEW MEGAN DIDN'T WEIGH MUCH, maybe one hundred and ten pounds. Too heavy to carry. But not too heavy to drag. Keeping my flashlight on, I stuck it in my sweatshirt pocket and planted my feet by her shoulders. I put my hands under her armpits and lifted, raising her butt and back. Her head lolled to the right and her chin dangled against her chest. I yanked and took a step backward. Megan's heels bounced over a root. I stepped back again.

After ten steps, I stopped to rest, turning around, gauging my progress. I didn't let go of Megan completely, but leaned over, releasing her weight. Her arms dangled outward and her torso concaved into a ball. I counted to ten, squeezed my legs and lifted, taking another ten steps. I kept my eyes trained on Megan's heels, wincing each time they hit a root or a stone. I wondered what had happened to her flip-flops.

I continued the pattern, another ten steps and a rest for ten breaths, followed by another ten steps and a rest. Every five steps I glanced behind me, just to make sure I was heading out of the forest and not farther in. When I reached the edge of the trees, I gently laid Megan down on the trail, making sure her head didn't hit the ground. I levered myself upright, trying to ignore the sharp pain that stabbed my lower back like a hot poker. I ran a few steps away, not wanting to leave her, but needing to find help.

I yelled, screamed, shouted myself hoarse. My voice was lost in the darkness and no one heard. I was too far from the trail.

Ten more steps. A rest. The fourth time I paused, I took stock. I was more than halfway across the meadow.

My breath was now loud and ragged, sounding like a chainsaw cutting into the night. My thighs burned and the muscles in my back felt like they were on fire.

The next time I stopped, Megan whimpered and stirred, trying to lift her head. I gently laid her down and cupped her head. "Megan?" She shifted, grunting, and her body tensed. From above I could see her eyes flutter open and loll back shut again. At the same time, her head collapsed downward and she relaxed into unconsciousness.

When we finally reached the trail that plunged down the steep slope to the marsh, I laid her down. Now would be a good time to get help. The initial part of the trail was steep, enough of a vertical drop that I would have to scoot down. I tried to shout, but my voice emerged in a muffled croak.

I cupped my hands around my mouth like a megaphone, took a few breaths, and shouted. This time, my voice emerged strong and true, clear as the clapper on a bell.

"Help," I shouted. "Help. I found Megan, but I need help. Shelby here."

I waited for the rescuers, for the thundering horde of saviors. But nobody came. Off to my left, in the distance, I could hear the faint roar of the ocean, the sound of the waves hitting the beach and then receding. Down the slope, in the marsh, a frog croaked. It was joined by another, and another.

I yelled again, but my voice scattered like a flock of crows, yanked and shredded by the wind.

The only thing to do was to leave her.

I rolled her on her side. The one thing I did know was not to leave an unresponsive person on their back.

"Megan," I said, placing my hand on her cheek, "I'll be back. Soon. I promise. I'm going to get help."

I ran to the cliff edge, dropped to my butt, and slid down the hill. About halfway down, I stopped, stood, and yelled, giving it all I had.

And this time, a faint voice floated back up the cliff. "Where are you?"

"Top of the cliff. Get help. I found Megan."

After I heard a reassuring return shout, "On the way," I scrambled straight up the slope, ignoring the trail. At the top of the cliff, I laid my flashlight down and left it on, pointing outward and downward. A marker.

Megan lay where I left her. Her breathing was shallow and rapid and her skin was still clammy. What did that mean? I smoothed her short hair and cupped her chin. "Stay with me, Megan. Please. Stay with me," I pleaded.

Five minutes later, a State Parks ranger arrived. Without saying a word, he rolled Megan onto her back, removed his jacket, and covered her with it. Then, he sat by her feet and placed them on his lap. An eerie silence descended, broken by static bursts from his radio. Suddenly, two paramedics burst over the cliff top, their heavy-duty flashlights as strong as a pair of spotlights. One carried a stretcher, the other slung a pack of supplies off her back.

One of the paramedics handed me her light. I trained it toward Megan, trying to shake the memory of the paramedics coming to Megan's rescue years before. It had been dark then, too, and I'd been trying to stop the bleeding. My hands had been covered in blood.

Seconds later, the beam from another powerful flashlight bounced up and over the rim of the cliff. As the person reached the cliff top, she aimed the light to the ground, so I couldn't tell right away who it was. But when she spoke, saying, "Good work," I could tell it was the ranger, Yvonne Sanchez.

Anne followed her, the beam from her flashlight bouncing over the ledge like a living creature, pooling into a wide circle and lighting up the dusty ground. "Where is she?"

I waved my light toward the dark tangle of bodies to our left, the two paramedics now hunched over her, talking rapidly.

Anne pushed past me and dropped her flashlight. She knelt by her daughter's head. Megan was now hidden from my view.

Yvonne turned to me, her voice cutting through the paramedics' urgent, clipped tones. "Where was she?"

"In the woods. Over there." I pointed. "I dragged her. I didn't want to leave her in there."

"You dragged her?" She sounded as if she didn't believe me. When I looked at the distance, I could see why. It was a lot farther than I'd thought. A quarter of a mile? A half?

I nodded. One of the paramedics shifted and I could see a stretcher, as red as a slash of blood, on the ground. A stiff brace held Megan's neck in place and the slender tube of an IV ran from her hand to a bag of liquid resting on her chest. I heard, "On my count."

"How is she?" Yvonne asked.

I shook my head, "Bad. Unconscious. Beaten. The side of her face is completely bruised."

As if one person, the paramedics stood and picked up the stretcher. The bruise was livid in the light, and I could see that Megan's nose was crooked and her cheeks were swollen.

Seconds later, Megan was gone. Anne followed, trailing the paramedics down the slope like a small child.

"What could have happened?" I asked Yvonne, bewildered, dazed, shocked. "Who could have done this?"

Yvonne laid her hand on my shoulder and said gently, "She might not remember." As she squeezed my shoulder, she added, "She'll be on her way to the hospital soon."

"Thank you for believing me," I said.

The ranger nodded in response. "I'm glad I listened. A sheriff's deputy along with an investigator will be up here soon. You'll have to walk them through everything, while it's fresh. I'll stay with you, okay?"

"Thanks," I replied.

37

TWO HOURS LATER, I was wrapped in a green blanket, a Styrofoam cup of hot chocolate in my right hand, while I held the corners of the blanket around my shoulders with my left. Everything from that long-ago afternoon came rushing back, from the heavy, musty smell of the crawl space underneath the cottage to the sparkle in the far corner that I'd mistaken for a bottle cap. I shivered.

But instead of Dexter comforting me, I had Cody propping me up. When I'd stumbled into the cluster of lights at the staging area, Cody had found me. He'd folded me into his arms, and then wrapped me in the blanket and forced the hot drink into my hands. Pure coincidence had brought him here. He was filling in for another deputy, on patrol in the northern reaches of the county, when the missing persons report had come through on the radio. Though he'd arrived hours ago, I'd missed him in all the chaos.

We'd walked away from the lights, the staticky radios, the shouts, the squawk of the sirens, and now stood across the road that led up to the visitor center. The darkness pressed against us and I could almost pretend that we were alone. Part of me wanted to pull him into the blanket with me, cocoon him in that closed space and shut out the world. The other part of me, though, was blubbering. "I shouldn't have let her walk to the car on her own," I cried. "I should have gone with her."

Cody gave my shoulders a small shake. "People walk around every minute of every day, all over this country, and they are fine. This wasn't your responsibility." Keeping his hands on my shoulders, Cody stepped back. "Hey," he said, as he cradled my chin in his hand and raised my face to his. "You had nothing to do with this. This was the work of some random perp. Some nut job. Unfortunately, the world is filled with them. Okay?"

I nodded, sniffling. "You're right."

On the cosmic, karmic level, he was right.

Absolutely. One hundred percent correct.

But what if, on the everyday practical level, someone had mistaken Megan for me? What if someone had wanted to snatch me, but had gotten her instead?

And why? Maybe it was related to the web of events that had started earlier in the week. Maybe I was getting too close to Justin's kidnappers. Maybe Randy Vinson had known I was following him and was exacting his revenge. Maybe someone had traced my computer searches and knew that I knew about The Stork.

Or maybe, it was just because we'd been to that rundown cottage.

I'd have to go back.

"Shelby?" Cody gave me another small shake. "Shelby? You okay?"

Hot chocolate sloshed out of my cup, just missing Cody's shoe.

I smiled, "Thanks, Cody. I'm okay."

My mind was on overdrive. I'd return to that house. Tomorrow. Maybe if I looked at it differently. Maybe if I saw it again, I'd notice something. Anything. A clue, an answer, a lead, would leap out at me. It had to.

And then, if I was right, I'd tell Cody. I'd tell him everything. From the surrogacy, to Jackson and Diane, to Frankie. And now to Justin.

I felt a light hand on my back. "Shelby?"

Kathleen reached out to hug me, and Cody took the cup as I leaned into her, cautiously, knowing that once I let my guard down, I'd turn into a blithering basket case.

"Thanks for coming," I said. "Do you know Cody?"

She nodded, smiled, and said, "We've met."

Cody smiled. "Hi again."

I tugged on her arm. "Were you able to reach Dexter?"

"Yes," she replied. "Finally. Just a few minutes ago. He'll meet Megan at the hospital."

"Will you take me there?"

"Sure," she replied, looking questioningly at Cody.

"I'm on patrol," he said. "I should be getting back to it." Giving me one last hug, he said, "I'll call you tomorrow. Instead of brunch, I'll meet you at the hospital, okay? Ten?"

"Thanks," I said, nodding, fighting back the sharp sting of tears. I reached back up to hug him, reluctant to leave that island of safety and security. When I stepped back, I asked, "Will you do me a favor and tell Yvonne that I went to the hospital? If the police have any more questions, they can reach me on my phone."

•   •   •

"How do you know Cody?" Kathleen asked as I settled myself into the passenger seat of her car. I dropped my backpack on the floor, made sure that my phone was still in the front pocket of my sweatshirt, and adjusted the blanket around me, trying to hide my filthy feet and sandals.

"I met him at the coffee kiosk in the parking lot. How do you know him?"

"A case I worked on a while back. He's a nice man."

"I like him." I tried to keep my voice steady, even.

"Are you two dating?" she asked.

"I'm not sure," I said. "We haven't updated our Facebook statuses or anything."

Kathleen laughed. "You're not sure? In my day, you just knew."

I picked at the blanket that I'd tucked around my legs. "It's been such a long time since I've been with someone, I don't remember how." My voice felt tiny and sad, twinged with regret.

"Does he know about you?" Kathleen's voice was quiet as she asked. When I looked at her, her eyes were fastened squarely on the road ahead. The headlights tunneled through the dense fog that now covered the road like a cloak.

"Not yet," I said. "I don't want to scare him off."

"Cody?" Kathleen laughed. "Believe me; that man doesn't scare easily."

A few miles down the road, she said, "He's a good man, Shelby. Talk to him."

I smiled and nodded, and said, "I know. And I will." Then, I pulled the blanket close to my chin and dozed.

DAY SIX

SUNDAY, JULY 22

38

W E REACHED THE HOSPITAL just after midnight. Kathleen drove to the ER entrance at the back of the building. I leapt out of the car, thanking Kathleen as I sprinted for the door. Once inside, I realized I'd left my backpack on the floor of her car, along with the blanket. Thankfully, my phone was still in my sweatshirt pocket. I could get my pack on Monday at work, but I regretted leaving that blanket. I knew it would be cold inside the hospital. Hospitals were always cold.

The waiting room was deserted. Bluish fluorescent light gleamed off the plastic chairs, the white walls, and the speckled linoleum floor. A custodian was mopping the entry and the sharp stench of Lysol hung in the air.

I hurried to the closed glass window of the check in station and knocked.

The window slid open and a young man with a buzz cut asked, "Can I help you?"

"I'm here to see Megan Fitzgerald. Where is she?"

The man replied, "Hold on." He turned to his computer and checked the monitor. "She was just moved to the ICU."

I leaned in. "Where's that?"

"First floor. Through that door, then to your right. Follow the signs. It's marked."

I hurried through the halls. The lights were dim; the corridors deserted. The soles of my sandals squeaked against the floor. At each turn, I checked signs for directions. I passed another custodian, pushing a cart piled with toilet paper and paper towels. He nodded and I nodded back. I dead-ended in an elevator bay and backtracked, then pushed through a set of double doors and jogged toward the bright lights at the end of a hall. I was stopped short when I tried to push through the next set of double doors. They didn't open.

A large sign read, "ICU. Family only. Push button." I stood, helpless, on tiptoes, trying to peer into the small window set high into the doors.

"Shelby." Next thing I knew, Dexter had his arm around my shoulders.

"I want to see Megan," I panted. "Where is she?"

"Back there." He pointed at the doors. "Only Anne is allowed back there. Only relatives. They're saying that tomorrow Megan will be moved to the CCU — the Critical Care Unit. We can visit her then."

"But I need to see her," I protested, panic rising. "I need to. I need to know she's alive. I need to know she'll recover." I jumped up, trying to look through the window. "What if she's dying and I can't say goodbye?"

Dexter put a hand on my shoulder, steering me away from the door. "Shelby, Anne promised she'd tell me the minute anything changes. Megan is alive. They're stabilizing her." He propelled me toward the small ICU waiting room and gently helped me lower myself onto a small sofa.

"Are you hungry?" Dexter pointed to a table laden with bottles of water, energy bars, a bowl of fruit, and a pile of pastries wrapped in individual plastic wraps. "Coffee, tea, hot chocolate are down the hall. And there's a fridge full of yogurt and pudding."

"Thanks," I said. The sight of all that food made me realize I was hungry. Starving. As well as exhausted. But I didn't want to sleep.

Not yet. I twisted the top off a water bottle, drained it, and asked, "Where did you say the hot chocolate was?"

"I'll get it," he replied.

Minutes later, Dexter returned balancing a large cup of steaming liquid on top of two small plastic yogurt containers. I took the drink. He peeled the top off one of the yogurts, stuck a spoon in it, and held it out to me, saying, "Eat. Then tell me what happened."

I sipped the hot chocolate, grateful for the warmth, and placed it on the end table. I grabbed the yogurt from Dexter. After practically inhaling it, I said, "Thanks. That hit the spot." I looked around the room, noticing how empty it was. "Are we the only people here?"

Dexter nodded. "Anne comes back every so often to fill me in, but otherwise, I'm the only person waiting."

"When did you get here?" Dexter handed me the second small yogurt.

"As soon as I heard."

"Have you seen her?"

"No. Not yet." He sighed and then plopped onto the sofa next to me. Air wheezed out of the cushion. One of the overhead lights buzzed. "Rules. But I'll wait."

He held his head in his hands for a minute, rubbed his eyes, and then looked at me. "So, what happened, Shelby? How did Megan end up in there?" He gestured toward the closed double doors.

Between bites of yogurt and sips of hot chocolate, I told him everything about our visit to the beach, every last detail. But I skipped any mention of our visit to the cabin.

I'd have a lot of time, later, to wonder why I'd omitted our exploration to Pescadero Creek Canyon Road. I was tired. I didn't want my brother to yell at me, or worse yet, blame me for what happened. I was already blaming myself. I didn't need external confirmation that it was my fault.

But just a few hours from now, I'd desperately, and without hope, wish that I'd filled him in.

The small room fell silent after I finished. I thought again about Megan's disappearance. How she just never came back. If I'd clued in on it earlier, would it have made a difference? How had someone snatched her, a fully functional adult, right from the beach on a busy Saturday afternoon? Had they stuck a gun in her side? Or had they lied, claiming they'd already taken me and Annie? With her limp and slow progress on the sand, she would have been an easy target.

Another thought crossed my mind, one that caused me to feel faint. An icy sweat beaded my forehead and I couldn't breathe.

"Shelby? Are you okay?" Dexter's voice was distant. "Put your head between your knees. Breathe."

I felt my brother's hand on my neck, prodding me down, folding me in half. "Breathe. Take a big breath."

A few seconds later, I pushed back up and looked Dexter square in the face. "Do you know anything about her injuries?"

Dexter shook his head. "Nothing detailed. I gather that she's in the ICU because they're watching her brain. It doesn't look like she has a brain injury, but they're being extra cautious. She was beaten, bruised. A nasty cut on her scalp. Broken arm. Broken nose. Scrapes on the back of her legs and heels."

"Was she raped?" I asked quietly. Outside, in the hallway, I heard the sound of footsteps running, hitting the floor in quick soft thumps.

"I don't think so. No one said anything about that."

I started to cry, weeping into my hands.

"Shelby, what is it?" Dexter put his hand on my shoulder, his touch as gentle as a child's. "Shel?"

If Megan had been beaten up because someone thought she was me and if she'd been raped on top of that ... I didn't want to think about it, let alone talk about it.

"I'm okay," I replied, getting my tears under control. "I'll be okay." Hands shaking, I picked up the now empty cup of hot chocolate.

"More?" Dexter held out his hand; I gave him the cup, saying, "Thanks."

He left the room, and I stared after him, wishing he'd return with Megan, saying it was all a mistake. A joke. That she was actually fine. That it had been some other girl in the woods. Someone who'd just looked like Megan. That Megan had run into an old friend, just like Yvonne the ranger had suggested.

But I knew that wouldn't happen.

Megan was lying in a bed, unconscious, behind those sealed double doors, with tubes, an oxygen mask, and IV drips. Beeping machines. Neck brace. Bandages. And pain.

A surge of anger coursed through me. I lifted my head and stared across the room. "I'm going to find whoever did this," I muttered out loud. "And hurt them."

My phone chirped a happy end-of-battery-life warning. Pulling it out of my pocket, I saw that a call had come in hours ago. I dialed voicemail and listened.

"Hi, Shelby." It was Ryan Boyd. His spoke quietly, gently. "I just wanted to check in and see if you had anything for us. Still nothing from the police." He sighed. "Call me." The voicemail ended and I turned off the phone to save what little battery was left. I slipped it back into the front pocket of my sweatshirt.

Dexter returned a few seconds later with my second cup of hot chocolate.

"Thanks." I took a sip. "We should call Mom and Dad. When did you last talk to them?"

Dexter squinted and angled his head up to the ceiling, thinking. "Last weekend, I think. I talk to them every weekend." He looked at me. "You?"

I shrugged. "Maybe a few weeks ago? I can't remember. I think that Mom said they were going to Mary and Richard's for dinner." Mary and Richard lived down the street from my parents. Their kids had been about the same age as Dexter and I and we had practically lived at each other's houses growing up.

"Mom told me about that, too, afterwards." Dexter started to fill me in on what our childhood friends were doing now. His words rolled over me, soft as silk, as warm and comforting as a down quilt and I felt my eyelids droop.

"Hang on," I interrupted him. "Let me get comfortable." I put the cup down, leaned my head on his shoulder, and said, "Keep talking." Before I knew it, my eyes closed, his voice faded, and I was fast asleep.

When I woke, I was alone in the darkened room. My neck was stiff and my throat was parched. I stood and stretched. I grabbed a bottle of water, drank it in one long gulp, and picked up another as I walked into the hallway to find the restroom. Dexter stood by the ICU doors, staring through the small window.

I hurried over to him. "Is everything okay? Any change?"

"No," he shook his head. "Anne came in while you were asleep. Megan is still out but her vital signs are holding steady." He turned away from the door and I could see the fatigue etched below his eyes. "Anne asked us to go pick up her car. It's still parked up at Waddell." He held up a set of keys. "You up for a drive?"

"Sure," I replied. "I'll be ready in five."

39

IT WAS ALMOST FOUR IN THE MORNING by the time Dexter and I left the hospital. Outside, the fog pressed down in a damp oppressive mist. A sheen of moisture covered the cars in the lot.

"I'm over there." He pointed to the right, toward the half-empty main lot, now dimly lit.

We hurried to the car, a newer Honda Civic. Dexter hit the remote and the lights on his car flicked on and off. We both slipped in and I locked my door, sighing in relief when the door locks automatically snapped shut with a final, definitive click. We drove in silence.

As we merged on to the highway, Dexter put his phone in the console between the seats. "I gave Anne my phone number. So she could let me know if anything changed."

"Okay," I replied, "but it won't work up there. No service."

"She'll leave a message. And I'll know before I go back in the hospital." His voice sounded grim and steely, as if he were preparing himself for the worst.

I refused to think about the worst, and instead, fixed my gaze on the approaching curve in the empty road, the notorious sharp hook that marked the end of the freeway portion of Highway 1. The headlights glinted off the "Curve Sharpens" sign and I remembered joking with Dexter when someone had cleverly graffitied the "Sh" in "Sharpens" into an upper-case "H", and the first "r" to a "p": "Curve Happens".

The car swayed as Dexter rounded the curve. As he hit the straightaway, he floored it, accelerating so fast I was pushed back in my seat. He slammed to a stop at the next red light, deciding at the last minute not to run it.

"You want me to drive?" I asked.

Dexter shook his head. "I'm fine."

He slowed as he drove down Mission Street, the Highway 1 connector through the westside of Santa Cruz. We passed restaurants, thrift stores, a grocery store, a few gas stations, and several small, deserted strip malls that looked tawdry in the yellow streetlights, the light now pooled into globs of misty amber in the dense fog. Dexter sped up again when we reached the Safeway on the edge of town, racing through the final two lights before we hit open highway.

We reached Wilder Ranch, the state park a mile north of the city limits, in record time: Dexter was going seventy in a fifty-five mile per hour zone.

I turned around to look behind us. A set of small, round white headlights swam out of the fog. But there were no flashing red or blue lights.

Dexter slowed when we reached the outskirts of the small town of Davenport, keeping to the speed limit as we passed the restaurants and galleries fronting the highway. Everything was dark, shuttered. People slept, cozy and safe.

Davenport passed in a blink and Dexter gunned the engine as we crossed the railroad tracks marking the northern boundary of the town. He took the car back up to seventy, and I knew he was eager to drop me at Anne's car and hurry back to the hospital. Even though he wasn't showing it, he was frantic with worry. I was too. But I needed sleep. My plan was to drive Anne's car back to the hospital, drop the key with Dexter, and borrow Dexter's car so I could go home, shower, and try to rest.

The road curved to the left, down to Scott Creek Beach and its wide pull out, where we hit a thick patch of fog. Dexter stepped on the brakes, swearing, and the car slid over the road's surface, as if we'd just hit an ice patch. The visibility was down to practically nothing. I rolled down my window. The cold air chilled me; waking me a notch.

"Can you shut that please?" Dexter asked. "I'm freezing." He gestured to his shorts, t-shirt, and tennis shoes. "I was building a bike on the patio when Kathleen called. You know how hot it is right there; the fence blocks the wind. And it wasn't foggy. I just picked up my keys and bolted."

I pressed the button to close the window, saying, "Sure."

We were on the cliff top straightaway now, the mile stretch that passed the Greyhound Rock parking lot before dropping down to Waddell Creek Beach, our destination. Fog swirled in patches and a car loomed in our rearview mirror, and then retreated as the driver put on the left turn signal, the orange light muted and splotchy through the mist.

I turned around in time to see the taillights disappear into the Greyhound Rock parking lot. "What's that person doing?" I wondered.

"Up to no good, I'm sure," Dexter returned. "State parks law enforcement should be out here, watching, checking."

I didn't think anything of it. But I should have.

A few minutes later, we reached Anne's car. The only remaining vehicle, it was parked on the right side of the road, next to the now locked access gate. Dexter pulled to a stop next to it, parallel to the highway.

As I opened my door, I aimed the key fob at Anne's car, and clicked. The lights on the car blinked and the car beeped. "Don't leave until I'm moving, okay?"

Dexter nodded.

"Thanks," I said. "See you soon."

"Bye, Shel. See you in twenty."

I climbed into Anne's car, locked the doors, and adjusted the seat. I started the car, inched forward, and then gave Dexter a thumbs up. He pulled a U-turn in the middle of the highway and his brake lights flashed as he crossed the small bridge. Then he zoomed up the hill, around the curve, taillights growing blurry as the car disappeared into the fog.

Accelerating, I followed Dexter as fast as I could. I shivered, a result of fatigue combined with the chill from the dense, pressing air, but more because I was terrified. A woman alone, on a deserted highway, at four-thirty in the morning — with a predator still on the loose.

The stuff of nightmares.

40

A FEW MINUTES LATER, I approached the entrance to the Greyhound Rock parking lot, where Dexter and I had noticed the car turning in not ten minutes earlier. A dark pickup was parked at the intersection with the highway, angled as if it were about to pull out and head north. I sped up. But the driver flicked the lights, from low beam to high, once, twice, three times.

I slowed. Was someone in trouble? The driver flicked the lights again, this time, leaving them on the high setting. The beam was like a warning, cutting through the dense fog in two brilliant shafts of light, illuminating the feathery plumes of pampas grass on the steep hillside opposite the parking lot entrance.

In trouble or not, there was no way I would stop. Not a chance.

But I would call. Later, when I was back at the hospital. I fumbled for the front pocket of my sweatshirt and felt the reassuring weight of my phone.

Just as I was about to sail by the pickup, the driver revved the engine. The sound cut through the night like the roar of a lion. A challenge. A threat.

My heart started to race.

Pressing my foot to the floor, I veered into the left lane and zoomed by, turning to stare. The driver flicked the lights again, throwing the high beam directly into my eyes, momentarily blinding me.

Automatically, I stepped on the brake and concentrated on the double yellow line, swerving the car back to the right side of the road.

I glanced in the rearview mirror. The pickup had pulled into the lane behind me and was following me. Close. Too close. Nearly climbing my bumper. The truck's high beams raked the inside of my car, boring into the rearview and side mirrors. My stomach cramped and a tight fear clamped the back of my neck, radiating upward, as scorching as a burn.

Suddenly, the car bucked with a shriek of metal on metal. I clutched the steering wheel, fighting to keep the car straight, but it veered into the opposite lane. I yanked the wheel and the car leapt back to the right.

Out of the corner of my eye, I saw the wide dirt pull out I'd noticed earlier in the day. Then, it had been like a parking lot, with RVs, cars, vans, and a vendor selling nuts, cherries, apricots, and avocados. A whole army of tourists had been standing on the small berm that separated the edge of the lot from the two hundred foot plunge to the sea below.

Another jolt, another wrenching screech of metal on metal.

I jerked the wheel back and forth, pumped the brakes, and then stepped on the gas. The car surged forward.

I glanced in the rearview mirror. In spite of the high beams, I could make out the truck's boxy outline. The grill across the front of the vehicle was level with the rear window of the sedan. Small, round lights were set on each side of the grill, below the high-set, imposing hood.

I flashed back to the dark pickup that had tried to mow me down a few days ago.

A low moan escaped my lips.

The pickup edged in again. The silver grill loomed against the back window and the truck's lights scoured the inside of the car. I felt exposed. Naked.

I was sure that the driver could see my fear, read my every expression.

And something about that infuriated me.

Still driving, somehow managing to stay in front of the truck, I held the steering wheel with my right hand and wiped my sweaty left palm against my sweatshirt, and repeated the process with my right. My eyes flicked between the rearview mirror, the speedometer, and the road. I jammed down the accelerator. The car leapt forward. The needle rose: sixty, sixty-five, seventy.

I streaked down the straightaway, my eyes fixed on the road ahead. I straddled the double yellow line, hoping, praying, that the road was empty. Mist spattered the windshield and I turned on the wipers. But the droplets smeared, making it even harder to see.

The car plunged over the crest of the hill as the highway swooped down to Scott Creek Beach. One and a half miles to Davenport; sixty seconds at the speed I was going. In the distance, I could see the light on the tower of the now-shuttered cement plant at the north edge of the small town. I was so close. Ahead of me, at the bottom of the hill, the highway and beach were swathed in a light mist, though a dense, heavy patch of fog covered the marsh to the left. The beach was deserted and both sides of the road were empty. There were no campers or cars; no motorcycles or RVs. Not even a bicycle. Not a single person around. No one to rescue me.

I'd have to do it myself.

But just in case I was wrong, in case there was a lone backpacker with a cell phone hidden in a sleeping bag below a cliff, I pressed the horn and held it down. The sound streaked back and cloaked the car. For a short-lived instant, I felt invincible. Behind me, the dark pickup crested the hill and caught some air, landing with a hard crunch. The driver continued to gain speed and within a second, the truck was almost on the bumper. Again.

I pressed the accelerator, trying to watch the speedometer, the side mirror, the rearview, and also see what was in front of me.

And then, I made my mistake.

Three pairs of eyes gleamed in the middle of the road ahead. The round, small disks caught the headlights full on and reflected the light, glowing like bright yellow stars against a black sky. One set of eyes was larger, and that animal was taller, its bright eyes standing higher off the road. A mother and two babies. Raccoons, perhaps, or skunks.

The animals had stopped, staring toward the cars.

Watching.

And I reacted, on pure instinct, doing what ninety-nine point nine percent of drivers would do.

I lifted up on the accelerator.

The car slowed. Time slowed along with it, bending from a straight trajectory into a tangled jumble that stuttered forward and bounced back. Seconds boomeranged and curved in on themselves. I didn't have time to think.

Ahead, the shiny eyes vanished. The animals had either disappeared or had been a complete trick of my imagination. My headlights picked up the double yellow line, the black tarmac, the white line marking the shoulder, and the guardrail.

I moved my foot back to the accelerator and pressed down. The weight of the pedal felt heavy and the car moved sluggishly, as if all its power had been used up, sucked dry. I lifted my foot and then stomped down on the accelerator again, but the car seemed to stay in place. Sound was muffled, as if I were cocooned in a giant wave. The truck's front grill filled the entire field of view in the rearview mirror, looming like the dull silvered teeth of a giant monster. Time leapt forward again and I heard a sickening wrench as my car was pushed to the right, toward the guardrail that gleamed like bones in the headlights.

Whimpers filled the car. Mine. I had to do something.

Lifting a hand from the wheel, I wiped my forehead and fumbled with the buttons on the door handle. But my hands were shaking, and I was able to only crack the back window on the other side of the car. Even so, a salty tang floated in through the window, bringing the bright smell of the ocean. For a second, I felt almost normal.

I hit the accelerator again. This time, the car surged forward.

Keeping my foot on the gas, I yanked the steering wheel from left to right, swerving across the road in wide arcs. I careened through a curve, feeling the wheels stutter on the pavement.

The road behind me was dark. Had I lost him?

But then, I froze. That icy pit of fear settled in my stomach again and sheer terror clamped my bowels.

The grill was right against the back window.

Just as I realized that the bastard had tricked me by turning off his headlights, the truck smashed into the rear end of my car with a shrill metallic screech that sounded like the devil's fingers playing across a chalkboard.

My car imploded. The back window disintegrated, collapsing into small chunks of glass that scattered across the back seat.

Cold air blasted into the car and wind whistled through the frame where the window used to be.

The truck backed off and then rammed the rear of the car again, this time hitting straight on in a direct shot that shoved me forward into the steering wheel. The seat belt retracted, skewering me to the seat with a searing pain across my chest and hips. The airbag exploded in my face. I couldn't move. I couldn't catch my breath. I couldn't see.

Again, the truck rammed the back of the car. Again, and again.

Each time, the tiny car was pushed forward, and each time, I was thrown forward into the airbag and viciously snapped back.

In sheer desperation, I slammed on the brakes. And everything went black.

41

M INUTES LATER, HOURS LATER, DAYS LATER, I pried my eyes open, wiping away the sticky layer that welded them shut. A dark surface loomed right above my face, squeezing me, as if I were in a box. I forced myself to close my eyes, to breathe, to hold the mounting panic at bay. My long-ago therapist's voice, her cadence soft and soothing, rung in my ears: "Shelby, breathe. Take a big breath. Count to ten. Take another big breath and count to ten again. And so on. It will help you calm down. I promise."

Taking shaky breaths in and out, I tried, but the fluttery feeling in my chest wouldn't go away. Bile rose in my throat. Sweat trickled into my eyes. A white-hot fire cinched my chest.

It was dark, so dark. I heard a scratching sound, like a small creature scrabbling across a hard surface, and I realized it was me, muttering, over and over, "Don't make promises you can't keep." Talking back to the therapist, who I hadn't seen for at least three years.

Down, into darkness.

When I swam back to consciousness again, the room was black slate. Obsidian. I'd been pulled into a black hole, where all light and sound had been snatched by an evil, wicked presence.

I lifted my head. Pain stabbed the inside of my skull. I rolled to my side and vomited. I tried to move and escape the rancid odor, but a rolling wave of what felt like knife cuts ripped through my temple and radiated down through my jaw. Deep breathing only made things worse.

Blackness. Again.

I was on my side when I woke, curled in a tight fetal position, cradling my head with my arms. Terrified of that stabbing, searing pain, I didn't dare move. I lay immobile, panting like a sick animal, ignoring the stench, intent on staying as still as possible.

But the smell was overwhelming. Slowly, I scooted away, keeping one hand under my head and pushing with my free hand while fishtailing my ankles and hips. The small measured movements were jarring, but the earlier stabbing pain had receded.

Time vanished. I could have blinked or been out for hours. Now, light seeped into my prison, bathing the room in dirty gray. The ceiling floated far above me, anchored in its center by an empty light socket. Cold air, rising from the tile, radiated through my clothes and chilled me. My eyes focused a yard out on a dingy tiled floor that might have once been shiny and pristine, but was now chipped, pocked, and stained.

I struggled to sit. My head throbbed, my chest ached, and a wave of nausea gripped me, forcing me to stop all movement and put my head between my knees. Light shallow breathing was all I could manage. When the nausea passed, I sat up, keeping my hands on the back of my neck for support.

I took stock, just moving my eyes.

Piles of shattered ceramic tile covered the floor of my prison. A long rectangular space, like an empty grave, gaped in the flooring to my left. A small round hole split the floor next to it. The empty wall to my left yawed with cutouts. Someone had dumped me in an abandoned bathroom.

I slowly swiveled, cradling my head, sliding on my butt.

The closed door was all the way across the room.

I had to get out.

I leaned forward and tried to crawl, but the headache throbbed and expanded until my head felt like it was about to explode. I collapsed, flat onto my stomach, trying to calm myself, trying to muster some reserve of energy to get over to the door.

Staying flat, I found that I could scoot forward by reaching with my hands and pushing with the tips of my toes. I moved, inch by excruciating inch.

By the time I crossed the room, sweat drenched my body and I was shivering.

How had I ended up here? And where was here? The last thing I could remember was sitting in a room with Dexter. The image swam into my mind's eye, and it was as if I was looking at a stage, seeing the two of us in a small space with taupe walls, institutional furniture, and a table laden with bottles of water.

Water. I licked my lips and ran my tongue over them. They were dry and cracked. I tried to swallow but nothing was there, just a lump. I'd never been so thirsty.

Suddenly, I flashed back to that room, where Dexter and I had been waiting. I saw myself reach into the large front pocket of my sweatshirt, pull out my phone, and listen to the message from Ryan Boyd.

My phone.

I deliberately pushed myself to my side, using my right arm to lever myself up and my feet to push against the smooth tile. As soon as my weight was off my stomach, I bunched the material in the front of my sweatshirt, hoping, wishing that my fingers would meet a hard, sturdy surface.

But the sweatshirt was soft, without any edges. The pocket was empty. My phone was gone.

I lay there, unmoving, on my back, no idea of how long I'd been here. Time had no meaning now. There was only my head, my breath, and the silence that enveloped me, pulsing in concert with the beating of my heart.

There were just two choices: I could wait. Or I could try to get out of here on my own.

42

I SHIFTED TO A SITTING POSITION and held my head, slowly turning my neck from side to side. The hammer no longer exploded inside my temple on movement.

I felt my neck, shoulders, legs, feet, and then checked both arms and hands for damage. All in one piece, just tender. Then, I gently probed my head, slowly feeling the crown and the temples. The sticky layer I'd felt earlier was now thick and congealed. I put my finger in my mouth and tasted something heavy and metallic. Blood. The trail spilled across my cheek; and I discovered a two-inch long, still oozing gash that ran from my right temple to my forehead.

I took off my sweatshirt, and then removed my t-shirt to hold against the wound. In the dim light I could see a blue-black bruise, as long and narrow as a seatbelt strap, splotching my stomach below my bra line. I imagined it ran from shoulder to hip.

Holding my t-shirt to my head, I took stock. I was alive and mostly in one piece. My clothes were all intact; as far as I could tell, I hadn't been assaulted.

Slowly, holding my sweatshirt with one hand and the t-shirt to my temple with the other, I scooted to the door and leaned back. I dabbed my temple a few times, then got dressed. The bloody part of the t-shirt was damp against my chest. I pulled my sweatshirt on, grateful for the familiar warm fabric.

I knew I had to stand up. I had to feel my way around the room, run my fingers over all the surfaces and find the cracks and fissures — the weak spots. There had to be a way out of here. There had to be.

Taking a deep breath, I leaned forward. I lifted my butt up in the air and carefully walked my knees around in a circle until I faced the door. Still on my knees, I reached for the doorknob, grabbed it, and transferred my weight forward. I planted my right foot on the floor and then my left. With all my strength, I pulled on the doorknob and lifted myself up. I sagged into the stiff door, fully expecting my body to protest, but other than a throbbing head and the searing pain across my chest, it didn't.

I rattled the knob. It didn't turn either right or left. And the knob was smooth. That confused me. A bathroom door would have a lock on the knob on the inside of the door, not on the outside. I wondered if the knob had been reversed, on purpose. Or if this place was so old, there wasn't one.

I baby-stepped across the room to the window. It was covered with plywood, nailed to the outside. I smacked it, but the wood didn't give. I tried the window next to it with the same result. I peered into the narrow crack between the plywood and the window. I could see the trunk and lower branches of a redwood tree. Needles littered the ground. It was sunny. Leaning my head against the plywood, I fought the panic that rose from my feet upward, making me feel light and ungrounded, making it hard to breathe.

There was no point in any more discoveries. I knew what I'd find — solid walls and impenetrable surfaces.

I'd have to concentrate all my resources on the door.

I shuffled to the middle of the room and stopped. I kicked a pile of tile out of the way, and then gingerly lowered myself to my knees. I took a tile and delicately pushed the vomit out of the way. Now on my hands and knees, I scoured the floor from the middle of the room to the door with the side of a broken piece of tile. I threw the tile across the room, and pulled myself slowly to my feet. I ran my hands along the margin of door and up and down the door frame. The knob was on the right side, and there were three three-inch long hinges on the left. I pushed against the middle of the door. It gave, just a little bit.

I walked back across the room, dragging my feet, pushing the remaining small bits of tile out of my way, making sure there'd be nothing to trip over. I turned toward the door, took a breath, stood on my tiptoes, and powered forward with as much energy as I could. I rammed the door with my right shoulder, like an NFL linebacker.

And I staggered back. Pain burst in my shoulder and reverberated down to my hip, eclipsing the pain I was feeling anywhere else.

The door shuddered, but held. I stood, stunned, massaging my neck and shaking my head.

This time, I gave myself more space, starting farther across the room. And I tried to focus, remembering the mental clarity I'd honed after years of pitching softball. Before each pitch, I'd run through the sequence in my mind, from my stance, to rocking forward on my front toe, to exploding off the back leg, to the arm rotations, the release. Now, I could see how I'd attack the door: a strong, short sprint, diving into it with my right shoulder, crumbling the wood to splinters.

I tried.

The impact rattled my bones and I bit the inside of my cheek, drawing blood. Instead of the door shattering, I bounced back and fell hard, landing square on my butt. The shock burst upward through my tailbone and spine, hammering my neck and skull like a gunshot. I sat for a moment and forced myself to stay upright, breathing.

I stood and ran my fingers over the door's surface. After all that pounding, there were no obvious cracks. Not even a splinter.

My heart raced, my shoulder burned, and I felt light-headed.

I flashed on a TV show I'd seen with Dexter and Dad, maybe it was one Christmas when we were home visiting our parents. It was a rerun of some old cop show, *Magnum, PI* or *MacGyver*. Something Dad loved to watch. There was a scene with someone kicking down a door, and we'd talked about it. If it were even possible.

Dad had said, "All it takes is finding the door's weakest point. Either the latch, the frame, or the knob. Then just give it a good strong kick with the sole of your foot."

Dexter had smiled, and then said, "You sound like you know what you're talking about, Dad."

He'd smiled back as he'd pushed himself out of his worn recliner. "I might," he'd replied. "I just might."

I ran my hands over the surface of the door, probing again for a crack or a soft spot, and then jiggled the knob. This time, I noticed that the door below the knob didn't quite fit into the frame. It was a little off. A small sliver of light crept through.

I stepped back a few feet, far enough to give my foot some maneuvering power, close enough to kick the door flat on, with the sole of my foot. Placing my right foot back, I swung my left leg up gently, making sure it would land underneath the knob. After doing this a few times, I leaned back, took a breath, and shifted forward, pushing from my right heel, transferring the energy forward to the kick. Just like pitching.

The door gave, buckling inward at the frame below the knob.

I kicked again and the door splintered.

On the third kick, the frame below the knob shattered, and the knob came loose. I could separate the knob from the latch.

The door swung inward and I walked out.

43

I FOUND MYSELF IN A DIM HALLWAY. I stopped, listening. There were no sounds at all and I was certain I was alone. The hallway ran from one end of the house to another, with two closed doors across the hall, another one to my right, and a closed door at either end. I turned to my left, moving quickly, reaching the end of the hallway in a dozen steps.

I twisted the knob. It turned easily. I cracked the door open and saw a vacant room. The windows here were also covered with plywood. Light filtered in through cracks at the edges of the window frames. Another door was directly across the room, though I couldn't walk straight across to it. A table-sized hole splintered the floor in the middle of the room. I slid my feet around the perimeter, not daring to hurry, terrified the boards would give out and I'd plunge through.

When I reached the door, I grabbed the doorknob and turned it, again, expecting resistance.

But to my surprise, it swung open. Whoever had locked me in had counted on me staying put.

Within a second, I was outside, on a small porch.

I was free.

The sun beat down, hot and bright. It had to be at least noon. I'd been imprisoned for seven or eight hours, if not longer. The accident had happened in the small hours of Sunday morning. Dexter would be frantic. Someone would have reported Anne's twisted wreck of a car by now. Kathleen would have called the police and I hoped she would have called Cody as well.

I shivered in the heat, remembering the screech of metal on metal as that truck had run me off the road.

I had to get back.

But the ground beneath me tilted and I felt like I'd just lurched off a roller coaster. I leaned over, put my hands on my knees, and breathed, sucking in the fresh air, as if my lungs couldn't get enough. The pain in my head had returned, insistent, localized, pounding in my right temple like a jackhammer.

Holding my neck with my right hand, I maneuvered slowly down the three stairs in front of me, clinging to the railing to avoid crashing through the rotten boards.

Part of me knew I had to move quickly. But the animal core of my brain prevented that. Each step jarred my spine and sent shock waves of pain up my neck. A few steps from the house, I saw a large branch on the ground that I could use for a crutch. When I leaned over to pick it up, I fell, landing with my hands straight out in front me.

I rolled over and pushed myself on to my hands and knees, facing down the slope, away from the house. I lifted my head, inch by agonizing inch, fighting dizziness and incessant waves of nausea. When the scene in front of me registered somewhere in the murky depths of my brain, I quickly squeezed my eyes shut and shook my head to clear it. I had to be imagining things. The car crash, the head injury. No way could I have ended up here.

But when I opened my eyes, nothing had changed. I was looking at redwoods, a pullout, and a creek across a road.

Dumbfounded, still on all fours, I twisted back to the wreck of a building. Behind it, the driveway ended at the aluminum-sided garage, locked with that enormous, shiny padlock.

I pushed myself up, picked up the stick, and leaned on it for support, staring in front of me, twisting behind.

My mind protested: it couldn't be. No way. No how. I was imagining this.

Except I wasn't. I was seeing the same structure. The same plywood tacked to the windows. The same slope up from the road. The same small boarded up ramshackle cabin that Megan and I had investigated. Before events had careened on each other and led to this.

It was the cabin at 789 Pescadero Creek Canyon Road. The address I'd checked out from Diane's list.

This made no sense.

Suddenly panicked, terrified that the driver who'd run me down would return, I stumbled down the steep slope in front of the cabin and crossed the narrow potholed road. If I could get to the creek, to the woods, I could hide.

But I was already too late. "Stop." A man's voice. Loud.

I took one more step, then lost my balance, and staggered, falling forward. Unable to catch myself, I pitched to the ground, face-down.

"Listen, bitch. I told you to stop." In the quiet after he spoke, after I hit the dirt, something clicked. Something metallic, abrupt, unforgiving.

He had released the safety on a gun. I froze.

"Stand up. Then, put your hands on your head and turn around."

I couldn't move, couldn't breathe. Couldn't believe this was happening. Maybe this was all a joke. A mix-up. A big fat mistake.

"Now." The voice cut through my terror. He took a step, his foot thudding square on the dirt. He must be on the other side of the narrow road. Maybe I could escape.

Another step. "Get up," he barked.

I rolled on to my side. Keeping my hands wide, well away from my body, I pushed myself up, eyeing the small puffs of dust that rose as I placed my feet in front of me. As soon as I was upright, I put my hands on top of my head. My back was to him. In front of me was the small embankment that led to the creek. It looked so inviting, the cool water flowing over the warm stones.

"Turn around."

Panic squeezed me, compressed my chest.

"Now."

I turned, baby-stepping in a circle.

A man wearing a blue-checked flannel shirt with the sleeves cut off and a pair of jeans stood in the middle of the road. He was in the full sun, booted feet planted at shoulder width, hands at his sides.

And he was smiling widely, as if he knew me. As if the two of us were old friends who shared a deep secret. As if we were lovers.

But the smile stopped at his mouth and his eyes were as flat as copper pennies.

Then, he raised his arm and pointed a handgun at me; a blunt-nosed black thing that gleamed in the sun like a shiny toy. The hand holding the gun trembled slightly.

That small tremor clicked me back to the moment.

Made me think.

I wondered if I could jump him. Maybe he was overheated in all those clothes. Maybe the exertion of getting me here had worn him out. Maybe I could exploit those small advantages.

Keeping the gun pointed at me, he ordered, "Get over here. Don't do anything stupid."

I hesitated, the panic making me slow, sick with fear.

He was on me in a second, quick as a snake, strong-arming me with one hand while holding the barrel of the gun to my neck with the other.

"Walk," he barked.

I took a small, shuffling step and felt as if I were falling backward. He gripped my right arm with his left, pulling it up, bending it so the palm of my hand was flat to my back. Lightning tendrils of pain shot up and down my arm, shoulder, and back. I stared at the sky. The cylinder of the gun, as round and hard and cold as a dime, dug into the tender skin of my neck, just below my ear. I held my left arm very still along my side, knowing that the slightest twitch might cause him to pull the trigger.

"Walk," he repeated as he ground the gun into the soft skin on my neck.

I nodded and a guttural moan escaped my lips. My heart hammered; I couldn't breathe. My legs shook and my knees felt like they were about to buckle.

The man leaned in, his body pressing against my back. His breath was hot against my ear as he whispered, "Go. Now."

What had I been thinking? Right then, I decided that if I ever made it out of here, I would be done. No more investigating. No more trying to figure out why Justin Boyd had been kidnapped. No more address hunting. No more obsessing over Jackson, Diane, or Frankie. No more Stork hunting. The police were fully, completely competent. Let them figure it out. I, obviously, was not good enough.

Surely, Dexter would remember my questions about Pescadero Creek Canyon Road. Maybe he'd think to turn on my computer and look at the browsing history. My phone, where I'd also searched for those addresses, was missing. Even though the envelope with the addresses was secure in my desk at work, Kathleen would know nothing. Neither would Cody. I'd tossed the map I'd printed out for directions. And Megan, probably still unconscious, wouldn't be able to say anything. If she would even be able to remember.

44

"GO." THE MAN SHOVED ME ACROSS THE ROAD, past my prison, the small cottage with the boarded-up windows. Past the brand-new garage I'd examined yesterday. Up the road I'd almost taken the time to explore.

Now that it was too late, I could see my mistake. There was a faint black tire tread on the apron of the garage, as if someone had recently parked there. Crisscrossing tire tracks led up the dirt road next to the garage.

If they had been there yesterday, and if I'd noticed them, when Megan was with me, I might have had a chance. I could have explored, and she could have waited and gone for help if I never returned. Or, we could have come back with Kathleen, or Cody, or Dexter. Or…

The man shoved me in front of him, gun to my neck. I gazed up at the blue, blue sky.

A few steps on, he jerked me to a stop. Still imprisoned in his iron grip, he leaned against me and ran his knee up and down the back of my leg. The stiff material of his Levis roughed my skin. He squeezed against me, too close, too close, and I tried to wiggle away.

If he was going to rape me, why now, out here in the sunlight? Why not attack me back in my prison, when I was captive and had nowhere to go?

I shuddered. Maybe he had other plans for me.

The man behind me tensed. I could feel his body go rigid, as if he could see himself doing it. As if in his mind's eye he was going through all of it. The tension on the trigger. The slow pull with his index finger. The point of no return; followed by the roar of the bullet as it exited the chamber, plowing through my neck, ripping my flesh, and exploding into me.

My lips moved, and I whispered, muttering quickly, reciting my childhood prayer, terrified I would run out of time. It had served me well in the past. I mumbled through clenched teeth, my jaws clamped together like a vice. "Please be okay. Please be okay. Please be okay."

Though there was no wind, a roaring sound vibrated in my ears, as loud and real as a whirling dervish. A pounding, as steady and regular as the beat of a drum, became louder and louder. My heart. I was hearing my heart.

"Maybe," he whispered, "we can stay here for a while. And play. Just you and me. What she doesn't know can't hurt her." His voice was sing-song, a light tone, feathery and high.

She? I thought. Who is she?

"She's been telling me to keep an eye on you. To watch you," the man continued, his voice a mere breath. "And I like that."

A tear slipped down my cheek, followed by another. My lips started to tremble. Snot flowed from my nose. Sweat slicked my fingers, making my palms greasy and oily. My hands shook, the tremor as severe and pronounced as if I were in late-stage Parkinson's.

In my mind, I could see it play out, in terrifying, slow motion Technicolor. Him throwing me to the ground, training the gun at my face. Ordering me to take off my clothes. Him pulling down his zipper. And then the playback stopped. I couldn't go any further.

Just then, a small thought breezed through my mind, like a welcome wash of fresh air. I thought of Cody. His smile. His eyes.

And I screamed. Long, loud, shrill. Effective.

The man stepped back, slightly easing his grip on my arm, just for an instant. Long enough for me to stamp on his boot and kick his kneecap. Not that it was enough. He bent back slightly, as if deflecting an ineffectual swat from a small child. Then, his grip tightened and he twisted my arm, hard.

I screamed again.

The gun ground into my neck.

"Shut up." His voice was low, menacing. "Shut the hell up."

I clamped my mouth shut and stood completely still, as motionless as a statue.

Suddenly, a woman's loud, commanding voice split the quiet. It was coming from above us, up the hill. "Erik," she yelled. "For god's sake. Bring her here. I told you to get her. Not assault her."

Erik. The man's name was Erik.

He immediately dropped the gun to his side and clicked the safety back on. Keeping hold of my arm, he shoved me forward, pushing me up the hill in the direction of the woman's voice.

Whoever she was, she certainly had a lot of power. I might be able to use that to my advantage.

I tried to wrestle my arm free, saying, "Look, you have a gun. I'm not going to take off." Erik still wouldn't let go. His hand clamped my arm so hard I was sure I would have a bruise.

The road curved upward, to the left. The bright light forced me to squint. I tried to walk slowly, measuring my escape. Redwoods beckoned to my left and right, a welcome canopy over an uncluttered forest floor. Dust motes hung in the still air as shafts of sunlight penetrated the shade. For an instant, I remembered sitting in the scooped out hollow at the base of a redwood, pregnant and big as a house, waiting for Jackson to bring me water and snacks. Back when I knew nothing. Back when everything was just as it appeared.

But Erik tightened his grip and shoved the barrel of the gun into my spine, yanking me out of my daydream, into a terrifying present.

I walked.

Past the curve, the road opened up into a graded gravel driveway.

At the top of the rise stood a well maintained, two-story log cabin, like something out of a suburban-rural western neighborhood. A porch, complete with sturdy beams, a porch swing, and two Adirondack chairs, ran the length of the house. Four large windows, covered with decorative wrought iron security bars, flanked the front door. The upstairs sported three small dormer windows. The structure had been stained recently and gleamed in a dark, rusty glow. All vegetation had been removed from the perimeter, replaced by gravel, confined by bender board. A shed was attached to the right side of the house and I imagined neatly stacked firewood, gardening tools, and bins for trash and recycling.

A large security light was attached to each side of the house, another hung above the front door. Three more were placed above the slope of the porch roof, in between the dormers. I wondered where the electricity came from. This place was way off the grid.

A black pickup with a dented and scratched front bumper was backed in next to the house.

A woman stood in the open front door, shaded by the porch roof. Her hands were on her hips, and she was shaking her head. Was this the woman Erik was scared of? A small grin was plastered to her face, as if she found the situation — my situation — funny.

That pissed me off.

"Bring her in," she said as she turned to walk inside.

I stopped short, somehow wanting to get the upper hand on things, knowing, at the same time, that it was impossible. There were at least two of them. They had one gun, if not more. Erik was built like a wrestler, a solid, stocky fireplug of a man who'd already demonstrated that he could take me out with one good jab.

I lifted my head to the sun, relishing the hot still air and the heat on my skin. I closed my eyes and breathed in, smelling pine and the dust from the road mixed with Erik's sweat and the scent of the oily fumes off-gassing from the newly applied stain on the cabin's exterior. A jay squawked, loud and noisy. I glanced up, Sunlight kissed the top of a redwood and it looked like it was on fire. A glossy black raven swooped across the blue sky, wheeling and cawing, while high above it, a small speck, probably a red-tailed hawk, circled up and up and up, rising on an unseen current. Free. My throat ached.

My gaze slid from the trees to the quiet, still house, a solid, squat prison. An executioner's lair. Images of Ted Bundy, Jeffrey Dahmer, and *The Silence of the Lambs* flit through my mind, washing me in an immense sadness.

But movement in a window on the second floor caught my attention. A tiny round face stared down at me from behind the glass, watching. A hand lifted, gave a small wave, and then, the person vanished.

45

"**H**EAD DOWN," THE MAN GROWLED. The pressure of the gun against my spine increased.

One more step and I had a decision to make. Go in the house, like a good girl, and likely get killed. Break for it and get killed. Or at least get shot at.

I stopped. I willed something to change, to be different. For him to trip. For a ringing cell phone. The blast of a car horn. The wail of a siren.

Something to take his attention off me for a split second.

But it never came.

And my decision was made for me.

Keeping the gun to my back, the man grabbed my shoulder and shoved me forward. "Inside. She wants you inside."

After the bright sunlight, the dimly lit interior made it almost impossible to see. The staircase rose up in front of me, bisecting the house in the middle. A closed door was to my right. Erik prodded me and I shuffled a few steps to my left and a few forward, finding myself in a large room that took up all of the interior space. As my eyes adjusted to the gloom, shapes emerged. Heavy drapes, like the kind you'd see in a cheap motel, were partially drawn across all the windows. A few metal folding chairs were placed around the perimeter of the room, cast-offs from the card table parked by the large front window. A wood stove sat on the hearth, squatting in the darkness on its four legs like some kind of demon.

An enormous wooden desk was the room's focal point. It was a solid piece of furniture, with the six-foot long desktop held up by two banks of drawers. The person sitting at the desk was completely in shadow. The only thing I could see was a pair of black, round-toed laced shoes underneath the desk, as plain and functional as those of a waitress in a diner or a nurse on shift.

Behind the desk, a bank of floor-to-ceiling filing cabinets flanked a long narrow table. A small lamp, with a brass pull and a domed glass lampshade, threw soft light onto the desk's polished surface, empty save for a pad of yellow legal-sized paper, reminding me of Kathleen. What advice would she have for me now?

"Here she is," the man stood next to me, the gun pushed into my ribs. "Just like you wanted. Not a scratch on her." He smiled at me, lips compressed and eyes tensed. Not a smile at all; more like a grimace. Even a threat.

"Thank you. That will be all." The forceful and commanding voice belonged to the woman I heard on the porch.

"You sure?" He kept the barrel of the gun shoved into my side.

"Yes. I'm sure," she said.

The man dropped the weapon, took a step back, and shook his head. "I think you're making a mistake."

The woman repeated, "That will be all."

"Okay, but she's sneaky. Tricky. I still think …"

"Erik, I don't care what you think." Her voice sharpened. "You don't think. I think."

The man breathed in through his teeth and walked past me, shaking his head as he stuck the gun into the waistband of his jeans at the small of his back. He strode into the open kitchen, opposite the woman's desk, and paused at the refrigerator. As he yanked it open and grabbed a bottle of beer, he threw the woman a sullen look. Beer in hand, he sauntered toward the far side of the kitchen, pulled open a door, walked through, and slammed it shut behind him. A TV flipped on, the sound low, with the unmistakable chatter of canned laughter and the rip of a machine gun.

The front door was only ten steps away and Erik was watching TV. I could try it: turn around, barrel out the front door. Run for it. I could head up or down the slope, sprint into the woods, or burrow into a thicket if I had to.

But there was the face I'd seen.

As if reading my mind, the woman said, "There's nothing out there. We're way, way off the beaten path. I bought the property about thirty years ago when no one wanted to live out here. That house you found yourself in, earlier," she said this delicately, "was the original structure on the property. I built this place about ten years ago. We run on solar and we have a generator. No wifi. No phone." She gestured toward a folding chair sitting a few feet in front of the desk, saying, "Sit."

I couldn't see her after lowering myself into the chair. The woman was still in shadow.

"Who are you?" I asked.

She laughed, a low guffaw, completely devoid of humor. "You might figure it out. Or not." Then, a second later, as if changing her mind, she called, "Erik. I need you." The door across the kitchen opened. "Take her upstairs," the woman said.

The man ducked back through the door and returned to the main room. The gun was now in a holster, with the strap dangling over his shoulder like a purse. For show, I suspected. But what an effective show. I could see the gleam of the barrel, the curve of the trigger, the handle's polished stock.

He gestured at me and I stood, quickly, facing the woman. The chair behind me fell to the ground with a thwack and for an instant, I wondered if I'd been shot, bracing for a quick pain, and then, the embrace of nothingness.

But the instant passed.

Out of habit, I leaned down to pick up the chair. As I stood, placing it upright, I caught a glimpse of her face. Plain. Cat-eye glasses. Gray hair parted in the middle.

I set the chair upright and turned around again, to stare. But Erik grabbed my elbow and steered me toward staircase, pushing me up the flight of steps.

Upstairs, a long hallway ran the length of the house. The bathroom door, across the hall from the staircase, was open. The other doors, four in total, two on either side of the hallway and opposite each other, were closed.

Erik turned to the right at the top of the stairs. He pulled open the door next to the bathroom, across the hall from the room where I thought I'd seen the figure watching me through the window.

But before my captor could shove me into my new prison, a voice threaded out from underneath the door. "What's going on out there?"

A child's voice.

Erik gave me a warning sign and I knew not to say anything. He grunted a return. "Nothing's going on out here. Everything is fine."

"But there's another person with you," the child said. "It's someone who's smaller than you. I can hear them walk. And breathe. It's fast, like they're scared."

"Hey," Erik growled, "be quiet."

He pushed me into the room, slammed the door shut, and rattled the knob, making sure the door was secure. I heard him whack the door across the hall for good measure. His footsteps receded down the stairs.

I lay flat on the floor and pressed my mouth to the crack between the bottom of the door and the floor. "Hello?" My voice was a tiny whisper. "Who are you?"

"My name is Justin," he replied, in a voice just as quiet. "Justin Ryan Boyd."

Justin? I'd found Justin?

"Who are you?" he asked.

"Shelby McDougall," I replied, my voice a small sigh, floating under the door and across the hall.

Maybe I was too loud, or maybe Erik had stopped at the bottom of the stairs to listen. He yelled up the stairs and his voice reverberated through the hallway. "You two. Shut up. No talking."

I waited a few minutes and then whispered, "Justin, I've been looking for you."

"I know. Justine told me," he replied, his voice soft, yet matter of fact. "She said you would find me."

"How many people are keeping you here?" I asked.

"Just two," Justin replied.

I paused and then said, "We'll have to figure out how to get you home."

Justin agreed, saying, "Good."

Bewildered, I remained outstretched on the floor for a few more minutes, trying to process what I'd just learned. How could Justin be here? And exactly how was I going to get him out?

I stood and surveyed my prison. The door, of course, was locked. A dormer window took up most of the opposite wall of the narrow room. It looked out the back of the house onto the forest, the idyllic view ruined by a set of bars. A single bed was shoved into the far corner of the room and a waist high plywood dresser with four drawers sat on the opposite side of the room, next to the door.

The springs gave when I tested the bed and the mattress sagged into the bed frame. Under the plain yellowish bedspread were two thin blankets, a top and bottom sheet, and a flat pillow with a white pillowcase. All freshly laundered, as far as I could tell, but worn thin, like they'd been well-used or bought at a second-hand store. The dresser was of the same vintage, with a fading finish and drawers that didn't quite fit. All were empty.

I took off my sweatshirt and threw it on the bed, and then seesawed the bed frame away from the wall, looking for anything that might help me escape. A dangling spring. A loose iron bar. A forgotten screwdriver. But there was nothing. I pushed the bed back against the wall, plopped down on it, sighed, and held my head in my hands.

I was stuck. I'd escaped from one prison, only to land in another.

Restless, I walked back and forth across the room, counting my steps. Twelve of them. Twelve steps. I'd counted ten stairs from the first story to the second. All pointless, useless information.

A sudden dizziness came over me. Saturday night I'd been hunting Megan and had slept a few hours in a chair in the hospital waiting room. Last night, I'd been out cold in an abandoned house. I hadn't had anything to eat since the two yogurts Dexter had brought me at the hospital, before my ill-fated trip up the coast to retrieve Anne's car.

And I was thirsty. I thought about water. How good a tall glass of water would be right now. I remembered the fluorescent light glinting off the bottles of water in the ICU waiting room, and wished I had one of them.

My head started to ache and the wound throbbed. I knew I needed stitches. I probably had a concussion. And the pain in my torso had returned — each breath felt like someone was pounding on my chest.

I pulled on my sweatshirt, then yanked back the bedspread and blankets and lay down on the bed, fully clothed. I decided to keep my sandals on, in case I had an opportunity to escape. They left a grimy trail on the white sheets.

Just before I fell asleep, I thought about the woman downstairs. I knew I'd seen her somewhere. Recently. But where?

46

HEAVY FOOTSTEPS OUTSIDE MY ROOM WOKE ME and I pried my eyes open. Light streamed through the barred window and a crack of brighter light squeezed in below the door. I had no idea what time it was. I tried to push myself up, but the headache was back, pounding and insistent. My throat was tight from thirst.

The handle on the door across the hall rattled and the man's voice barked, "Dinner. Here's your food."

I remembered. I was a prisoner; taken by the same people who'd taken Justin — the man named Erik and that woman.

Suddenly, I had it. I knew where I'd seen her.

She was the woman in the photograph with Diane. The picture I'd puzzled over, the one where Diane had been standing with an older woman on the front porch of a house. Their arms had been linked, but neither of the women looked relaxed. The middle-aged woman was so plain as to be invisible. Her glasses looked like they were from the seventies. Add to that her graying hair, cut in a blunt, unflattering style, her ordinary clothes, her black round-toed shoes that reminded me of the shoes my mother, a nurse, wore to work.

That photograph had been taken almost ten years ago.

Lying on the bed, cradling my head, I tried to figure it out. Diane was somehow connected to the woman in the photograph, who was also the woman downstairs. Diane was connected to me. Justin had been kidnapped by the same woman. And Justin was connected to me. Diane and Justin were connected, tangentially through the woman, and directly through me.

But my brain was too fuzzy to go any further.

Out in the hall, I could hear the murmur of voices and the sound of a heavy door opening. Something rattled: dishes on a tray? The door shut and the steps faded, methodically clomping down the stairs, followed by the boy's voice, surprisingly loud, ricocheting through the walls: "Hey," he yelled, "Hey. I need meat. Give me some meat. I can smell it cooking down there. I want some." He banged his fist against the wall a few times, and his insistent tone reminded me of Justine's urgent need for animal flesh.

A few minutes later, the footsteps clomped back up the stairs and stopped. Justin began his tirade again, "Did you bring me some meat? I'm dying." The word was stretched to two syllables, and I could almost imagine the accompanying eye roll.

In return, his door opened and closed. The child was silent, and I assumed he'd received his ration. Again, the footsteps retreated down the stairs. A few minutes later, they returned and stopped by my door. I struggled to sit as I heard something being placed on the floor and the sound of the key in the lock. Then the door swung open.

My jailor stood there, tray in hand. The hall light fell on him like a spotlight. I sized him up — he was not tall, but he was built like a brick wall with a neck the size of a small tree trunk and thighs the size of my waist. His biceps bulged out of his shirt sleeves like Popeye in those old cartoons I used to watch with my brother. I might be able to outrun him, but I sure as hell wouldn't be able to knock him out. I'd be like a child trying to swat a giant.

Without glancing at me, he placed the tray on the dresser.

As he started to back out of the room, I asked, "Could I use the bathroom?"

Ignoring me completely, as if he hadn't heard, he closed the door.

I ran over to examine the food. Three sixteen-ounce bottles of water lay on their side. I immediately picked one up, twisted the top off, and chugged. I swallowed until I choked, stopped to breathe, and then drank until the water was gone. I sank to the floor, leaned against the door, and held up the empty in celebration.

I cracked open another bottle, took a swig, then pulled off my sweatshirt and t-shirt and poured water on a corner of the fabric. Using slow, circular motions, I slowly swabbed my face, hoping to remove some of the blood. I didn't dare touch the gash on my temple; I could feel that it had mostly closed up and I didn't want to risk it bleeding again.

In the light from the window, I could see the livid, purple bruise radiating across my torso like a rash. I poked at it, winced, and then pressed it gently with the palm of my hand, probing. The searing pain had dulled now into a generalized deep ache. I didn't think I'd bruised or broken a rib.

I pulled my clothes back on and eyed the tray of food. A bunch of grapes sat on a paper plate next to a banana, five sticks of string cheese, a few Oreos, and a long packet of saltines. It was an interesting assortment, the kind of food that Megan had in her kitchen. The kind of food that Dexter took to the park for Ashley. Kid food.

I peeled the banana and scarfed it, my stomach suddenly full, almost bloated. I stumbled back to the bed, collapsed, and fell asleep again. When I woke, the room was in complete shadow. I stretched and sat up, swinging my feet to the floor, feeling like I'd aged fifty years during my nap. Every muscle was tight. My head pounded. Each time I breathed in, a sharp pain seared my ribcage. Maybe I had damaged a rib after all.

But I was still hungry, and there was food across the room. I baby-stepped over to the dresser and fumbled for a light switch. I found one adjacent to the door, but when I flipped it, the room remained dark.

My foot banged into something that had been placed just inside the door. I picked it up and found myself squinting at a five-gallon bucket. A roll of toilet paper lay unfurled at the bottom. I carried the bucket to the far corner of the room, set the toilet paper on the floor, squat and emptied my bladder, wondering about the outside world. Was Megan out of the ICU? How was the search for me progressing?

Don't go there, Shelby, a quiet voice inside me warned. Just don't go there.

My eyes were adjusting to the dark now. I picked up the tray and walked slowly back to the bed, where I removed all the food and set it in tidy rows. Then, I set the tray aside and sipped from the second bottle of water. I slid my hands over the grapes, the string cheese, crackers. Hoard it or eat now?

Without thinking, I popped a grape into my mouth. The small squirt of juice reminded me of our beach picnic just a few days ago and I thought of the succulent green grapes that Annie had delicately bitten in half. I remembered the way Cody had torn into his sandwich, obviously enjoying every bite. How Megan had eaten a few bites of her sandwich and handed the remainder to Dexter.

As I ate another grape, I concentrated on what had happened since I'd been summoned to the Boyd's house after Justin's kidnapping.

First of all, there was the Boyd twins themselves. Genius IQs, their mom had said. What was it exactly? Two hundred ninety and three hundred? Only a few people in the entire recorded history of the world had that caliber IQ.

I thought about Justine's physical traits. The child, my offspring, resembled me somewhat, what with her hair and freckles and her body shape, but not enough to claim me as a parent. And there were her eyes, those ringed eyes that sucked in light, flat as a cat's. Where had those come from?

Added to that were Justine's traits: her uncanny conversational ability and her sophistication with words and sentences. Her imperious nature as she'd perched in her small armchair, dictionary in her lap, expecting people to serve her. Her insatiable appetite and craving for meat.

Then there was her body's denial of a basic biological need: sleep. How was that even possible? I'm not a scientist, but I know that all mammals need sleep.

Where had all these super-human abilities come from?

I thought of Justine's mysterious phone call from her brother. Plus my brush with a dark pickup truck earlier in the week, one that looked suspiciously like the truck in the driveway.

Megan getting snatched — that piece still made no sense to me. Had someone, most likely Erik, gotten the wrong person? Had he confused Megan for me? Could he have wrestled Megan into his pickup, and driven her all the way here, only to discover that he'd gotten the wrong person? Then, he would have had to drive her back to Waddell, lug her up the cliff, assault her, and dump her. That seemed unlikely. More likely, he nabbed her, discovered his mistake, and then strong armed her across the road, through the marsh, and up the cliff.

I shuddered, remembering what he'd threatened to do to me. I'd been saved — my screams had alerted the woman and Erik had backed off.

Megan had not been so lucky.

My breath quickened and I vowed to exact revenge. To get Erik arrested, to let the slow wheels of justice churn him into prison for the rest of his life. Attempted manslaughter for starters, then add two counts of aggravated assault, possibly a rape charge, and three counts of kidnapping: Justin, Megan, and now me.

I assumed I'd been the one Erik had been after. If that were true, why hadn't he just captured me earlier in the week? There'd been plenty of opportunities. The morning he'd almost run me down, he could have just as well sidled up to me, stuck a gun in my side, and ordered me to come along. When I sat in the park in Corralitos, drinking coffee, pondering what kind of games Justin would play. And that long evening when I'd watched Randy Vinson's house and followed him to Marina. No one knew where I was then; it would have been easy to snatch me. Or the morning I'd been on my early walk at Davenport Beach before driving to Ice Cream Grade.

Why on Saturday?

Because I'd found the house. This house. Because I'd come snooping. They assumed I was putting the pieces together; that I was on to something. But what were the pieces? What was I on to?

And just who were they, Erik and the woman?

A woman old enough to be my grandmother. A woman I'd seen in a photograph dug out of the wall in what used to be Jackson and Diane's soundproofed office.

I stared out the window, my eyes unfocused. What was the connection? What was I missing?

My mind drifted to Jackson and Diane, how I'd first met them, through an ad in *Rolling Stone*. Now, all those ads for surrogates or gestational carriers had migrated online. The agency ads, the non-agency ads, the money. My spreadsheet.

Had the ad I'd seen earlier in the week also been part of this? The one that included the dangerous and seductive phrase, "First time moms encouraged." The ad I'd responded to and never heard back from?

Ignoring my stiffness and my aching head and torso, I started to pace the room, from the window to the far wall. Maybe I was looking at that packet from Diane's house completely wrong. Maybe the individual pieces were not important. Maybe the collection of photos and addresses, the entire packet, was what mattered.

Diane had thought that collection was enough to incriminate someone. Or, find someone.

Or maybe both.

I sat back on the sagging bed and leaned against the wall. I picked up a grape and bit into it, thinking. Wishing. For a laptop. A cell phone. Even a tiny scrap of paper and a stub of a pencil to write it all down. If I could capture all of it, people, places, dates, and times, I might be able to draw connections.

For now, I'd just have to do it in my head.

Picking up the water bottle, I took a small sip, and then realized I had to pee. Again. I walked over to the bucket and relieved myself. When I stood and glanced down, I was astonished by the amount of bright yellow liquid that sat in the bucket. And I got an idea.

47

WORKING IT OVER, EXAMINING IT FROM ALL ANGLES, I sat back on the bed, peeled open a string cheese, chomped, and obliterated it in three bites. I ate another and then another until I only had one left, discarding the plastic wrap on the floor. I needed fuel to clear my head, to give me energy for the job in front of me.

Leaving the crackers, knowing they would make my mouth pucker with thirst, I eyed the Oreos. I hadn't eaten Oreos since the night I'd first met Frankie, Jackson and Diane's delivery man. The night he'd come to my cottage for dinner when I lived on Jackson and Diane's property. When Dexter had hired him to look around. To protect me. That had been long before I discovered the baby-brokering scheme, or even imagined such a thing was possible. Before I met Megan. Before I'd ever heard of The Stork or discovered the monster lurking inside Frankie. I decided to give the Oreos a pass.

I strode across the room to the bucket, picked it up, carried it to the door, and set it down. I sank to the floor and pressed my back to the wall, pulling the bucket close, trying to ignore the acrid smell by breathing through my mouth. After five minutes, I stood and lifted the bucket on to the dresser, and then walked to the far wall, trying to keep myself awake and limber. I tired after twenty trips across the room, and returned to my seat by the door. I wanted to be close. Ready.

I didn't have long to wait. Footsteps thud up the stairs and stopped across the hall. A door opened and then clicked closed. The footsteps receded.

A few minutes later, the same methodical, measured gait tapped up the stairs again and stopped in front of my door. Silently, I picked up the bucket and stepped back until I stood a foot away from where I projected the edge of the door would swing into the room. I gripped the bottom of the bucket with my right hand and the top with my left so hard that the plastic edges bit into my palms.

Time stretched. I imagined Erik fiddling for the key, pulling it out of his pocket, fingering the keychain, finding the right one.

The key slid into the lock. The lock turned. Pins and tumblers rolled and engaged and fell into place.

A second later the knob twisted and the door angled open. The toe of a black shoe appeared in the door frame.

My palms were slick with sweat. The sharp stink of urine was making me gag. My right hand started to twitch. Sweat dripped down my forehead. My heart battered my rib cage, pounding like a jackhammer. My ears rang.

A dark figure loomed in the doorway, lit from the dim bulb in the hallway.

I took a step and swung the bucket, heaving it up and forward, aiming for where I thought Erik's head would be.

The yellow arc of pee looked like a waterfall.

In return, I heard a long drawn out shriek of surprise, disgust, anger.

I threw the bucket.

And then, I jumped.

But instead of landing on a bulked-up body, hard with sculpted ridges and firm muscles, I landed on a soft, rounded shape. A flabby cushion. Air escaped in a sharp exhale, followed by a rasping sound, as if whoever it was couldn't catch their breath.

We fell to the ground. I landed on top; my body fully extended, pressing down. The person below me struggled, reaching around me to pummel my back. I pushed myself up to a sitting position, straddling the person, leaning in.

The woman was trapped beneath me. Even though I was blocking the light and her face was in shadow, I knew it was the woman who'd spoken to me earlier.

Defiant and angry eyes peered at me. Her glasses must have fallen off in the struggle. Wrinkles etched her face, drawing down her features. As I stared, her face turned from red to dark red, purpling her lips. Her mouth was opening and closing in fish-like gasps. She couldn't breathe. I scooted back, taking my body weight off her sternum.

Within seconds, she caught her breath in one rasping gasp. "Erik," she yelled. "Erik, I need you."

I clamped my hand on her mouth. The woman struggled, trying to get free, grunting and trying to bite my hand. She started to hit me.

"Hey," I heard Justin yell from behind his closed, locked door.

"Not now, Justin," I yelled back.

"Listen," he shouted. "Erik's gone. I heard him leave. Thirty minutes ago. I heard the downstairs door open and close and the truck drive down the hill. Don't worry about him."

The woman's eyes opened wide for just a second and I knew it was true.

Still straddling the woman, I lifted my hand off her mouth and held down her arm. I squeezed my legs, enough for her to be uncomfortable, but not enough to cut off her air. "I know you," I said. "I've seen you before."

"That's nonsense," the woman replied, her voice sharp. "Never seen you before in my life."

"No, I haven't met you in person," I replied. "I've seen your photograph."

I felt the woman tense her legs as if she was going to try to stand. "Who are you?" I asked.

She shook her head and didn't answer.

In one swift motion, I grabbed both of her arms and swung off her, so that I was on my knees next to her. I squeezed her forearms. She writhed and twisted, trying to snap free. In return, I increased the pressure.

"Stop that," I warned. "Time to get up," I said, yanking her wrists.

But she resisted, turning herself into a dead weight. Every time I pulled, she pushed her body into the floor, actively opposing me.

"Okay then, we'll do it your way," I said as I pulled her arms up, over her head, rotating her shoulders until her arms were straight out on the floor. She grunted and kicked, trying to gain leverage so she could roll over.

Justin started banging on the door across the hall. "Hey, what's going on out there? Is everything okay?"

I didn't answer.

The woman was now actively resistant, kicking her legs like she was in a swimming pool, twisting her torso, flinging her head from side to side. I didn't like dragging her by her wrists. The way her arms were contorted over her head made me wonder if her shoulder was about to be dislocated. And it was hard; I had no leverage. I sank to the floor, planted my heels next to her shoulders and pulled, trying to fishtail her body in a circle. But my feet slipped, and I swore, panting.

I got on my knees, the hard surface of the wooden floor drilling into my kneecaps. I yanked. No more polite tugging. She moved, a small inch. I yanked again. Another inch. She tensed and squeezed the length of her body against the floor, jamming her heels down, as effective as a brake.

The doorknob across the hall rattled and I glanced up. The high-pitched voice shouted, "What's going on? Tell me."

"We're still here, Justin," I replied, my eyes fixed across the hall. "I'll be with you in a few minutes."

I looked at the woman now. Her face was stony and her lips were compressed in a hard, thin line. Her eyes bored into mine.

"You really think you're going to be able to get me in that room?" she asked.

"Yes." I replied as I yanked again, moving her another inch.

"I don't." She was as rigid as a plank.

Now what? I had her hands over her head and my back was against the wall. I had boxed myself in.

There was just one thing to do.

I dropped her hands and backed up. I needed room.

She pulled her hands to her side and sat, scooting her back to the wall, just a few inches to the left of the open door. Bewildered, she looked at me. She should have run.

Without replying, I strode back toward her, drawing back my fist. I didn't like it. I really didn't. Punching an older woman seemed sacrilegious somehow, against the natural order of the world. It was like decking my beloved grandmother.

But soon enough, I wouldn't feel the same way at all.

48

I HIT HER ON THE SIDE OF HER JAW and her head snapped to the side. Quickly, I dragged her through the puddle of pee, past the overturned bucket and the soggy toilet paper, into the room where I'd been imprisoned. I lay her on her side against the far wall of the room and rifled in her clothes for the keys. But she didn't have any pockets. I felt around her neck and found a silver chain with two keys. Two standard-issue brass keys.

One for this room and one for the room across the hall. I yanked the chain. It broke and the keys tumbled into my palm.

I leapt to the door, turning around to glance at her. She was still out. There was one bottle of water in the room, the packet of saltines, and the Oreos. That would hold her. The police would be here soon enough. I slammed the door and made sure it was locked, leaning over to catch my breath. My heart was pounding and the swoosh of blood pumping through my body throbbed in my ears. I felt a trickle against my temple and raised my hand, feeling something sticky. The cut was starting to ooze again, and a heavy pain radiated across my head, down through my neck.

"Hey." That voice again. "What's going on?" The words filtered muffled and small through the heavy door as if the person had almost given up.

"It's me. Shelby," I said. "I have the key to your room and I'm going to open the door."

His matter-of-fact "Okay" was followed by a question. "So how do you know my parents, anyway?" he asked. "Who are you?"

Who was I? I could answer that question in a million ways, but I stuck to the easiest one. "A friend. I'm here to take you back home. Are you ready to see your sister?"

"Yes." Justin's voice grew excited. "Yes. I miss her."

I took a breath, inserted one of the keys into the lock, and turned. The door swung open.

Light streamed from a bulb in the ceiling. A small boy sat on a bed, his right hand resting protectively on a stack of textbooks. He stared at me, sizing me up. His eyes were just like his sister's, those flat rings of color. I remembered their milky blue eyes in the hospital and wondered how old they'd been when the bands had developed.

"Justin?" I asked.

He nodded.

"Come on, let's get out of here. Before Erik comes back." I held my hand out. "Sound good?"

He nodded again and stood. His head was no taller than my waist. His blue button-down shirt and jeans were crisp and fresh, as if they'd just come from the wash. "Okay." He looked around the room. "But I have to collect some things."

"What?"

"These textbooks." He pointed to the books on the bed. "College-level math. They cost a fortune. Auntie told me that Ryan and Lisa would not be able to afford them."

"Auntie?" I interrupted.

"The woman in the hall," he answered.

Nodding, I said, "I don't think we're going to be able to carry those textbooks. We're on foot. We need to hurry. We have to be out of here before Erik comes back."

Justin sighed and said, "Okay. Can we look for the notebook, though? We can carry that."

A chill ran through me. "What notebook?"

"Every time she came to play with me, she wrote notes. I always asked her what they were and she would never tell me. I'd like to see what she wrote down."

I crouched down so I was eye to eye with him. "Who are you talking about?"

Justin pointed to the hallway. "Auntie. The lady who was picking up the tray."

"Does she have a name?"

The child nodded; his eyes serious and thoughtful. "Auntie Helen." He swiveled those eyes toward me. "I saw her once before I came here."

"You did?"

"At the park one day, with Lisa and my sister. I never forget a face."

I flashed back to Lisa telling me about the older woman who'd been watching them at the playground, who'd given her a business card. Helen?

I placed my hands on his shoulders. My eyes drilled into his. "Did she hurt you or threaten you?"

"No. I didn't like her though. She was always writing down everything I did. Even when I went to the bathroom.

"Another thing," he said, pointing to the far corner. "Cameras."

I looked up and saw a tiny black recorder hanging from the ceiling.

"It's on all the time. I can hear it."

I cupped my hand around my ear and shrugged. "I can't hear anything."

He looked at me like I was an idiot. I remembered that look from his sister. "I know," he said. "I can hear things most people can't."

"Like what?"

"Auntie Helen and Erik talking downstairs. The TV in Erik's room. The truck coming up the driveway."

Nodding, I held out my hand. Justin took it. His hand was so tiny, so fragile. "Let's go see if we can find that notebook, okay? Maybe we can find where she keeps all the recordings."

We walked to the door and I peeked out in the hallway.

"Where is she?" Justin asked.

I pointed toward the opposite room. "Over there. She's sleeping."

Something creaked downstairs and I stopped. I knelt down, placing one finger to my lips. I put my other hand on his shoulder and leaned over. "Erik?" I whispered.

Justin shrugged and whispered back, in the way of a child who doesn't know how to be quiet. "No. The truck didn't come back."

We exited the room and stepped carefully down the stairs, taking it slow, just in case something was down there waiting for us. But the downstairs was empty, dark. The main room was bathed in the dim light coming from the single bulb recessed into the ceiling above the kitchen sink.

"Did you ever come down here?" I asked in a whisper.

Justin shook his head. "Never. I was upstairs all the time."

"Have you been here since they took you?"

"Yes."

"Did Erik take you?" I asked.

"Yes." His eyes were wide, and in that instant, he almost seemed like a kid. "Justine left to use the bathroom. Erik came into the room, pointing a gun at me. Never said a word. He just walked over to the bed and put a wet rag on my face. It smelled bad; sweet and chemically. Like cough syrup tastes. Then I woke up here."

"Have they been nice to you?" I asked.

"Most of the time," Justin shrugged.

"How did you use the bathroom or get a bath?" I asked.

"Bucket. Like the one on the floor upstairs. They took me to the bathroom down the hall every morning and every night. I took a bath every day."

I nodded. "Well, let's see if we can find that notebook."

49

T HE YELLOW PAD WAS STILL IN THE MIDDLE OF THE DESK; the pen in its same place. Justin pulled the chain on the desk lamp and it flickered on, throwing a circle of light across the desktop. An old-style flip phone sat by the base of the lamp. I picked it up and slid it into my pocket.

The table behind the desk held two metal boxes. The one on the left was labeled In. Its companion on the right was labeled Out. Both were empty. A set of matching journals, held upright by two polished stone bookends, stood between the two boxes. Justin swiveled the chair toward the table and climbed up. I reached for the leftmost journal, handed it to him, extracted the next one, and flipped to the first page. The rule was thin and the handwriting was small and precise, never straying outside of the lines. "Day Two" was written on the first page, followed by:

Justin slept well and woke before dawn. He banged on his door until Erik arrived exactly three minutes and twenty-two seconds later. He told Erik he needed to use the bathroom. Erik escorted him down the hall and waited by the door. When Justin returned to his room, he told Erik he was hungry. He did not ask where he was or demand to be taken home. Instead, he walked to the bookshelf and pulled down *Multivariable Calculus Principles, Edition Two.* Erik had to help him since the book was so heavy.

I quickly scanned the pages. Each entry recorded Justin's every move, from when he stood up to stretch or drink water, to which books he pulled off the shelf, to how long he studied a page of text. The journal also included several pages of formulas. I couldn't understand them, they appeared to be proofs for a math problem. I angled the journal toward Justin and pointed.

"Hey," he protested. "That's my work. She stole it."

Justin took the journal and I pulled another one from the shelf. "Day Five" was written in the middle of the first page. The words "IQ Test" were at the top of the next page, followed by a series of questions, scribed in the same precise handwriting. Justin's answer followed each question. In addition, Justin's notes and scribbles had been cut out from other pieces of paper and taped below each answer. Very low tech.

A sudden bang upstairs made me jump and I glanced toward Justin, who'd picked up another notebook and was slowly turning the pages. "We need to get out of here," I whispered. "Grab as many of these as you can. I'll figure out how to carry them."

"Wait," he muttered, his voice low. "Here are the notes she took when she gave me some calculus problems. She wrote everything down. Even when I talked to myself." He dropped the notebook and reached for another one, saying, "Erik is usually gone a long time. For hours. Sometimes she would complain about it. Don't worry," he said as he turned his attention to the notebook, "I'll be able to hear the truck when he turns off the road."

He flipped through the journal, and I realized that short of picking him up and carrying him, I wasn't going to get him to move. I pulled open the filing drawer on the right side of the desk. It was stuffed with hanging green files, neatly labeled with month and year. I found a few for the year I was pregnant and quickly flicked through the folders.

In the file labeled "September 2006" were four nine-by-twelve inch manila envelopes.

My pulse quickened. Trembling, I reached in and pulled out one of the envelopes. Angling it toward the desk lamp, I read the dates scrawled on the front of the envelope: September 15-22.

I turned it over and unfastened the metal tab holding the flap of the envelope in place. Slowly, I upended the envelope to shake out its contents. But I already knew what was in there. Pieces of a puzzle that had haunted me for years were starting to click into place.

I stared at the desk. Photographs and pieces of paper were scattered across the blotter like leaves.

Suddenly, everything was crystal clear. Where this had come from. When it all began. Where it was going. And just what would happen when Erik returned.

Justin's voice came to me from a long way away, small and tiny, interrupting my focus. "Hey. Hey, Shelby. You there?"

I ignored him and reached for a photo. But Justin pulled on my arm. "The truck. Erik's back. I hear the truck. He just turned off the road. We need to hide."

Reluctantly, I shook my head and willed myself back to the present. Then, I crooked my finger, leaned over and whispered, "So here's what we're going to do."

50

JUSTIN AND I STOLE TO THE FRONT DOOR and I inched it open, leaving the porch light off. Justin squared his shoulders and slipped outside into the darkness. I knew that Erik would be able to see the small child standing on the porch in the lights of the truck as he drove up the road.

I shut the door and threw the deadbolt. I didn't like leaving Justin outside as fodder for Erik, but knew I would need as much time as I could get. I sprinted back across the room to the table, picked up the journals we'd been looking at, grabbed a few more from the bookshelf, and then reached into the desk drawer and pulled out five of the manila envelopes.

Just as I was pushing the drawer shut, a flash of red, the spine of a journal, caught my eye.

I heard the truck skid up the road and slam to a stop. The engine cut off and the truck door creaked open. Heavy footsteps crunched against the gravel. I imagined Justin standing on the top step of the porch, drawn up to his full height, his chest puffed out and arms crossed like the lord of the manor.

Justin and I had talked about it. Justin would claim that I had pushed him out of the house. If Erik had that gun, Justin was supposed to do whatever Erik asked. Hopefully, Erik wouldn't overthink it and try to piece together why Helen was a prisoner and Justin was free.

Erik wouldn't shoot Justin, I was sure of that. He'd just hold the gun to his head and force him, and me, to do his bidding.

But not yet. I still had a few minutes.

I grabbed the pile of journals and envelopes, ran to the kitchen, opened the cabinet under the sink, and found a box of garbage bags. I retrieved a bag, dropped the evidence inside, pulled out the plastic white trash can, and shoved my plastic bag to the bottom of the can, beneath the bag filled with string cheese wrappers, naked grape stems, wet coffee filters, chicken bones, banana peels.

When Justin shouted, just like we'd talked about, a wave of relief washed over me. "Some lady forced me out of the room and shoved me out here," he said. "I could hear Auntie across the hall, banging on the door, but I didn't have the key to open it."

Erik said, "Dammit, kid. Get back here." His footsteps clomped off the porch and I knew Justin had run for it. All according to the plan.

I wished I had more time. What was that flash of red I'd seen in the filing drawer? The bank of filing cabinets surely held enough incriminating evidence to put Helen away for several lifetimes. I needed the laptop, the videos, all of the notebooks.

But it would have to wait.

Fighting panic, I opened the door to Erik's room and wasted precious seconds fumbling for a light switch. In the harsh glare, I could see a bed, a chair, and a table with a small flat screen TV. I checked under the bed, pulled out the desk drawer. There were no weapons. I scrambled through the closet. A shotgun leaned against the wall in the corner. I lifted it and was surprised by its heft. I eyed it briefly, wondering for an instant if I should hold on to it, but I had no idea how to use it. I didn't even know how to figure out if it was loaded.

With the shotgun in hand, I sprinted from Erik's room back to the kitchen, yanked open the cabinet under the sink, and shoved the thing to the back.

But that handgun was somewhere. Until I knew differently, I had to assume that Erik was pointing it at Justin.

I heard the handle on the front door rattle. Hoping Justin could hold Erik off a few seconds longer, I yanked open one of the kitchen drawers. It held a few pieces of silverware. I dumped the contents of the drawer next to it, scattering wooden spoons, pasta tongs, a garlic press, and spatulas across the floor.

The front door clicked. I ransacked the counter, shoving pots, pans, the dish drainer, salad bowl, mixer, paper towels, and the coffee pot out of the way. The half-full carafe spilled and dark liquid pooled on the white countertop. I opened the small cabinet above the sink: plates, bowls, glasses, mugs. My eyes traveled along the edge of the counter. And there, right behind a box of cereal, next to the red canister of Folgers coffee, I found it: the butcher block.

I pulled out two knives: a big-assed one, the size of the knives heroines use in horror movies; then, a smaller knife, about six inches long, with a sharp point. I ran into Erik's room, shut the door behind me, locked it, and turned off the light. Erik would have a key, of course, but forcing him to unlock it would give me a few more seconds. But for what?

Just as I thought that maybe locking myself in a maniac's room wasn't such a good idea, that maybe I should have run upstairs, I heard the front door open. Erik's heavy footsteps pounded into the living room.

"Where are you?" he roared. "I have the kid. Come out, now."

Justin called, "Don't worry, He doesn't have..." but his words were cut short.

I hid the smaller knife under the pillow and flattened myself against the wall next to the door, the wide slats of knotty pine smooth and cold. I chose the side that would be open when the door swung into the room. I didn't want to take the extra seconds to dodge around it.

Holding my breath, I watched the spear-shaped door handle move up and down as Erik tried to open it. I heard a loud and distinct, "Shit," followed by, "You better not be in there, bitch."

Keys rattled. In my mind's eye, I could see the chain that stretched from his belt loop to his pocket, the type of setup you'd see on biker bad boys in the movies.

A key clicked into the lock.

I crouched and pressed my butt against the wall, angled to spring.

In the few seconds I had left, I took a breath and squeezed my eyes shut, willing Erik to walk in with his hands at his sides. Without a gun.

Erik pushed the door open. He paused for a split second, surveying the room, his attention focused toward the bed. He didn't notice me.

And he wasn't carrying the gun.

Had I missed it in my frenzied search? Was it still in here, somewhere?

But I couldn't worry about that now. I had to concentrate on what was right in front of me.

I waited, my heart in my throat, gripping the handle of the knife with my right hand, my left, angled out for balance.

I needed him to take one step. I willed him to take one step.

He did.

And I jumped.

I landed on his back like a cat on a scratching post, arms around his neck, squeezing. The enormous knife was clutched in my right hand pointing up, the long sharp edge right in his face. The effect I'd hoped for, scaring him, forcing him to back off, wasn't working.

Erik raised his arms, placed his hands on my wrists, and pinched.

In return, I crunched my knees into his rib cage, hoping to cut off his air.

He turned in a dizzying circle and increased the pressure on my wrists. My legs splayed outward and I lost my grip. The knife clattered to the floor.

Erik kicked it under the bed. Good.

Now that the knife was gone, he eased up on my wrists.

I dug my thumbs into the hollow at his throat, remembering my self-defense teacher. "No hesitation," he had instructed us. "No thoughts. No mercy." We'd practiced over and over again on Bob, the dummy. Bob would beep when we'd hit the mark.

Erik gagged.

But instead of collapsing, he shook me off. I fell to the floor. Keeping his hands on his throat, he staggered into the wall and bent over, his breath raspy and ragged.

I leapt across the room to the bed and slid my hand under the pillow, confident once I had the knife with the six-inch blade in my hand.

With a roar, he was at me again, this time with a murderous ferocity in his eyes that hadn't been there before.

Just as he was on me, I crouched, holding the knife steady with both hands. Angling the knife downward, I drove it into his right thigh. It sliced through the thick denim of his jeans as if it were butter, and then slipped through his flesh into the muscle, where it met resistance. I pushed down until only the handle of the knife was visible, then scrambled backward toward the door.

He collapsed, grabbing his leg, bending and straightening it, rocking from side to side, howling in guttural animal-like shrieks. Sitting on his butt and leveraging with his good leg, he fishtailed across the floor, leaving a trail of bright red blood behind him. He pulled himself up on the edge of the bed and tried to stand, lunging for me. But his leg slid out from under him and he fell, hands circling the knife handle protruding from his thigh. He stared at me, his face flat and furious.

"You bitch," he muttered through clenched teeth. "I'll get you for this."

51

M Y HANDS WERE SHAKING as I ran out of the room and slammed the door behind me, almost plowing into Justin. The child stood right in front of the door, wide-eyed. He'd seen everything. But there was no time for soothing words.

Instead I said, "We're not clear yet. We should get out while we can."

Behind the door, we could hear hoarse breathing, interspersed with moans of pain. Rushing now, the terror of what I'd done catching up to me, I opened the cabinet under the sink; pulled out the trash can; turned it over on its side, dumping trash on the floor; and yanked out the bag I'd hidden there. Justin trailed me, bouncing on the balls of his feet like he was dancing, and then he jumped, punching his fists in the air.

"What's that?" he asked.

"Evidence," I said, adding in a whisper, "so we'll have something if they torch the place."

At the front door, I paused on the porch, breathing deeply, inhaling the cool night air. I felt a small measure of relief. But it wasn't over yet. We were miles from civilization. I likely had a head injury and my body was bruised and battered. Justin was a small child and wouldn't be able to walk far. I had a phone that might or might not work. It was pitch dark, with no visible moon.

I took Justin's hand and we sprinted down the porch steps, past the truck parked in the middle of the driveway. As our feet slid along the gravel, I felt like I was dragging the child; with two or three steps to every one of mine, he would not be able to keep up for any length of time. When my eyes adjusted to the dark, I could make out the contours of the driveway, the low bushes on either side, the redwoods beyond. A sudden, pungent piney odor made me want to cry. An owl hooted off to our right, low and mournful, and was answered by another, farther away in the depths of the forest.

Suddenly, a loud crack tore through the night, shredding the fabric of the silent evening. Gravel scattered, kicking up into a rooster's tail a few yards from us.

Placing my hand on Justin's back, propelling him forward, I turned to glance back. Erik stood on the front porch, swaying like a drunk, the handgun in his right hand. The knife still stuck out of his thigh.

I grabbed Justin's hand and we ran.

Another explosion tore through the air. The shot was wide.

I reached over to pick up Justin, yanking him up and resting him on my hip, holding him with both hands. The plastic bag whacked my legs, but I didn't consider dropping it. Not for an instant. I sensed, rather than felt, something tearing inside, around my ribcage. I squeezed Justin to me. The weight of his body against mine was holding me together. Literally.

"Put your arms around my neck," I instructed Justin. "And put your head down." His head burrowed into my shoulder and I hurried to the trees, pushing my way through the brush into a small, open circle of redwoods. Justin lost his grip and jabbed his foot into my side for purchase. A sharp pain slivered through me. My head pounded and I could feel a trickle of warm blood as the gash opened up again.

The darkness was absolute. I helped Justin slither to the ground. Turning downhill, I led the way, clambering over logs, scouting out low-hanging branches with my fingertips, dragging my feet through the duff, dodging rocks and roots. When we reached the road, I turned left toward the locked gate, rather than right, toward the neighbors' houses and possible help. Although heading towards people was the obvious choice, Erik or Helen would be able to follow us in the truck. Heading in the other direction would force Helen and Erik to go on foot. And Erik wouldn't be able to walk far.

A third crack. I glanced back. Behind me, Justin had stopped, frozen. I ran back to him, hand extended. "Are you okay?" I asked. "We need to run."

He nodded, lowered his head, and started to run in the choppy, ungraceful way of kids. After ten steps, he stopped, put his hands on knees and bent over. "I'm tired." He looked up at me with a plaintive expression. "I'm sorry. I'm going to slow you down. You go ahead. I'll catch up."

"Are you kidding? And have him snatch you again?" I crouched down, placed the plastic bag on the ground, my back to him. "Hop up. Grab my neck and put your feet around my waist. Piggy-back. Ever ridden piggy-back before?"

"No," he replied.

Once Justin was clinging to my back, hands on my shoulders, I leaned over and scooped up the plastic bag, grabbing it like a Santa Claus bag stuffed with toys. Then I took off, settling into an unsteady jog. With each lurch forward, my head throbbed and a jolt of pain squeezed my chest.

"Your job," I said, "is to listen. Tell me if you hear footsteps."

I ran a few more steps, taking us to the gate. The dirt road hooked to the left. As I wondered if Erik had a key to the gate on that key ring, I turned around, facing the direction we'd come from. The road was empty.

Either he was going for his truck, or he'd given up and had made his way upstairs to release Helen.

"Do you hear anything?" I asked.

Justin paused for a second and replied, "No. Nothing. Just you."

I dodged to the side of the chained gate, with Justin bouncing up and down on my back and the plastic bag hitting my leg. The road beyond seemed well-graded, the dirt compacted. It angled up, away from the road and the creek. My breath labored in and out and my feet thud against the packed dirt surface. Each step was agonizing. After a few minutes of an all-out sprint, I slowed and eased Justin to the ground. I dropped the plastic bag and sank to my knees, reaching into my pocket for the cell phone I'd grabbed off the desk. I flipped it open, hoping I had service, praying I had service. I punched 911. Nothing.

"Come on," I said. "Let's keep moving."

I stood and picked up the bag. We walked in silence for a few more minutes as the road continued to climb, eventually reaching a flat spot where the trees thinned out. Above, the sky was blue-black, a velvety darkness that would have been beautiful in other circumstances. Now, it was just dark. Too dark to move quickly. Too dark to see something coming.

"Try it again," Justin said, pointing to the phone in my hand. "I need to rest." He plopped down on the ground and crossed his legs. I sat down next to him, lifted the phone, and punched the three numbers again. This time, a miracle. The call connected. A voice, small and staticky, responded, "What's your emergency?"

"I need help," I panted, my voice rapid, my breathing shallow. "I'm at the end of Pescadero Creek Canyon Road. I've found Justin Boyd."

"Who?" The operator asked.

"Justin Boyd. The boy who was kidnapped last week from his home in Watsonville."

"Ma'am, are you safe?"

I eyed the road behind me. "No. I need help. I have the boy with me, but we're in danger. And they might get away."

"Who?"

"The kidnappers. Please ..."

But I was talking to dead air. The call had dropped.

"Are they coming?" Justin asked.

I looked up the road. It curved to the right. If we continued to walk, we'd be directly above the house.

And suddenly, I remembered that flash of red I'd seen before slamming the desk drawer shut. I knew what that was. I'd seen it dozens of times before. And I needed to go back and claim it.

52

"HOLD THE PHONE in case the operator calls back. Keep it open so you'll have some light. And wait here. Just for a second, Justin. I'm going to run up ahead. Five minutes, max." I crouched down and looked him in the eyes, at his level. "If they call back, just repeat that you're at the end of Pescadero Creek Canyon Road and that you're the boy who was kidnapped. The police will come." I pointed to the plastic bag on the ground. "Can you watch that?"

Justin nodded, his eyes wide, as I walked away, backward, watching him. When I reached the curve in the road, I waved. Justin gave a small wave in return. Then, I turned around and ran. A few yards beyond, the road pinched against the hillside. A portion of the flat surface had slid down the cliff to the left, making it almost impossible to squeeze past. I pressed my back against the rough dirt of the steep road cut and side-stepped past the slide. From the other side, I could see the slide's damage — it had toppled trees and pushed bushes into piles as it tore down the hill, leaving a direct view of the crumbling cottage and the lower part of the driveway up to the house.

I inched back past the slide and sprinted back. Justin was where I'd left him. Panting, I placed my hands on his shoulders and said, pointing in the direction I'd come from, "You're going to wait up there. Erik can't drive there. Part of the road is missing. He won't be able to walk that far even if he can drive here in the truck."

Holding out my right hand, I picked up the plastic bag with my left. We jogged to the slide and slithered past it. I coached Justin across, telling him to keep his back to the hillside and take baby steps. Once across, I motioned for him to sit. "If anyone comes, just start sliding down the hill and head for the road. Start walking down the road, by the creek, keeping out of sight." I gestured to the phone. "Keep going until you get a signal and then dial 911." Picking up the bag, I slid a few yards down the steep slope and shoved it under a bush. "Don't worry about this. I'll get it later."

"Where are you going?" He eyed me suspiciously and, in that moment, I could imagine him as an adult. Wary, not trusting, and in spite of being the smartest person in the world, convinced that everyone was trying to get the better of him. Which might be true.

"I need to go back."

"Why?"

"I need to get something."

"What?"

"Something I saw there."

"What about Erik? The gun?"

"I don't think he'll be getting up for a while. He's injured."

"You're sure you don't want to me watch your plastic bag?"

"No," I said. "You should be separated from it. Don't come out until you hear the sirens." I put my hands on his shoulders and stared at him. "Okay?"

He rolled his eyes, and in that moment he looked exactly like his sister: same annoyed expression, with the same *I'm-not-even-close-to-being-stupid* look.

"I know," he said.

•　　　•　　　•

Ten minutes later I was crouched behind the garage, wondering if Erik been able to stagger up the stairs to jimmy open the locked bedroom and free Helen. Or would I find him collapsed on the driveway from blood loss? At least I'd have the element of surprise. I was sure Erik would not have locked the door after he'd stumbled back in, blinded from rage and pain. In his wildest dreams, he wouldn't imagine that I'd be back.

I ran, keeping low, the adrenaline kicking in like I'd just had a shot of epinephrine. I kept my breath quiet and controlled, breathing in and out of my mouth in restrained puffs that whistled through my teeth. If Erik heard something, he'd assume the noise came from an animal.

When I saw the log cabin, I stopped, ducking behind the truck. The front door was closed and the place looked deserted. I circled the house along the left side, keeping far away from the structure, remembering the security lights. At the back of the house, I gently tossed a small stick against the foundation, fully expecting a motion sensitive light to turn on. But it stayed dark. Two more tries in different places. No lights.

Taking a deep breath, I hunkered against the house, keeping my head below the window frame. I stopped beneath the living room window and popped up like a prairie dog scoping its surroundings. Helen sat in the swivel chair at her desk, head bowed, looking at something in her lap. The lamp on the desk spotlighted the journal Justin had been looking at when we'd heard Erik's truck. The drawer I'd ransacked was still open. By now, she must have realized what we'd taken.

I squat back down, duck-walked to the small window in Erik's room at the far end of the house, and cautiously lifted my head to the window. Erik lay on the bed, not moving. The knife had been removed and he now wore a pair of sweatpants. I wondered if the woman had given him something for the pain. No matter, Erik seemed to be out of commission. I couldn't see his handgun and I wondered if it was on the bed next to him, or if he'd given it to Helen.

I ran to the front of the house, leapt up the porch steps, grabbed the door handle, and yanked it open. Two quick steps and I was inside.

I stopped.

Helen stared.

I flipped the light switch by the door and an overhead light snapped on, dim, but effective.

I could see her clearly now. Helen. Auntie Helen.

She placed a closed journal on her desk on top of the open one. It was red.

"I'm Shelby," I said, by way of introduction, keeping my distance.

"I know," she replied. "I know who you are."

"And you are?"

"My colleagues call me Doctor Helen."

I gestured toward her. "I know who you are and what you've done."

She looked at me pityingly and a chill entered her voice. "You had to come all this way back just to tell me that?" Keeping her eyes on me, she called out, "Erik. I need you."

His voice floated thin and thready from his bed. "I can't get up, Mama. I can't move. Hurts too much."

Mama? I glanced over to Erik's room, and then back at her. "Your son?"

The woman smiled. "My baby."

"Lucky you." I couldn't help but wonder if he was her biological son, or one she'd stolen from some luckless birth mother.

"Ms. Shelby McDougall." She stood, walked to the front of the desk, and leaned back, arms crossed. She was not a formidable presence as she stood there, and if I could ignore the expression on her face, one of pure venom, she looked almost professorial. "The *famous* Shelby McDougall." Her voice lilted on the last three words, goading me.

I didn't take the bait. Didn't need to. I knew who she was. And given time, I'd be able to work out all the details. I'd be able to reconstruct all the ins and outs of her operation, figuring out who, where, when.

But I still had some questions to ask. Questions I didn't know the answers to. And would never be able to figure out unless she told me.

"Why?" I asked simply. "And just who, or what, are Justin and Justine?"

53

S HE DIDN'T REPLY RIGHT AWAY. Instead, she stared at me, as if debating whether to say anything at all.

"Mama," Erik shouted, his voice raspy, "keep quiet. We can still get out of here. All we have to do is pop her and drive away."

"We are not killing anyone," she called in return.

"At least not yet," Erik said.

She shushed him, waving her hand in a go-away gesture, as if she were talking to a misbehaving child. Then, she pointed to the chair across the room. "Pull up a chair. Erik can't hurt you now. You took care of that."

I held my ground.

"Erik," she hollered, "can you walk?"

"No Mama. That bitch fucked me up good."

"Language," she said in a loud voice. "Watch your mouth." She stared at me. "Though you did," she held up her hands and air

301

quoted, "fuck him up good." She pointed toward the back room, where her son lay. "His injury is rather serious. Not fatal, but bad enough. He should see a doctor.

"I won't bite," she added, her voice light. "Come over here."

I approached carefully, now wondering at my brash decision to return here. I could run. But, I was drawn to her, unable to prevent my feet from sliding across the floor: one step, then the next, and the next.

I stopped a few feet from her desk and stood. No way would I sit. Our eyes locked.

"Have it your way," she shrugged. "I'll tell you everything," she continued, "if you first tell me how you found this place. No one, and I mean no one, knows we're here." She leveled her gaze, waiting.

I explained the list of addresses. And then, unable to stop myself, I relayed all of my suspicions — my doubts that Jackson and Diane were operating alone, Diane's acknowledgement that a Stork existed, my conjecture about the clinic in Los Gatos. As I talked, I looked for some reaction on her part. Anything. But her face was smooth and she remained calm, showing no hint of surprise.

She pushed herself up from where she'd been leaning against the desk and walked to the kitchen. I tensed; but she just pulled a mug from the dish drainer, opened the refrigerator, and poured herself a glass of apple juice. After she drank it in one long gulp, she rinsed the mug and returned it to the drainer, saying, "The Stork. Me. What a funny name." Shaking her head, chuckling, she moved back around the desk, and sat down, watching me, her eyes large behind her glasses.

I couldn't breathe. My vision narrowed to a pinprick and my pulse raced. I had been right. My suspicions had been correct. All my years of research and data collection weren't just a ridiculous hobby.

There was a Stork.

"Let's start with the easy part," she was saying. "How it all worked. I'm sure you've figured most of it out, Shelby. It was a hierarchical organization, just like any company. Me. The intended parents. The delivery boys. I didn't know a lot of my delivery boys, but I did have the pleasure of meeting Frankie. Once." She shuddered. "He made Erik here look like a babe in the woods.

"I worked with a few sets of intended parents. Once they were in, they could not escape. I haven't yet reached the point where they might age out. I'll have to deal with that in a few years." Her use of the future tense didn't escape me. As if she thought she had a future.

"I had one set who wanted out after a birth mother got a little too close and we had to take care of her. But they saw the light. In fact, they're still working for me, up in Marin County.

"The parents collected the money. A big cut was funneled to me. I hoarded my share, waiting until my research was at the right point." She smiled, her eyes fixed on the desk blotter, as if remembering. "We planned for you years in advance. I had it all worked out — the clinic, the eggs, the fertilization, the DNA."

"DNA?" The three letters squeaked out of me, as if of their own accord.

"You hadn't figured that out yet?" She waved her hand. "Well, you're not as smart as I thought." She threw me a sharp look. "You don't think Justin and Justine are the way they are by chance, do you?

"They're mine. Purely my invention. My creations. My human germline redesign. Think about it. Here's a kid who's five years old. He already knows numbers. He feels numbers. He breathes numbers. When I asked him what the next number in this sequence would be — zero, one, one, two, three, five, eight, thirteen, twenty-one — he answered thirty-four, fifty-five, eighty-nine, and one hundred forty-four without even blinking."

She glanced at me. "I bet you didn't know it. Most people don't. It's the Fibonacci sequence. Each successive number is the sum of the previous two numbers. Despite all those books he'd been reading at the Boyd's," she sniffed, "he'd never heard of it. But he knew the numbers. And the equation. He rattled off the next thirty numbers without even having to think about it. The kid is a genius. More than a genius." The woman picked up a pen and started rolling it between her fingers.

"You know their IQs, right?"

She stared at the pen and didn't even glance up at me as she continued. "Higher than the highest ever recorded. Higher than Einstein. But no one knows." After a beat, she added, "Yet."

His parents do, I wanted to interject. But she kept talking.

"Synthetic DNA. It's the future. I inserted synthetic DNA into the embryo that was then implanted in you." She pointed at me. "I was the first person on the planet to do it." She stretched her arms over her head, leaned back in her chair, and laughed, a long, happy chortle of a woman completely satisfied with herself. "I still can't believe it," she added. "I'm like a kid. I have to pinch myself."

Helen leaned forward, into her desk, placing her hands on the blotter. "Did you ever hear of that book, *Remaking Eden*? It came out in 1997 and caused such a stink. About how the market would evolve a new species of humans, the GenRich. Genetic aristocrats.

"I was light years ahead of that. During the day, I developed synthetic DNA for medical applications. Why not transfer that knowledge to humans? Why not design the next step in human evolution? An uber-human, engineered for intelligence and longevity. A being who innately understands abstractions. Ideas. A being who is logical. Whose brain is on fire, who can't stop thinking. And a being who is on the cusp of a new biological truth.

"Imagine not needing to sleep. Just think about it. Resting, yes, but sleep not required. You could spend those extra seven or eight hours a day learning, thinking, synthesizing, inventing. Advancing the field of mathematics. Developing new theories of quantum mechanics or physics. Redesigning democracy. Or space travel. Fixing the climate."

She waved her hand in the air in a circular motion, and then threw her arms out, as if embracing the world. Her voice rose, and her eyes burned with the fever of a madwoman. "Justin and Justine represent the first in a biotechnological human revolution. And the next step in human evolution. I did it. I made them."

I stood rooted in place, clenching my fists so hard that my nails dug into my palms. Bile burned in my throat, leaving a coppery taste, like I'd just swallowed water laced with heavy minerals.

"Once I reached a certain point in the lab, I had to take the experiment to the field. At first, I thought I'd just kidnap young women, insert embryos, and keep them for the length of the pregnancy. After the babies were born, I'd dispose of them. But that proved much too complicated. I'd have no way to determine if a woman was suitable. I needed to know her genetic, physical, and psychological history. And keeping a woman captive for ten or so months, feeding her, making sure there were no medical problems was very complicated. Besides, people would be looking for women who disappeared off the street.

"My scheme was so much easier. Convince a young woman to become a surrogate, go through the IVF process, with some modifications, of course, and pay her. No one's the wiser." Pride gleamed in her eyes. "You were my first success, Shelby. The first one." Her voice rose with excitement. "I was so proud."

She shook her head, and for an instant, I almost believed she was remorseful as she said, "There were plenty of miscarriages before you came along." But her mouth turned down as she spoke, and I knew I'd mistaken scorn for remorse.

"I'd perfected the technique and the process by the time you entered my life. With each of the surrogates, we had two chances, since our contract stipulated that a potential birth mother would only sign up for two in-vitro cycles. I didn't want to send up any red flags. We had to transfer your eggs from the fertility clinic to my lab in San Francisco. I inserted the synthetic DNA there and then had to return the eggs to the clinic so they could be implanted in you. It worked, with the help of a few insiders at the clinic."

I wondered if the closure of the fertility clinic, The Reproductive Health Center of Los Gatos, was somehow related.

Helen smiled, and her voice was light and full of excitement as she continued; as if she'd been waiting for years to tell someone, anyone, her story.

Panic rose in my chest, but I fought it, fists curled, arms rigid, knees locked. I wanted to run. I had to stay.

"I'm in constant communication with other like-minded scientists across the globe," Helen continued. "Scientists are racing to be the first. But I've done it. Me. Dr. Helen Brannon." She lifted her head and gestured proudly, outlining a marquee.

"It was so easy, Shelby. That was the fun part. So easy. Everyone thought it was something else. Even Diane."

My expression must have given me away, for Helen added, "Diane didn't know any of this. She did know something was different with you. She had to chart everything. And I mean everything." Helen picked up the red journal and waved it at me. "You remember this. Right?

"I had to know what you were doing, all the time," she continued. "I bet you didn't know there were cameras in that cottage, did you? I couldn't believe it when Frankie showed up at your house for dinner. But he was good. Very good."

I wanted to throttle her. I imagined leaping, crashing to the ground on top of her.

"The cameras allowed me to be able to factor out all environmental aspects of your pregnancy, so I could just focus on the genetics. We had to remove the equipment shortly after Jackson and Diane were arrested."

Helen slowly rose and circled the desk, still talking. "All those other birth mothers funded this grand scheme. I'd decided that you were the last one, though, with the DNA strand I was using. If you had miscarried, I decided I'd return to the lab and continue tinkering." Her gait was heavy and I realized she was limping. A huge bruise shadowed her jaw where my fist had slammed into her.

Her ankle turned and she leaned back against the desk for support, taking a quick breath. "And you had to screw it all up," she said.

I stepped back.

"Those babies were going to end up with me," she continued. "They were going to live here with me. I could have raised them and studied them, using pure methodologies and research, introducing them to the world when they were ready and the world was ready for them. Instead, by your actions, you relegated them to freak status. Because of you, those brilliant twins, the first of the uber species, are living with completely incompetent parents who don't have a hope of ever understanding them."

I took a step backward, then another and another. I continued walking backwards until I stood in the middle of the room, leaving plenty of space to maneuver.

"And now that you're here, and Justin is out there," she pointed toward the door, "there's nothing I can do. I could go outside looking for him, but you've probably got him stowed in some small hiding place that he'll never come out of."

I imagined Justin, crouched on the dirt road past the slide. I hoped he was safe.

"You win, Shelby. You've trumped me." She turned her hands up in a gesture of hopelessness. "My career. All the work I've done to create drugs that shrink brain tumors, to understand why transplants are rejected. All my research. My carefully designed experiments." She snapped her fingers. "It will all be discounted, because of you. My results will be questioned. I know how this goes. I've seen it before. One misstep and your life's work is suspect."

This was more than a misstep. This was not the same as fudging results for profits or mixing up lab specimens. As far as I was concerned, this was a global crime. A crime against humanity. A crime of epic proportions, on par with chemical warfare or genocide. A crime that could go no further.

54

KEEPING HER EYES FIXED ON ME, Helen continued to talk. "The scientific community loves me," she said quietly, almost longingly, as if she were trying to convince herself. "Everyone in the field of synthetic biology reveres me — researchers, professors, scientists, entrepreneurs, and investors. Of course, my colleagues in the United States will never be able to go on record with their support. But my colleagues in Russia, Eastern Europe, and China will be able to speak up."

"Human cloning is banned almost everywhere on the planet," I objected.

She shook her finger and snapped, "This is not cloning. These genes are completely synthetic. Brand new. All engineered. I completely replace the maternal and paternal genomes.

"The physical attributes were easy, like Mendel and his peas. But the mental ones," she tapped her temple with her index finger, "not so easy.

"One hundred years from now? Two hundred? There will be a completely new human species. The ruling class. Based on my pioneering work. If you were a parent, wouldn't you be proud to give birth to such a child? Of course, those children would have to be raised in completely sterile environments. Modern-day children's homes run by scientists."

She was crazy. No doubt about it. In her dystopian future, parents would give birth to children who weren't children at all, but members of a synthetic, manufactured species. Children who would only resemble humans in the fact that they had two arms and legs, a torso, and a head. They'd be smarter, quicker, and brighter than their parents by quantum leaps. This new genius race might be able to solve our world problems, rescue the planet, and colonize the universe, but what would we become? Without empathy, compassion, joy, humor, and love, what was left?

"Questions?" she asked.

My mouth went dry. Knowing what I did now, I could think of plenty. But there was one question she hadn't answered. One question that had sailed through my dreams, causing nightmares. One question that had burned itself into my psyche; one that I promised I would ask if I ever got a chance.

And I asked it.

"Why me?"

But once I uttered those two tiny words and saw her small lopsided smile of pleasure, I wished I could take them back.

"Why you?" she replied. "Why you." She limped back to the desk chair and dropped heavily into it. Her face was shrouded again. "Why you," she repeated.

"Well, I could answer with an obvious question: why not you? You were just as good as anyone else." She shook her head. "But that's not entirely true. When I saw the videotape of your interview ..." here my eyes must have widened of their own accord, for she said, "Yes, we did tape the interview. All of them. You were one of ten we interviewed."

She continued, "There was something I liked about you. And I still do, even though that very quality brought you here in the first place, and has now brought you back. You had some..." she paused and looked upward, as if sifting through all the words in her vocabulary for just the right one, "some moxie about you. Some kind of spirit.

"Even though I was replacing all the genetic material in your eggs, I couldn't use just anyone. I had to rule out the obvious: past genetic familial disorders, no drugs, no alcohol, no mental illness. I was also looking for intangibles. I had to find out everything about my candidates. Probably more than the young women knew about themselves. Take family history, for example. Did you know your mother's great-grandfather was a physician? And a professor? And did you know that your father's grandfather was a mathematician? That gene did not get passed down to your father or to you or your brother, but I found it an interesting trait."

My mouth must have dropped open, my jaw hanging in the wind. "Didn't know that, did you?" she asked. "There's more. Your maternal grandmother was a nurse, passed that to your mother. Noble profession. And your paternal grandmother was a stay at home mother. But your paternal great-grandmother was an outspoken suffragette. I liked that family trait." She laughed. "That did get passed to you.

"No mental illness to speak of, though your parents and brother are all prone to situational depression. That's more and more common, so I was able to discount that. No genetic, physical, or emotional abnormalities in your family tree that I could find. No Down's, autism, or delayed development. No developmental disability. No criminals, no jail time.

"No," she paused, and then continued, "sickliness. No one died in the flu epidemic. No TB or pneumonia deaths. My other top candidate had two ancestors who died from lung diseases back in the twenties.

"So you come from hardy, if a bit boring, stock. But if I had given it more thought, I should have avoided you. I should have picked someone without any family ties in this area. It would have been better for my candidate to be completely alone."

She paused, calling, "Erik, are you okay?"

A faint, "Yes, Mother," floated out from the bedroom.

"Get ready then," she said. "It's almost time."

I took another step back and glanced over my shoulder. The solid wooden front door was just a few steps away. I could sprint to it, pull it open, and escape. Run back to Justin. I could outrun Helen any day and Erik was out of commission. But I first needed a few more answers.

Taking a breath, I asked, "Jackson and Diane?"

Pushing herself up, Doctor Helen shrugged and shook her head. "You really aren't as smart as I took you for." She smiled, small, quick, almost regretful. "My daughter," she said.

"Your daughter?" I repeated, disbelieving.

"Who better?" she returned.

Filing this away for later, I shook my head and stared at her for a good long minute.

"Now what?" I asked.

Keeping her eyes on me, she walked to the middle of the room and called, "Erik? It's time. I need you."

Helen stared toward the kitchen, her eyes bright and expectant. She pressed her palms together in front of her, as if praying. Seconds later, Erik seesawed into the room, dragging his injured leg like the broken wing of a bird. His face was shiny with sweat and he reeked of blood, body odor, urine.

That handgun dangled from his right hand.

He stopped in the middle of the kitchen, two yards from his mother. The side of his face was lit by the bulb over the sink, and what I'd assumed to be sweat was actually tears. The man was crying.

Like a moth, I was stuck, mesmerized. Bewitched. My legs would not move even if I ordered them to. I had to see what would happen. What was Helen asking Erik if he was ready for? To run? But Erik wouldn't be able to go anywhere, unless it was on a stretcher. Surely, she would know that the police were on the way. Soon, the driveway would be swarming with cop cars.

Then, I grew rigid, each cell shot through with fear.

Had her confession made me a dead woman?

But Helen stared at Erik, gaze fixed, focused, as if I weren't in the room. As if she were expecting something.

"It's time, son," she said quietly, keeping her hands up, in prayer. "I'm ready."

Planting his injured leg to steady himself, Erik raised the pistol. As he stared at his mother, he pulled back on the safety. I stopped breathing. The sound, loud and unmistakable, echoed in the small room.

Erik held the gun on his mother for an instant, and then slowly turned. He aimed it at my forehead.

I stood completely still and stared at him, trying not to blink. Trying to appear strong and steady. Trying to stay alive.

He stared back, tears streaking his cheeks. His hand shook and the gun trembled.

Just I tensed, ready to dive to the ground, to do something, his mother said, "Son, that's not what we talked about. She doesn't matter anyway." The woman's voice was quiet, soothing, so unlike the mocking, arrogant tone that had been directed at me. She dropped her hands from their prayer-like position, opened her arms, and raised them to shoulder height. She stood completely still, as commanding as a cross.

"Leave her alive to tell the story. Do it, son, just like we agreed. I'm ready. There's nothing here for me anymore." She gestured with her hands, as if inviting death to her, "Please. I'm ready."

The gun swung toward Helen. But Erik's eyes were full of tears and his hand was shaking so hard that the barrel of the gun was wavering, making it impossible for him to fix on a target. His mouth was pulled into a grimace. Between the pain that must be coursing up his leg in fiery pulses and the terror of what his mother was asking him to do, he looked like he was about to pass out.

"Do it, son," she repeated. "We talked about this. This is better for you. You'll be declared mentally incompetent. You'll be put in a place with enough food and TV to last you the rest of your life. Please. I can't get caught. I'll be crucified. Do this for me. Please?"

She looked at him with love, her eyes shining.

Erik took a breath that squealed between his teeth like the wheels of a train straining to stay on a set of broken rails. He placed both hands on the pistol, cocked his head, and stared down the barrel. His fingertips were white from the pressure of his grip. Then Erik lifted his eyes and, for an instant, fixed them on his mother. She gazed back in return, and gestured with her head, like a priestess giving a blessing.

Erik squinted, sighting again down the barrel. The skin on his face grew taut as he concentrated. He grasped the trigger with his index finger. The touch of the smooth metal must have grounded him, for the tremors stopped and he stood without shaking. He crooked his finger against the trigger and pulled back slowly.

Helen's eyes were fixed on her son. She mouthed, "Thank you."

One second, two seconds later, the sharp, deafening sound of a single gunshot rocked the small room.

55

I SLAMMED INTO THE FLOOR, landing with my hands stretched out in front of me, palms flat. A wave of bright, fierce pain pulsed across my right shoulder and down my arm. The gash on my head felt like it had opened up again and the bruise across my torso throbbed. My ears rang.

Taking a deep breath and using my left arm for leverage, I pushed myself to my knees and rose to my feet, trying to figure out what had just happened. Erik stood across the room in the middle of the kitchen, frozen in place, paralyzed. His hand hung at his side and the pistol was by his right foot, where he'd dropped it.

Tears streamed down his cheeks and he was weeping.

Where was Helen? She should be here, lying on the floor, right where I was standing. Wounded or dying, the life passing out of her with every breath.

But there was no body. Not even any blood. No drops, spatters, or sprays.

I scanned the room. The front door was still closed. The drapes still hung over the windows, motionless. Helen wasn't crouched under the desk or hiding behind it. She wasn't standing on the stairs looking down at us. She wasn't in the kitchen.

The woman had vanished.

Then, an anguished roar split the quiet, a keening cry of grief, loss, disbelief. It was followed by another and another.

I had to move, to get out before Erik noticed me.

I turned and sprinted for the door. But a loud boom ripped the air and a gash appeared in the floor between me and the way out. My ears buzzed. I could smell that odor again.

I stopped.

"You're not going anywhere." Erik's voice was low and guttural, huffing out each word as if his life depended on it. I didn't turn, I didn't need to. I knew that gun was pointing right at me.

I had one second to figure this out. Likely less than that. The front door was out of the question. Even if I reached it, the time it would take me to open the door would be my last moments on this earth. The windows were impossible; there was nothing to break the glass with, and even if the glass miraculously disappeared, I would not be able to squeeze through the decorative wrought iron security bars. Upstairs would be a deathtrap.

The only option was the desk.

Not looking at Erik, hoping to catch him off guard, hoping to run so fast he wouldn't be able to get me in his sights, I sprinted to the desk, sliding under it as another gunshot rocked the room. I hit my right shoulder again, the pain momentarily taking my breath away. I held my right arm across my torso to cinch my shoulder in place and scrunched into the small cavity below the desk, curling my head to my knees to fit.

I heard the thud of a single footstep, followed by the scrape of Erik's heavy work boot as he dragged his injured leg behind him. Then another thud and another scrape.

He was coming.

Taking a deep breath, steadying myself, I slowly leaned over and peered around the side of the desk.

Erik was less than five feet away. In just a few more steps, he would be on me. All it would take was another squeeze of the trigger to finish me off.

I pulled back under the desk and held my breath. Staying glued to the floor, as fixed in place as the desk, pretending this wasn't happening, would be so easy. If I shut my eyes, maybe it would all go away. If I didn't see him, he wouldn't be able to see me.

But I knew that course of action would be my end. Carefully, quietly, I pressed my hands to the floor, feeling the rough wooden planks.

Another thud, followed by the dragging scrape.

I clenched my fingers, drawing them up so my knuckles were on the floor.

Erik stopped. "Mama?" he called. "Mama?"

The room was still.

"Mama?"

Still crouched below the desk, I kept my head low and slowly shifted my weight forward onto my knees. I twisted to my left and exploded upward, out into the room. I shoved the desk chair out of the way, doubling over in pain as my right hand slammed into its rigid back, sending a jolt up my arm into my shoulder. A second later, I stood. And ran for my life, taking leaping strides across the room.

But my slight delay cost me. Erik reached the door first.

I stopped, halfway across the room.

Darkness shadowed the man's face. He lowered his head and stared at me, a murderous vicious intent clouding his eyes. A cry, a cross between a full out battle shout and a furious gasping lament, erupted from him.

He took a step toward me, dragging his right leg. His face reddened and he muttered, "You bitch. She made me do this. Because of you. It's your fault."

I took a step back.

"I'm going to strangle you with my own hands." His voice was quiet, with each word spoken in a whispering hiss.

He dropped the gun. It clattered to the floor and he kicked it behind him. It skittered across the floor and slid to a stop by the door.

He took another step, placing his hands on the top of his right thigh, pulling his game leg forward.

Now, we faced each other.

My body was rigid, braced in anticipation.

Erik breathed hoarsely, clenching and unclenching his fists, as if readying for the task ahead — putting his hands around my neck and squeezing the life out of me.

The sharp smell of blood hit me. Fresh red blood had seeped through his sweats.

Erik lifted his left foot to take one more step.

But before he could place his foot back down, in that in-between state when he was balanced on his injured leg, I raced for him, head down. I screamed, the sound starting in my chest and rising upward, an explosion of anger, hate, and terror.

I connected with his injured thigh, square on, the top of my head butting the wound, driving him backward.

He screamed and fell, hands grabbing, scrabbling to catch on to something, to keep him upright. His hands landed on my upper back and I could feel the weight of them as he squeezed, pulling me over on top of him.

But his skull cracked against the hard wooden floor when he landed, and his hands relaxed, long enough for me to slide off and wiggle away. I kept one eye on him as I leaned over and breathed, trying to control the nausea.

Erik moaned, lifted his head, and then collapsed back down.

I had to get out before he woke.

I ran around him, keeping my distance, terrified he'd reach out, grab my ankle, and wrestle me to the ground.

I yanked the door open in the same second I noticed the gun. I leaned over for it, but my training kicked in and I knew not to touch it. Instead, I used the corner of my shirt to pick it up, holding it in front of me.

Leaving the door open, I ran across the porch, jumped down the steps, and stopped.

I gulped in the fresh night air. It was over. All over. I looked up. Small pinpoints of stars poked through the velvety blackness. The silhouettes of redwoods cut sharp points into the dark sky. An owl hooted, possibly the same one that I'd heard when I'd fled the first time, escaping with Justin.

I turned around and glanced back. Light spilled out onto the porch and cast a warm glow.

I shuddered. Things are not always what they appear.

Then, I looked down the driveway, toward freedom. I took a step, the sound tiny and quiet in the immensity of the outdoors. Then another step and another. Heart hammering, suddenly so eager to get away that I almost fell, I ran, flying around the slight curve and down the hill. With each jarring step, I could feel the gash on my head, the pain in my shoulder, the throbbing in my torso. I was glad for it, all that pain reminded me that I was alive. That I was still breathing and moving. That I hadn't been shot.

Ahead of me, the aluminum siding of the garage glowed dully, like pewter. I stopped there and leaned against it, the surface cooling my skin. I carefully placed the gun on the concrete apron.

It was only then that I realized Erik's truck was gone. The driveway had been empty, open, a yawing blank spot where that pickup had been parked when I'd foolishly returned to confront Helen.

And Helen must have driven away in it, abandoning her son. Leaving him to take the fall and face the police alone. To face a lengthy trial and a life-long jail sentence.

What kind of mother would do that?

I vowed that I would keep looking. That I wouldn't give up until I found her.

I heard a thread of sound. I cocked my head, listening intently. Willing the sound to be my salvation.

It was.

The long undulating wail of a single siren shred the night, followed by a second and a third.

I walked to the road where I would be standing upright, shoulders back, when the police arrived.

EPILOGUE

MONDAY, DECEMBER 31

EPILOGUE

T HE NIGHT WAS SURPRISINGLY CHILLY, even for the last day of
December. Dexter, Megan, Cody, and I stood outside on the
small patio of our apartment, glasses raised, counting down: ten,
nine, eight, seven, six, five, four, three, two, one. At exactly midnight,
we leaned in, clinked our mismatched champagne glasses, and
welcomed 2013. It wasn't exactly a good riddance to 2012. I had met
Cody after all, and Dexter and Megan were now intertwined and
inseparable.

We slid the patio doors open and hurried back inside. I curled on
the futon next to Cody while Dexter and Megan squeezed into the black
leather recliner Dexter had found at a yard sale. Ashley and Annie had
fallen asleep hours ago, tucked on an air mattress in the entryway.

I held up my champagne glass, a relic from a Pebble Beach golf
tournament, and stared at the bubbles. "Anyone have any wishes for
this year?" I asked.

"Sure," Cody said. "I wish I get all holidays off, so I can spend them with you all."

I leaned over and kissed him on the cheek. "Me too," I said. Somehow, Cody had managed to get tonight off, probably because he'd worked both Thanksgiving and Christmas.

"Dexter?"

He glanced at Megan and she gave him a little nod. "Megan and I have something to tell you." He paused and took Megan's hand. "We're moving in together."

"What?" I asked. "When?"

"Not sure how, or where, but we've decided," he said. "By April, we'll be living together. The lease here is up at the end of April, so ..." his voice trailed off.

"That is great," I exclaimed, pushing myself up and clapping my hands together. "I'm so happy for you." I walked over, leaned down, and gave them both a clumsy hug. I wondered where I'd end up, but decided there'd be plenty of time to figure that out. Besides, this might catapult my relationship with Cody to the next level.

"Congratulations," Cody said. "I'm happy for you."

I sat back down, snuggled next to him, and smiled as Cody put his arm around me and drew me close.

"Megan? Anything to add?"

"Well," she paused. "I can't say I'm sorry to see 2012 go. It was hard, all the way around." I nodded. I knew. Not only did she have to skip the fall quarter, she had to retake the summer biochemistry seminar. As for our relationship — she and I had been over this so many times. She didn't hold me accountable. At least she said she didn't. She acted like she didn't. But subconsciously? I'd never know. I was careful with Megan now, overly solicitous, guarded, as if waiting for that nugget of blame to leak out and poison our friendship. I hoped this would pass, in time.

Erik had gotten the wrong person. He'd thought that Megan was me. It was that simple and that terrifying. He'd stuck a gun in her side as she'd stood by the car in the busy parking lot at Waddell Creek that Saturday afternoon — at the moment she realized she didn't have the car keys. He demanded she come with him and keep quiet. She froze. He prodded her with the pistol and she walked. Once he figured out that she wasn't me, he marched her through the marsh and up the steep hill to the cliff top, where he'd beaten her senseless and left her. To die.

By some miracle, he hadn't raped her.

"My wishes for 2013?" Megan was saying. "A 4.0." She laughed. "And that Dexter and I find a cozy, affordable place to live somewhere near campus, so that Annie can continue at the same school and I don't have to drive to class."

"How about you, Shelby?"

I smiled. "That's easy. I want to keep hanging out with Cody." I felt him squeeze my shoulder. "I wish that I get a 4.0, too. And that I keep working for Kathleen, and that Randy Vinson continues to get the help he needs." Cody, Dexter, and Megan nodded. I stared past Megan and Dexter, remembering what Kathleen and I had seen when we'd finally completed our surveillance work. All we'd found was a singularly depressed man, enamored with his Sig Sauer and Glock, playing a serious, solo game of Russian Roulette.

Other morbid thoughts shimmered at the edge of my mind, about to roll across my landscape like a thundercloud. I shook my head, willing them away, saying, "That's all. The most important is Cody,"

Later, Cody and I left the light on by the side of the bed and threw a scarf over the lampshade. His torso glowed in the dim light and his skin was so soft to touch, with his muscles forming a dense, solid wall beneath. Our kisses started slow, gentle at first, teasing. We lay in bed, touching, caressing each other, staring into each other's eyes. Cody ran his hands up and down my back, and pulled me to him. He groaned, so quietly, that I felt the sound rather than heard it. That low moan vibrated though my core and my need for him was urgent and essential. Overpowering.

Afterwards, I'd tried to sleep, but at two in the morning, I'd risen, restless. My therapist was encouraging me to develop new habits for my insomnia. No more internet during the small hours. No more research. No more spreadsheets.

Instead, I was trying to read. Not contemporary fiction, but the classics, the books I'd been forced to read in high school and college.

The tomes I'd stuttered through, eyes glazed and mind in a fog. *Pride and Prejudice. The Grapes of Wrath. Catcher in the Rye. The Great Gatsby.* My therapist thought such a dramatic shift in how I spent the sleepless hours would be good for me. Transformational, even.

I picked up the book I was reading now, *1984*, but within ten minutes, my mind had circled back to Helen Brannon and Justin and Justine Boyd. As usual.

My Stork had proved to be not so mythical after all. Everything she'd told me in our short time together had turned out to be true. Her full name was Helen Brannon, and she was the director of research and chief scientist at Neuro Pharmaceuticals, a biopharmaceutical company specializing in drugs for reducing the size of brain tumors. Diane and Erik were her children. Diane, the older sibling, claimed she had no idea her mother was the one orchestrating it all. And Erik refused to speak. Despite offers of reduced sentences, both Jackson and Frankie claimed ignorance.

Helen Brannon's record had been dazzling. After graduating with honors from Johns Hopkins Medical School, she'd completed her residency in neurology at the University of San Francisco. While there, she'd married, and immediately given birth to Diane, with Erik following a few years later.

She accepted a fellowship in a lab at the university, running clinical trials. Later, she'd earned a PhD from Stanford in Epidemiology. Her marriage had fallen apart and her husband, a Polish scientist, had returned to Poland with no apparent interest in her or his children.

Helen had moved from corporation to corporation heading up labs, leading pharmaceutical development and managing clinical trials, landing at Neuro twelve years ago. Somehow, somewhere Helen had gone off the rails.

Stress? Ambition? Megalomania? In one of her prestigious research positions, she studied immune responses to liver transplants by activating and silencing different genes. Her goal was to discover the magic genetic combination that would allow an organ, say a heart or a liver, to be better tolerated by the recipient. At that point in her career, she had decided to use her lab for her own DNA tinkering. During the day, she ran a competent, professional lab that met federal standards for genetic research. After the scientists and graduate students cleared out at night, she did her own private work.

She'd struck a deal, one that probably began as a blackmail threat, with a doctor at The Reproductive Center of Los Gatos. Helen was given the frozen embryos that were left over from IVF cycles. Of course, there was no record of how many or who the embryos belonged to. From there, she experimented, editing genomes by adding or deleting DNA strands in pursuit of specific traits. She'd inject her embryos with her synthetic DNA and examine them after they'd replicated. Over time, her technique improved — her replacement genes survived, and the rate of mutations was low.

And then, she leapt from the lab to human subjects. Just as she'd said, there were miscarriages before me. At least ten. I was the first where the embryo with the synthetic DNA survived in utero and grew to a viable pregnancy.

Justin and Justine were products of biotechnological eugenics.

The investigators found her personal manifesto on her computer. Right there, clickable from the desktop. A two-thousand word treatise that stated her goal, clearly, unequivocally: To create the next species of humans. Not a select few individuals with beyond-genius IQs. Not children selected for traits like looks, height, intelligence, or athletic ability. But to create a whole new species where super high IQs were the norm. Where intellectual pursuits were all that mattered. Human attributes we take for granted — love, sleep, empathy, compassion, humor — would be a quaint relic of evolution, as extinct as the dinosaur.

And the existing human species, all of us, would become slaves to this uber race, feeding it, housing it, cleaning up after it.

DNA tinkering was the first step. Over time, Helen was sure that evolution, with her assistance, would work its magic to create this new species.

Luckily, she was stopped. I stopped her. For now, anyway.

But I would find her. And stop her for good.

They never did find her or the truck. That night, when Erik had raised the gun to shoot his mother, as they'd planned, he swears that I leapt and pushed her out of the way. That explains how I ended up on the floor with a separated shoulder. But that leap? I have no memory of it.

That instinctive reaction on my part allowed Helen Brannon to escape, leaving her son to take the fall.

And it makes me lose sleep, question my judgment, and wonder if I'm in the right profession.

Would the world have been better off if I hadn't pushed her?

As for Justin and Justine — the press has been merciless, branding them as freaks, mutants, sociopaths. The government and scientific communities are fighting over them. Talk shows can't get enough of them, and like a bad politician, they come up in every conversation.

The children still live with their parents, but their lives have changed completely. Courtesy of our tax dollars, the Boyd family moved to Fairfax, Virginia, where some spooky branch of the US government regulates their every move. Lisa and Ryan are now government employees. They care for their children, as best they can, and coordinate their schedule of appointments with scientists, professors, researchers, doctors, psychiatrists. A Secret Service agent guards their house at all times and accompanies them on any outside excursion. A nutritionist fixes their meals. A doctor monitors them daily. Their house is infiltrated by cameras and spy equipment.

Just what the doctor wanted.

They tried to run experiments on me; biopsy this and that, take blood, and subject me to MRIs and CAT scans. But I refused, giving them five vials of blood and, in return, receiving orders from the NIH to report yearly for testing. I am supposed to wear a special ID bracelet, to alert paramedics and ER surgeons to my potentially compromised state. And, I've been warned to never ever think of a pregnancy. Adoption might be a better course, they'd told me. I'd filed all that away for later.

Helen had stored plenty of incriminating evidence on the computer at her cabin. Scanned copies of contracts with birth mothers, including mine. The first contract was dated twenty years ago, long before she started at Neuro.

Tragically, there were no records for the infants. All those babies. Lost.

The doctor still had six sets of phony intended parents working for her. Five of the couples were arrested immediately. But the couple in Marin County got away. Someone alerted them, and they vanished overnight, leaving behind a very relieved birth mother, days away from her due date, who decided to keep the baby after all.

The addresses I'd received from Marie at Lavender Farms, the new owner of Jackson and Diane's property, could all be traced back to Helen, to a fictitious corporation registered in Erik's name. Diane, I was sure, had kept the addresses as insurance. I knew they were all locations where Frankie had delivered babies, but nothing could be proven.

I assumed we found what Helen wanted us to find. Enough to keep diligent investigators busy for a long, long time. I was sure she had a whole second, or third, or even fourth identity available, with enough cash to start over, in some other country, where genetic redesign was encouraged, even praised.

I'd find her. I didn't know how, but I would find her.

I put the book down and went back into the bedroom, pulled back the covers, and slipped in next to Cody, spooning my body into his. He stirred and, in his sleep, threw his arm over my shoulder and pulled me close. I could hear him breathing, slow and steady. After escaping Helen and Erik, and freeing Justin, I'd told Cody everything. He didn't question me, or judge me, or feel hurt that I hadn't told him earlier. He listened. He understood. And he was still here, still with me.

I smiled, snuggled close him, and fell into a deep, deep sleep.

ABOUT THE AUTHOR

Nancy Wood grew up in various locations on the East Coast and now calls Central California home. Recently retired, she spent thirty-five years as a technical writer, translating engineer-speak into words and sentences. She likens it to translating ancient Greek — when you're not too familiar with the Greek part.

Since retiring, she and her husband have been traveling the world. So far, they've visited France, Spain, England, Sri Lanka, New Zealand, Belgium, the Netherlands, India, and Vietnam. They are not anywhere close to done and have many more trips planned. Nancy is also a passionate photographer, focusing on macro photography and blur.

For more information about the world and works of Nancy Wood, visit *nancywoodbooks.com*.

BOOKS BY NANCY WOOD

DUE DATE

Surrogate mother Shelby McDougall just fell for the biggest con of all: a scam that risks her life ... and the lives of her unborn twins.

THE STORK

It's been five and a half years, and Shelby McDougall is finally on track. But a late-night phone call puts Shelby's perfectly ordered life into a tailspin.

THE FOUND CHILD

Private Investigator Shelby McDougall is out for revenge.

TREASURE HUNT

When ten-year-old Tyler signs up for a Saturday afternoon treasure hunt sponsored by the city's Parks department, he discovers much more than he bargained for.

Available from Paper Angel Press in
hardcover, trade paperback, digital, and audio editions
paperangelpress.com